A FIELD GUIDE
TO HOMICIDE

A FIELD GUIDE TO HOMICIDE

LYNN CAHOON

KENSINGTON BOOKS
www.kensingtonbooks.com

KENSINGTON BOOKS are published by

Kensington Publishing Corp.
119 West 40th Street
New York, NY 10018

All Kensington titles, imprints, and distributed lines are available at special quantity discounts for bulk purchases for sales promotion, premiums, fund-raising, and educational or institutional use.

Special book excerpts or customized printings can also be created to fit specific needs. For details, write or phone the office of the Kensington Sales Manager: Kensington Publishing Corp., 119 West 40th Street, New York, NY 10018. Attn. Sales Department. Phone: 1-800-221-2647.

Kensington and the K logo Reg. U.S. Pat. & TM Off.

First Kensington Books mass-market printing: February 2020
ISBN-13: 978-1-4967-1685-9
ISBN-10: 1-4967-1685-X

ISBN-13: 978-1-4967-1686-6 (ebook)
ISBN-10: 1-4967-1686-8 (ebook)

10 9 8 7 6 5 4 3 2 1

Printed in the United States of America

To my Facebook Buddies—Karen Rochetta-Ellis, Gerri Smith, Joan Varner, Betty Tyler, and Mary Kay Aldridge, who played the "name the writers visiting Cat during this retreat" game.

Acknowledgments

Naming characters is a hard thing for this author. Especially in this series, where I have to have at least seven new characters a book. The four writer retreat guests plus the Covington student attendee, plus the victim and the killer. So if I've met you, I'm probably going to steal your name or a version of your name at some time or another and make a character out of it. It doesn't mean I'm putting "you" into a book. Or even killing you off in a book. But sometimes . . .

One more note on a personal matter: I was writing this book when I lost my Homer. He was a great writing companion and kept me company while I played with my imaginary friends. And he insisted I get up every couple of hours to let him and his doggie buddy out in the backyard. I'll be dedicating a book to him soon, and creating a doggie spot for him in one of my series so he can live forever, but not quite yet. I miss you, little buddy.

Chapter 1

Late October can be the best or worst time to schedule a hike. Right now, the jury was out on Sunday's activity for the participants of this month's Warm Springs Writers' Retreat. Seth Howard—Cat Latimer's boyfriend, retreat driver, and, for this retreat, hiking guide—sat glued to his laptop. Cat watched him over her coffee mug. He'd been sitting at the kitchen table staring at the computer for more than fifteen minutes without saying a word. She glanced at the clock. "You're going to have to leave soon if you're going to make it to Denver before the first plane arrives."

Seth grunted.

Cat looked at Shauna, who was busy on her own laptop working on the final, final draft of her *Warm Springs Writers' Retreat Recipes for Brunch* cookbook. In Cat's opinion, the title was way too long, but Shauna would have to be told that by a publisher or an agent. Mostly because she wasn't listening to Cat right now. "Hey, help me out here.

We've got guests expecting to find a ride to Aspen Hills when they land. You know Shirley took a cab from Denver because she hadn't told us she was coming and it cost her a fortune."

"Seth. Go get the writers." Shauna didn't even look up from her manuscript. "Cat's getting nervous."

"I'm not getting nervous. It's called project management. I'm just trying to keep us on schedule." Cat stood and refilled her coffee mug. "Do you want a travel mug to go?"

Seth closed the laptop. "I guess. Although there's two hours in between flights, so I'll probably just wait around for the second group and bring them back together. Will the retreat pay for lunch for three of us?"

"Sure, but don't take them to some upscale place," Shauna answered Seth's question. "I'm on a strict food budget until the first of the year. We want to make sure we put as much on clearing the debt from the remodel in the next three months as possible."

"I thought the loan had over a year left on it." Cat searched her memory to try to remember the terms of the bank loan.

"It does, but I was talking to my brother, Jake, when I visited and he said the sooner you get the business out of debt, the more secure you'll be in the retreat. I think we should save up for the rest of the remodel and not get another loan." Shauna shut down her laptop and stretched. "Do you know how much money we could save by not paying interest?"

"Now don't get crazy on me. That remodel project is on my work schedule for next year and I'm counting on the revenue." He took the travel mug Cat had filled and grabbed the keys to the SUV. "It looks like that storm is going to hold off, so the guests won't need snowshoes for the hike tomorrow."

"That's good news." Cat kissed him and handed him a bag of cookies. "Don't break into these until you're on your way back from Denver. There's plenty for you and the guests."

"I might get hungry on the way there. You sure you don't want to come with me and make sure I stay out of them?" He smiled and for a second, Cat's heart stopped. They'd had a great week alone when Shauna had visited her brother and then a week lying on tropical beaches at a Mexican resort. They'd just gotten back last Sunday, so they'd been busy getting the retreat together and hadn't had much time to spend together.

"You two need to get a room. Or just cool it until the guests leave." Shauna picked up one of the field guides Seth had made and gotten printed at the office supply store. "Don't forget to give me your receipt for the printing."

He pulled a wrinkled receipt out of his jeans pocket. "I forgot I had it."

Shauna took the paper and set it on the table, trying to rub out the wrinkles. "What does this even say? Don't tell me you spent over a hundred dollars on the printing."

"I think one twenty. I got the glossy cover paper." He held up one of the booklets. "*A Field Guide to Aspen Hills Hiking* by Seth Howard. Now Cat isn't the only author in the room."

"I estimated out my cookbooks if we go self-published and they were less per book than what you paid." Shauna took the receipt to her desk and tucked it in the top drawer. "Next time, let me handle the printing. Hal down at the shop is a friend."

"I went to school with him. You think he's going to give you a better deal than he gave me?" Seth glared at Shauna.

"He could charge me full price and give me a better deal than what you paid." Shauna shook her head. "He must have seen you coming."

Cat pointed to the clock again, hoping to stop the argument. Sometimes Seth and Shauna sounded more like siblings than just friends.

"Yeah, yeah, I know. I need to leave." He shrugged into a jacket and kissed Cat. Before he left, he paused at the door. "Hal and I are going to have a talk Wednesday at the Vet's Hall."

"Call me when you get back on the road. We're ordering pizza for the welcome night dinner," Cat called after him.

Instead of responding, Seth held his hand in the air to let her know he'd heard. Cat sank back into her chair. "Man, he was hot about the printing."

"Actually, I think he's been worrying about something else. He's not looking forward to that reunion next week at the Vet's Hall. He got an e-mail from an old buddy in his unit who wants to talk to him about something. He wouldn't tell me what, but I overheard him talking to someone on the phone."

"Why wouldn't he tell you?" Cat sipped her coffee. Seth hadn't told her anything except that he needed to be out of the retreat Wednesday night. Since there wasn't a need for a driver that night, she hadn't pressed for an explanation. Now, she wished she'd pushed a little more. Relationships were hard. If you didn't push, you were weak. If you did, well, then you were a word that rhymed with hitch.

"I think the bigger question is why he isn't confiding in you." Shauna walked back from her desk and sat next to Cat. "You two aren't fighting, are you?"

"No . . ." Cat sighed as she thought about their week away. "However, Seth doesn't talk about his time in the army. He never did, even when we were together back then. He'd change the subject when I asked. So I just stopped asking."

Shauna reopened her laptop and searched for a file. "Well, I say next week, after the retreat is over, we knock him over and sit on him until he gives and tells us what's going on."

Chuckling at the imagery, Cat said, "Or we could just ask him nicely."

"Party pooper."

Cat set her cup in the sink and moved to the door. "That's my signal to go upstairs and get some writing done. I love this being uncontracted thing. I can write anything or everything. It's surprisingly freeing."

"Your agent will call any day now with a new contract," Shauna said, not looking up from her work.

"Yeah, but by the time she does, I might just have another book finished and ready for her to shop." Cat waved and moved out to the hallway. Climbing the two flights to her office gave her time to think about Seth and his secrets. Was it better to let sleeping dogs lie? Or, as a good girlfriend, should she dig into the issue even if he made it clear she wasn't welcome in that part of his life.

Relationship road mine. She opened her office door and sank into her couch instead of going over to the desk to write. She had some thinking time to do before she could move forward for the book. Characters needed a clear path, or they'd wander around the page with no goals. Kind of how she felt right now. Wandering and lost. A lethal combination.

When five p.m. came around, she and Shauna were in the kitchen finishing up a double batch of chocolate chip cookies. It had become an arrival night tradition. Cat turned the heat on the tea kettle and sat down with a couple of cookies to wait. "He didn't call me when he started heading back."

"He texted me." Shauna put the last tray of cookies into the oven to bake. "Which leads me to ask one more time, are you sure you're not fighting?"

Cat shrugged. "I didn't think so. I mean, typically when we disagree, it's on the table and I know when I tick him off. But lately, he's been moody. Do you think he's reevaluating agreeing to do this hiking day? It can be a little overwhelming to be in charge of a full-day activity like that."

"I don't think so. He's been so excited about the hike and the trail guide he made up for the group. He told me that he's going to offer to take them out again on Thursday as long as they don't have a seminar." Shauna turned off the screaming kettle and poured two mugs of water. She sat one next to

Cat and pushed the basket filled with tea options toward her after grabbing one for herself. "So if it's not you, and it's not the seminar, it has to be this army thing."

"Probably." Cat knew Seth didn't like to talk about the time they were apart. And she felt uncomfortable bringing it up, especially since she'd been married to another man. But she couldn't change the past. A door banged in the foyer and Cat stood. "Speak of the devil and he appears."

Seth opened the kitchen door and poked his head into the room. "We're here. I'm glad the flights weren't delayed."

"I'll be right out to get them checked in." Shauna glanced at the oven timer. "I've got five minutes left on this last batch."

"Come when you can. I'll handle it until you do."

Seth grinned. "It won't take much. Did you know you had two couples signed up?"

Cat glanced at Shauna. "I didn't check the listing this month. We were so busy with the trip and then getting ready. Is it true? Are they couples?"

Shauna shrugged. "I guess so. I mean, we don't have a couple's rate, so they signed up individually. Maybe that's something we should look into. We could book more writers if we had people sharing rooms."

"And I'd have more writers to deal with." Cat laughed as she finished her cookie. "I'll have to think about this whole thing."

"I've got two waiting in the lobby and I'll run out and get the other couple now. They wanted to stretch their legs a minute." Seth held the door open for her as she walked out to the foyer. "They're really nice. One couple writes a travel blog. You should hear some of the stories they tell."

"You're making my ears burn." A tanned blonde smiled at Seth and Cat. "I told Tristin he shouldn't tell that story. People don't get the right impression of me when they hear about my obsession with skinny-dipping."

"Cat Latimer, meet Sydney Evans." Seth nodded to the woman standing by the double dozen of red roses on the desk in the foyer. "Sydney and her husband, Tristin, are writing a travel book on the Pacific Islands."

"We adore the Philippines. Tristin never wants to go anywhere else. I guess we should capitalize on his obsession." Sydney touched one of the roses. "These are lovely. I can't believe you go to the expense of two dozen for a retreat."

"Actually, those are a gift from a former guest's widow. She loves celebrating the retreat every month with us." Cat took in the overwhelming smell of the cold roses. They'd only arrived a few minutes ago and every time they arrived, Cat thought of Linda Cook and her husband. "Let me get you checked in."

"Well, the retreat must have changed this world for her to send such a lavish gift." Sydney put her arm in her husband's. "Tristin, this is Cat Latimer, she writes those witch schoolbooks I'm so crazy about."

"Nice to meet you. My wife has read every book more than once." He flashed a wicked smile at Sydney. "I'm supposed to ask you, casually, if the series got picked up for another contract. She's dying to know but didn't want to fan girl."

"Way to be casual." Sydney slapped his arm. She turned toward Cat. "But I am dying to know."

"Me too. My agent says she believes they'll pick up more, but we haven't heard anything yet. So I'm writing a new idea. It's still young adult paranormal, but it's a boot camp for the school's graduates who have joined the army. Not the US Army, but the other world's troops. So they are learning all about their powers and how to protect the ones who are gifted in that way." Cat laughed as Seth stared at her. "Or something like that. I've been meaning to get this guy alone and talk about his boot camp experiences, but we've been busy."

"I think you'll find it's a different world." Seth nodded to the luggage. "What room are you putting Tristin and Sydney in? I'll take these up for them. Pizza should be coming any minute, right?"

Cat handed Tristin a key. "Two-oh-one. It's one of the bigger rooms on the floor. I'll have Sydney fill out the registration, and you and Tristin can drop off the luggage."

She handed Sydney the card just as the front door opened and the second couple walked in. Archer and Jocelyn Winchester were an older couple, probably in their sixties from what Cat could guess. Jocelyn sat her quilted flowery bag on the bench, along with a leather purse, and took one of the pieces of luggage from her husband.

"I was just heading out to get your bags." Seth hurried over to take another case off of the pile.

"We're good. Josh and I travel a lot, so we've got this down to a system." Breathing a little hard, Archer stacked the other bags near the door.

"We didn't have to do this in one load," the

woman snapped at him. "We have all week to start researching."

"You know me, Josh." He looked down at his wife in amusement. "I don't want to waste any time. I can't believe we're actually in Colorado. Google doesn't do this place justice."

Jocelyn's, or Josh's, as her husband called her, face softened as she reached up and touched his face. "You're living the dream."

Cat smiled and waved them over to the desk. "Seth will be right down to help with the luggage. I've got your key ready if I could get someone to fill out the registration?"

"I'll do it." Jocelyn set the luggage next to her other items. Archer was busy checking out the beams in the foyer and the construction of the house. "My husband, Archer, here is too busy freaking out since we're in the land of his dreams."

"I take it this is your first trip out west?" Cat handed her a card and a pen. "I see from your registration that you're both writing western historical fiction?"

"Add romance to my genre and you've got it. We met at a writer's group in Pittsburgh twenty-five years ago and we've been making up stories about western expansion ever since. I'm hoping that we'll be able to talk a little about publishing this week because I'm tired of all the agent rejections saying westerns aren't selling." Jocelyn focused on the card, then handed it back to Cat. "There you go."

"We'll definitely have a lot of time to talk about your concerns. This is your retreat. We structure a lot of the sessions around your needs."

The door opened and a tall, handsome, twenty-something man walked inside. He grinned at the three women standing at the registration desk. "Well, this retreat is just getting better and better. I didn't know I'd be surrounded by such beautiful writers."

Cat glanced down at the last name on Shauna's list of attendees. "You must be Brodie Capone."

He dropped a tote bag at his feet. "In the flesh. The party can begin."

Chapter 2

Sitting around the dining room table, Cat could already see that Brodie wasn't fitting in to the group. In fact, no one seemed to enjoy the larger-than-life stories the kid told. Hopefully when the retreat started, he would focus on his writing and calm down, but for today, he was falling flat with his stories.

"So you're probably all wondering if I'm related to Al. Well, I don't want to drag the story out . . ."

"That would be the first story he didn't drag out in the last twenty minutes," Seth muttered low enough so Cat was the only one who could hear him.

She pressed her lips together and tried not to laugh, but she got his message. This group was going to be more of a challenge to facilitate. "Brodie, I'm sure the story is fascinating, but we have a tradition of letting everyone speak at the first night's dinner and I'm afraid you've used up your allotted time. Sydney, tell us about your goals for the week?"

Most of the writers let out a sigh as Sydney outlined her very impressive list of to-dos over the seven-day retreat. "Of course, tomorrow it's all about the hike. I'm so looking forward to seeing the nature of the area."

"Seth made you all field guides. I think you're going to have fun."

"Hiking is fun, but it's a lot more than that, especially in this area. You have to be aware of your surroundings at all times. People can get hurt if they aren't careful."

"I knew a guy who got lost fall semester and they didn't find his body until spring," Brodie added, shaking his head.

"We won't leave anyone behind," Seth promised.

"Are there any old mining cabins on our planned route?" Archer asked, his eyes bright. "I'm writing a story about a mining camp, so it would be amazing if I could see some actual artifacts."

"There's a ghost town a few miles from here. Maybe sometime this week Seth could drive you up. The town's closed for the winter as it's a tourist site with reenactments during the summer, but you can still walk around. You just can't get into any of the buildings." Cat thought about the writer's group that had spent their extra day experiencing Outlaw. It hadn't gone exactly how she'd planned it, but then again, when did a retreat go as planned?

"That would be awesome. I'd even buy the gas." Archer watched Seth's reaction.

He glanced at Cat. "Then it's done. We'll set up a plan and if anyone else wants to go, just let Cat or me know."

"I'd love to." Jocelyn patted her husband's arm.

"I'm better at taking pictures than Archer. He gets so excited, he forgets."

"So we know what Sydney has planned." Cat looked at Tristin, trying to change the subject before Brodie jumped in again. "What's your goal list for the week?"

"Man, I'm just in it for the experience." He smiled at Sydney. "Besides, my lovely wife has enough goals for the both of us."

"You're not getting away with that." Cat shook a finger at him and laughed. "This is your retreat too. Seriously, what do you want to get done? Word count? Planning?"

"Honestly? I'd like to try my hand at some short stories." Tristin's gaze darted to Sydney. "I loved writing short stories in college, but since we've started the travel book, it's been put on the back burner."

"Well, not this week. Our visiting professor is not only an expert on Hemingway, he teaches the short story class at the college. I'm sure he'd be willing to adjust his lecture to add in some discussion." Cat made a mental note to give Professor Turner a heads-up e-mail before his Tuesday talk. "And it will give you something to work on during the word sprints we like to do in the afternoons."

"Awesome." Tristin turned to Archer. "What are your goals besides soaking up Colorado history?"

Cat loved it when the group started to meld together. This one was going to be different, not only because of the overtalkative Brodie, but because of the fact the other four were couples. Cat decided she needed to watch this play out and see if she needed to adjust anything on the marketing side or the scheduling. Maybe after they remodeled the other wing, they could do a Valentine's Day retreat where they were all writing couples. Shauna could do a couple's cooking class and . . .

"Earth to Cat." Seth nudged her. "Jocelyn asked what your plans for the week are."

"Oh, sorry, I was thinking about a future session." Cat laughed at the stares she was getting. "A February session, just for couples. You all have me dreaming."

"Maybe we should just sign up now." Jocelyn patted her husband on the arm. "Archer is horrible at remembering holidays and anniversaries. This way he'll be a captive audience."

"I'm sitting right here, you realize that, right?" Archer kissed his wife on the cheek. "Just look at what you and Cat have in store. Wives are like elephants. They never forget."

Seth put an arm around Cat's shoulders. "Man, I've already learned that lesson."

"Okay, you guys, not all of us are coupled up here." Shauna glanced around at the empty boxes of pizza on the table. "Are you ready for some dessert? I have fresh-baked chocolate-chip cookies and a gallon of premium vanilla ice cream. It's made by a local dairy."

"Using virgin cow milk, I suppose," Sydney added.

The group erupted in laughter.

Tristin leaned over. "Cows make milk to feed their young. They have to have sex to have a baby." He looked at the group. "We haven't gone over the birds and the bees lesson yet."

"And you're married?" Brodie asked, raising his eyebrows.

"Okay, kids, keep it PG. We have a young one here." Archer slapped Brodie on the back. "Son, you're going to realize someday there's a lot more to marriage than just a little booty call every once in a while."

"And twice on your birthday," Tristin added.

"Lalalala." Shauna laughed. "So seriously, dessert?"

"Why not? My diet is on hold until we get back to Pittsburgh." Jocelyn grinned.

Archer leaned close. "I love you just the way you are."

"I'm heading up to my room to write. You all continue down here." Brodie stood and saluted the group. "What time are we on deck for breakfast?"

"Since you're hiking tomorrow, we'll have breakfast ready from seven to nine, when you're scheduled to leave." Shauna paused at the door. "You sure you don't want to take a couple of cookies with you? And there's drinks in the fridge in the cabinet."

Brodie opened the door and grabbed two bottles of water. "This will work. I'm still running cross-country on the college team, so sugar is off-limits."

"There will be fruit available all day, but you may want to rethink the no-sugar rule. Especially when Shauna makes brownies. Man, they're to die for." Seth leaned back in the chair and watched Brodie. "By the way, you didn't say what you write?"

Brodie stared at his feet, color filling his face. "I'm working on something new."

"Oh, like what?" Now Brodie had Cat's and the rest of the group's attention.

His blush intensified when he answered. "Just something new." He bolted out of the room with his water.

The writers around the table were silent. Finally, Sydney spoke. "Romance. My money's on romance."

"Erotic or Regency. Something got him blushing," Jocelyn added. "It's definitely not a thriller or what he considers an appropriately manly book."

"Leave the kid alone. At least he's not chatting our ears off," Archer added to the conversation.

Shauna came back with the cookies and ice cream, and the rest of the night was spent talking about life and writing and histories. Cat enjoyed the conversation, but when the writers had gone to their rooms and she was cleaning up with Shauna, she sighed.

"What's got your goat?" Shauna broke a cookie in half and gave part to Cat.

"I hope Brodie didn't just blow his chance to bond with the group. You know we've been really lucky that the Covington student has been brought into all the groups easily. This time, the odds are stacked against him coming in."

"He didn't help his cause tonight. The kid has an ego." Shauna bit into the cookie. "The other four have already gotten comfortable. I think they'll be fun."

"I agree. I'm just concerned about Brodie." Cat ate the cookie and wondered if there was something, anything, she could do to stop the train wreck she saw coming.

* * *

When Cat got downstairs the next morning, both Seth and Shauna were already in the kitchen. Seth was paging through the field guide and making notes while he tracked his progress on the computer-generated image of the hiking trail. Cat grabbed some coffee and looked over his shoulder. "Did you leave Shauna the trail information in case we don't show back up?"

He grinned at her. "This means you've decided to come with us?"

"Of course. What kind of host would I be if I stayed back?" Cat sat and grabbed a muffin from the basket on the table.

"You've checked the weather then. A balmy sixty-seven degrees."

Cat shrugged. "My weather app predicted low seventies. I think this will be the last warm day we see until spring. The weather guy says it's going to snow next week."

"As long as this hike is done before the snow falls, I'll be happy. Next year can we plan the hike the months from late spring to early fall?" He closed his computer. "I think I'm ready. I've gone over the trail three times already this morning."

"I'm just looking forward to getting out. I've been spending way too much time in my office this last week." Cat sipped her coffee. "I kind of outed my new book proposal. Do you think you'd be willing to read three chapters before I send it to my publisher, and let me know where I got it wrong?"

"It's fiction, it doesn't have to be accurate." He stood and refilled his cup.

"But you know that's not true. You of all people

get upset when someone gets something totally wrong when you're reading military thrillers. I know this will be the softer, gentler side, but I want some authenticity. I think it helps the reader relate."

He set his coffee down. "I need to go check the SUV and make sure we have the hiking packs ready."

Cat watched as he left the kitchen via the back door. "Was that a yes or a no? I couldn't tell."

"I think that was a skillful avoidance of answering the question at all." Shauna shook her head. "Maybe you should ask one of his friends from the military to read it. I don't think Seth wants to go down that path."

"Yeah, I'm getting that feeling." Cat glanced at the clock. "If you don't need me, I'm going to work for an hour in my office before I take off for the day. I've got some planning for the next release to finish."

"I'm fine. I'm sending you all with a cooler full of sandwiches, snacks, and a bag of cookies that Seth has already put into the backpacks. I gave you a bag of peanuts as well. I know you need your protein or you get grumpy. I guess I'll see you all this afternoon? Do you want late lunch or just an early dinner?" Sasha opened her laptop as she talked.

"Can we have potato and sausage soup? That will work for me for both. Then if Seth's still hungry, he can make a grilled cheese or heat up soup for dinner."

"Sounds good. I'll be baking this evening anyway to get ready for day one." She peered at her screen. "How do you know when it's ready?"

"When what's ready? Oh, the book? I guess now it's when I hit deadline or when I realize I'm just moving words around. Then your editor will let you know if you're off base. But I'm not writing a cookbook." Cat put a hand on Shauna's shoulder. "I know they are going to love it."

"Who are they? Right now, it's just you and me." Shauna blushed. "And my beta reader."

Cat stopped by the door. "You never told me who that was."

"Didn't I?" Shauna peered at the computer screen lost in the book. "I'll come get you when Seth's ready to go."

Cat paused for a minute, but when she realized Shauna was lost in the book, she gave up. Either Shauna didn't really have a beta reader, or it was someone she thought Cat didn't approve of. Either way, it wasn't her business. Cat had enough on her plate to worry about. Like where she was going to tour with her next release.

Her publisher had agreed to fund four stops. She had twenty bookstores or libraries that had expressed interest in hosting her. She needed to be smart with the marketing budget she'd been given. She opened the e-mail again and read the parameters and the deadline for a response. Then she started listing her top ten and a reason behind each choice.

By the time Shauna knocked on her door, Cat had narrowed the list down to six stops and made a runner-up list for the next release. She'd mixed it up by different parts of the country. Now she just needed to cut the list again and she'd be done by Friday. It would be a painful choice, but she thought if she just let things simmer, she might even make the decision earlier.

She turned off the computer and went to meet the others downstairs.

The hiking trails were less than thirty minutes out of town, but it felt like they were in the middle of the forest. The trailhead had a small parking lot. Cat had hiked this trail many times in the summer and used it to cross-country ski in the winter. It should be challenging enough for the Evans couple, but not too hard for the Winchesters. Especially Archer, who had a bit of a tummy on him. Brodie had decided to stay back for the day. Cat didn't know if he thought the cost of the extra day wouldn't be covered by the college or if he just didn't like hiking. Either way, she was glad for the quiet Brodie's absence would allow.

They all gathered around the car, their backpacks on. Seth held out his trail guide. "I asked you all to bring a watch. Did you?"

Hands went up and everyone showed their watch.

"Good. Now look at this. You all have one of these and a pen. Take them out and as you're walking, see how many of the flora and fauna you can find and put a check mark by them, as well as what time you saw the item. That way we can compare when we get back. I'm hoping we'll see some wildlife too. So don't be surprised if we come up on a deer or an elk on the trail. Hopefully you won't see a bear, but if you do, stay still until they move out of the way. We scare them as much as they scare us." Seth glanced around the group. "Any questions?"

"Yeah, since you brought up a bear, can I just sit in the car and write until you all get back?" Jocelyn smiled, but Cat could see her hand reach for Archer's.

"Don't worry, honey, you can run faster than I can so the bear will stop at me." He kissed the top of her head. "We're ready to go."

"Stay close and don't drag behind." Seth waved Archer and Jocelyn to the front. "You two after me, Cat, you can be in the middle, and, Tristin, can you and Sydney bring up the end?"

"Works for me." Tristin circled his arms around Sydney and kissed her neck. "But we might lag behind a little."

"Perv." Sydney stepped out of his embrace, but her smile didn't waver. "Don't worry about us, we'll keep up."

"Great. Then we're off." Seth started up the trail, and Cat waited for the first couple to follow.

The first hour went fast with a few stops to take pictures, as well as compare plants with the pictures in the book. By the time they'd reached the first outlook, where Seth was already stopped and waiting for them, Cat's legs ached. She leaned on a tree and stretched out her calves. "Too many hours sitting at the desk."

Jocelyn plopped on the bench that the Forest Service had set up near the lookout. She took out her water bottle and took a long sip before talking. "I haven't done anything like this since college. I used to be on the cross-country team and ran for miles. I guess I should pick back up that hobby."

"I can't believe they have a full setup here."

Archer glanced at the outhouse. "Tell me that's functional."

"The Forest Service maintains this trail year-round because it's also a cross-country ski trail. For most of the hiking trails the maintenance is shut down November first or at the first snowfall," Seth explained as Archer made his way to the small building.

"Great."

Watching the now-trotting Archer, Tristin laughed. "I guess when you got to go . . ."

Sydney slapped his arm. "Don't be mean. Give Cat your camera and come over here so we can get a picture of us by the overlook."

Tristin took his camera off from the lanyard that kept it around his neck. "Do you mind? We have at least one couple picture from every hike we take. And Sydney's right, this is a perfect spot."

"Not a problem." Cat glanced at the expensive camera and pointed to a button. "This one?"

"Yep, just point and shoot. The camera will focus in on our faces so it will set the correct angle and background for you." He grinned as he made his way to stand by his wife. "It was pricy, but our photo quality for the blog has gone up at least by ten times."

"He's always about the picture." Sydney put an arm around him and a hand on his chest.

Love, Cat thought. It was apparent that these two adventurers loved each other. She took several pictures, then looked at the camera to make sure she got a good photo. Frowning, she looked closer and when Tristin came back for the camera, she

shoved it in his hand and rushed over to the overlook.

"What's wrong. Did the pictures come out bad?"
Tristin stopped and thumbed through the shots.
"These are great."

When Cat reached the edge of the lookout, she
saw what she'd seen through the lens. A man's leg
stuck out from a huckleberry bush across the val-
ley to the closest mountain. Seth joined her.

"What's going on? What did you see?" He lowered his voice.

All Cat could do was point toward the bush. She
knew when he'd seen the same thing when he
took a quick intake of air.

"See if you have cell service and call your uncle.
I think our hike is over for the day." Seth turned
and looked at the three guests who were gathered
around the bench watching them. Archer came
out of the outhouse and frowned.

"Are you all waiting for me?"

Chapter 3

U ncle Pete met them at the bottom of the trail-head. "You know, I should have realized it was retreat week and not scheduled Shirley to come out for some R&R."

"Just because it's retreat week doesn't mean that someone is going to die." Cat felt defensive. "We could have just ignored the man's leg hanging out of a tree so you could spend time with your girl-friend."

"That's not polite." He shook his head at her. "You need to be nice to Shirley. She might wind up being your new aunt."

"Really? You two are that serious?" Cat was curi-ous. She'd known that her uncle was dating the re-tired Alaskan deputy, but she hadn't thought they would be making wedding plans yet.

"Gotcha. You should see the look on your face." He motioned to one of his deputies. "Run up with Seth and have him show you what they found so we know where to start looking."

The deputy nodded and her uncle leaned against his Charger. "You want to take the guests home? Seth should be back down in about ten to fifteen minutes."

"We'll wait. I think they're a little shook up, so having some time to process might be a good thing. Do you really think that my retreat is the issue?" Cat tucked a wayward curl behind her ear.

He pulled her into a hug. "I was kidding. Although Shirley is going to be a little bummed when I have to work all the time. Do you mind putting her up at the house? She made a reservation with Shauna for the bed-and-breakfast part of the retreat, but she might be hanging out with your writers more than we expected."

Shirley Mann was a retreat graduate. That's how she and Uncle Pete met. "I'm fine with her staying at the house. I didn't really plan for us to be a B-and-B, but Shirley's almost family, right?"

He grinned. "I'm afraid I'll have both of you sticking your nose into my investigation this time. But maybe you all can rein yourselves in a bit."

"We'll see." Cat nodded to the SUV, where the four writers stood, looking shell-shocked. "I better go entertain our guests. I am sorry about the body."

"As long as you didn't kill him, there's no reason to be sorry." He waved her away. "Go do your job, I'll do mine. I was planning on coming over for dinner tonight. Is Shauna cooking?"

"Soup and sandwich night. But you know you're welcome."

He shrugged. "We'll see how this goes. I was hoping for Sunday fried chicken. I've been trying to hear how her trip to New York City to see her brother turned out."

Cat frowned. "She's been pretty quiet about it now that you mention it. I've been busy since she got back and hadn't noticed that she hasn't been talking about her visit. Not at all."

"That's not like our girl. Especially a visit with a long-lost brother. Maybe you should feel her out."

Cat watched as Archer pulled Jocelyn into an embrace. "I better get over there. I'll check in with Shauna as soon as we get back to the house."

But when they did get back to the house, Shauna wasn't there. A pot simmered on the stove with their soup and a note said there were sandwiches in the fridge, but Shauna had checked out on the board.

"Our guests took off to The Diner for lunch. And Brodie isn't here; I checked his room." Seth wandered into the kitchen and went right to the fridge to grab a soda. He pulled out the tray of sandwiches as well. "Roast beef and turkey. Awesome. Where's Shauna? Should we wait?"

Cat shook her head. "Let's eat. The board says she's working at the library this afternoon. I can't believe she's taken to writing so quickly. She loves the process. I'm going to head upstairs and do some work before they get back. I know today isn't an official retreat day, but I like hearing about what they're going to work on this week."

"And see if they are traumatized from finding a dead body. Too bad this wasn't one of the groups of mystery writers. They would have loved the day's activities." Seth shook his head. "I can't believe I spent so much time on the field book and we only got to half of the hike."

"You can't foresee a death. I hope Uncle Pete finds it was just an accident. Shirley's coming in tomorrow, and they won't have any time together if he has a murder investigation to solve." Cat dished two bowls of soup. "She'll be staying here. I'm going to have Shauna put her on the second floor since we're only using three rooms this week."

"How are you dealing with her visit?" Seth set the sandwiches in the middle of the table and put the sodas he'd gotten from the fridge near the soup bowls.

"Shirley? I'll be fine. Look, I know I had a mini pity party last time her name came up, but Uncle Pete was talking about dumping everything and moving to the farthest place away from home." She took a spoon and sipped the soup. Just what she needed after the shock of the morning.

"He might still move; you need to prepare yourself for that. Pete's close to retirement himself. And although your folks went south to Florida, I think Alaska would fit your uncle's personality a bit more. I can't see him in a pair of Bermuda shorts sitting around some pool." Seth dug into the soup. "This is the best soup that Shauna makes. Which is saying a lot. Maybe she needs to write a soup cookbook?"

"Shauna wants to write all the cookbooks. I think we created a cookbook-writing monster." Cat laughed as she took a turkey sandwich off the platter and moved it to her small plate. "I'm happy she has something to keep her busy. Has she said anything about her trip to see her brother?"

Seth shook his head. "Lots about the city, but

Jake is still a mystery. I hope she didn't feel pressured to let him help with her inheritance."

Shauna had received a large sum of money from the death of her fiancé a few months ago. From what she'd told Cat, Shauna's plan was to leave it for a year until she decided what to do with the funds. Cat knew that her friend was still dealing with the emotions of Kevin's death. She didn't need to be pushed to do something rash with the gifts he left her. "I know, I'm worried too. Uncle Pete says he hasn't been able to get her to tell him anything about the trip either."

"We might have to have an intervention after the retreat on Sunday. If that brother of hers is causing trouble, we need to be a united front to make sure she knows that no is a complete sentence." He stood and refilled his bowl with soup. "I don't think I've heard anything about a missing person lately, have you?"

Cat felt shocked at the quick change of subject, but she should have known that Seth was still thinking about the body they'd found on the hike. "No, but that doesn't mean anything. A lot of people live alone in those woods. I'm sure Uncle Pete's going to be able to find out who it is quickly and get this solved. Or he will if he wants to see Shirley this week. Speaking of Shirley, can you pick her up tomorrow at the airport?"

"Already on my to-do list." He grinned when Cat appeared surprised. "You're not the only one your uncle talks to, you know."

"That's true." Since they were talking so easily about so many things, Cat decided to dive in. "Tell me about your meeting Wednesday night. Will it be people from your group, or just everyone who was in the army who lives nearby?"

"We're having a platoon reunion, so it will be people I was stationed with when I went over to Germany. A lot of the guys stayed in and got their retirement, so I'll get crap for jumping after the first post." He kept his head down as he ate his soup.

"I never understood why you left after four years. When we talked in high school, you were planning on making a career out of the service. Twenty years and done. You wanted to have it tattooed on your wrist." Cat smiled at the memory.

He pushed the empty bowl away. "Seriously? You don't know?"

Surprised, she shook her head. "Sorry, no clue."

He stood and put the bowl and his plate in the sink. Then he grabbed a second sandwich and wrapped it in a napkin. Cat thought he was going to leave without telling her, but he paused at the door to the basement. "I left the service because that life was our dream, Cat. Yours and mine. When you married Michael, I quit."

"Seth . . ."

"I'm going to stow the hiking stuff for the winter. I think the time's past to plan anything now until spring comes along." And with that he was gone.

Cat stirred what was left of her soup, but her appetite was gone. Had Seth gone into the service to start a new life for them? Had that been the plan all along? Cat remembered she'd been planning on teaching, hopefully at the college level. That's why she'd applied for her master's degree at Covington, along with the Oregon school where Seth had been stationed. Michael had convinced her to take the Covington offer, saying that it mattered where she got her degree, especially if she wanted to work at a good college. Michael, who had been her advisor, then her friend, her lover, and finally, her husband. Had Seth had plans of a life together, even before she'd fallen in love with him?

She heard the kitchen door open and turned to try to explain, but it wasn't Seth who came through the door. It was Uncle Pete.

"What are you doing sitting here alone? The only one I usually find in the kitchen by herself is Shauna, but that's because I think she actually sleeps here. I'm starting to think you're treating our girl like poor little Cinderella who slept near the ashes in the fireplace."

"We don't have a fireplace in the kitchen." Cat peered at her uncle. "Hey, remember back when Seth and I were in high school?"

"Of course, I do. Your mom would call and ask me to go find the two of you because you'd missed curfew again. I usually found you at the ice-cream shop, sitting in the car, talking about the future." He poured himself a cup of coffee. "Why the trip down memory lane?"

"When Seth started talking about going into the army, about his future. Was it because of me? Because he thought he had to take care of me?" Cat felt the tears behind her eyes and she blinked them away. She wasn't going to cry over something that happened years ago. It was just time to find out the truth.

Uncle Pete sat next to her and patted her hand. "Seth wouldn't want me to tell you this, but I know that's why he went into the army instead of going to school. That boy wanted the two of you married and having babies as soon as possible. But he wanted to have a job so if you stayed in school, he'd be able to support the two of you. I thought you knew this."

"Maybe I did, or at least, I suspected." Cat glanced at her now-cold soup. "I kind of messed everything up then, didn't I?"

"The heart wants what the heart wants." Uncle Pete patted her hand again. "And maybe both of you needed some time away from each other to figure out what you really wanted out of life. You were both so young. Things are good now, though, right?"

She smiled and stood with her bowl. "Yes, yes, they are. Can I get you some soup? There's an extra sandwich there too."

"Soup would be nice. It got a little chilly out on the mountain before we got the body out and over to the morgue." He took his hat off and set it on the table. Then he ran his hand through his thinning hair. "That's why I'm here. I need to talk to Seth."

"Why do you need to talk to me?" Seth came out of the basement door. "I didn't kill the guy."

"Well, we've got a bit of a dilemma. The body, we ran his fingerprints through the databases and we got a match."

Cat set a filled soup bowl in front of her uncle. "That's a good thing, right?"

He nodded. "Thanks. Yes, it is, except our results tell us that the man died over ten years ago. He was in your platoon, Seth. Name of Chance McAllister."

Chapter 4

Seth dropped his spoon and stared at Pete. "That's impossible. Chance died in Germany. He was part of an undercover mission and he didn't make it. They brought back his body. It must be another Chance McAllister."

"There's no doubt of who this guy was. I knew him as Chance, but I don't think he ever gave me his last name. He was living on one of the old mining claims up near Deer Creek. The guy's lived there for maybe ten years now. He did most of his shopping either online or at the store, as soon as it opened. I'm heading over to the post office now because he had a box there. I'm not expecting to find anything, but you never know. At least we'll know what name he was living under."

"Seriously, there is no way this guy is my Chance." Seth looked over at Cat. "It doesn't make sense. You remember him from high school, right? He played football."

"Kind of. He's the guy who dated Sherry Flood.

I thought they got married." Cat moved closer to Seth. His hand shook on the table and he quickly tucked it underneath when he saw it.

"They were planning to. But Chance, well, he was killed. In Germany." Seth leaned back in his chair and ran a hand through his hair. "We always joked it was bad luck that put us in the same platoon since we were from the same little town in Colorado, but he was a stand-up guy."

"I'm pulling his military records and verifying what occurred. I'm assuming that he must have faked his death back then. But fingerprints don't lie. He's definitely dead now and in the county morgue. I'm sorry for your loss. Again." Uncle Pete watched the emotions run over Seth's face.

"What about Sherry? Have you told her?" Seth glanced at his phone. "I might have her number here. We ran into each other a few times after I got back."

"Sherry Flood moved to California a few years after Chance's death. She's back in town now, married now with three little girls. Since Chance's parents are both gone, I made next of kin notification to her. She seemed a little shocked to hear he was still alive." He took his bowl to the sink and ran water into it. When he finished, he went back to the table to get his hat. "I need to head back to the station. I just didn't want you finding out through the grapevine about this. I know you and Chance were tight as kids."

Cat spent a few minutes cleaning up the kitchen and watching Seth, who hadn't said anything since Uncle Pete left. Finally, she grabbed the box of cookies from the counter. "Do you want one?"

He smiled as he looked at the open box. "Emotional eating is your thing, not mine."

Cat picked out a cookie. "What can I say. Food makes everything better. So . . . are you okay?"

He shrugged. "It's weird. I've already grieved for him once. I went to his memorial in Germany on the base and talked to his mom when I came home on leave. I'd said my goodbyes years ago. But now to find out he was really still alive? I have to admit, that has thrown me for a loop."

"Maybe one of your buddies can shed some light on what really happened. You're all getting together Wednesday night, that can't be a coincidence."

Seth paled as he stared at Cat. "What are you saying?"

"I'm saying that the universe is sending you exactly the right people into your life to help you make sense of this. Maybe he went AWOL and staged his death. Whatever it was, you're not going to know anything until you ask around." Cat narrowed her eyes at him. "Wait, what did you think I meant?"

"Exactly that." He stood and kissed her, soft and slow. "I'm going up to my room for a while. Let me know if you need something."

"Are you sure you want to be alone?" Cat tried to stand, but he put his hand on her shoulder, motioning for her to stay seated.

"I've got some things to think about. Look, I'm okay. It's just weird, that's all. And you know I don't like weird. It's been a bad day all around." He paused at the door. "If you want to delete the hiking trip from your list of offerings, I'd understand."

"Are you kidding? I mean, yeah, if we find a dead body every time we go hiking with guests, then I may rethink my decision, but for now, we're keeping it on the list of options." She broke her cookie in half. "You have to admit, it brings a bit of excitement to the week."

"Again, I'd rather have boring." He winked at her and left the kitchen.

By the time Shauna returned to the house, so had the writers. Cat paused at the kitchen door. "Look, I've got to tell you something, but it's going to have to wait. Are we doing dinner?"

"I thought you all wouldn't be back until late." Shauna glanced at the clock. "I guess I can make something. Maybe I have something frozen I can heat up."

"Let's do that." Cat watched as the group moved into the living room. "I'm going to go check in with the group and see what their plans are. Sunday's are a free night so I don't want them to think they have to hang around."

"Brodie went back to his dorm before I left. He said he'd be here about nine but not to wait up for him." Shauna shook her head. "He really needs to be here to bond with the other participants. I tried to tell him, but he insisted he had things to do. I believe he wasn't totally honest with me. And I think he's lonely."

"There's probably a good reason for that. I'll be right back in. I want to hear about your day after I tell you about our crazy outing." Cat waved and then moved into the hallway. She paused at the door to the living room. The two couples were sitting on the couches, talking. At least these guys had bonded. Even if it had been over finding a dead body.

"Hey, Cat, come on in." Sydney waved at her. "We're just talking about lovely Aspen Hills. We're thinking about taking a short walk around town since . . ."

She paused and Cat filled in the rest in her head, since the hike had been called off short. "That's a great idea. I was just coming in to tell you that Sunday afternoons are a free time so you're welcome to do anything. I'm going to talk to Seth and see if we could reschedule the hike for Thursday, if you want."

"That sounds great." Tristin nodded. "I still want to get some video of the area for our travel blog. I looked at The Weather Channel and it's supposed to be warm all week."

Archer narrowed his eyes. "What exactly are you calling warm?"

"Fifty-two during the day. We won't be out at night when it goes below freezing." Tristin slapped Archer on the arm. "Weren't you saying you wanted to be more active? This is what 'being active' looks like."

"Me and my big mouth," Archer grumbled.

Jocelyn laughed. "I guess we're all in then. I'm so glad you were able to reschedule. I enjoyed the hike right up until the end."

"Yeah, that was a surprise," Cat admitted as she moved into the room.

"Did they find out who the guy was?" Archer

watched her as she leaned against one of the wing-back chairs.

"They did, but they aren't releasing the name yet. Next of kin notification, I guess." Cat tried to play dumb on the subject.

"It would be so cool if any of us actually wrote mysteries," Jocelyn added, then seemed to dismiss the topic. "We walked through the campus on the way to lunch and the library is so beautiful. I can't wait to get busy in there tomorrow. I don't think you'll be able to pull me away from all the research sources I've read that the library owns."

"We'll go over just before nine. Our librarian has a little orientation for you before you use the library and then you're free until Tuesday morning when Professor Turner will be here to discuss Hemingway and short stories." She realized she hadn't updated the professor yet, so that needed to be on her list today if not right when she walked out of the room so she wouldn't forget. "We'll meet on Wednesday morning to talk about the business, Thursday will be the hike, and Friday is packed with a visit from the local bookstore owner, planned word sprints, and a wrap-up of the retreat. Then we celebrate Saturday night with a dinner at one of the local restaurants, my treat."

"It sounds like it's going to go so fast." Jocelyn sighed. "I guess I better be on my game and working when we're not in sessions."

"I would hope so. I want to start living the high life off your royalties." Archer leaned over and gave his wife a kiss. "Kidding, not kidding. I'm sure she's going to be the one who gets published first.

My books are a little history-dense to make it with a wide audience."

"Well, it looks like if we're going to see the sights, we better get going." Tristin stood and pulled his wife up off the couch. "Do you want to come along and be our tour guide?"

Typically, that had been the Covington student's unofficial job, but Brodie had made himself scarce. "I think you'll be fine. Take a picture of anything you don't understand and any of the three of us can explain or give you history on the house or building. I've got some things to take care of before we start tomorrow."

Cat waited for the group to leave and then went into the study on the other side of the stairwell. It had been her ex-husband's den, but she thought, with a little pride, she'd made it a part of the retreat and a more generalized area since she'd moved back. Michael's desk still sat in the middle of the room, but now, it held her stuff. She took a laptop out of the side drawer and booted it up. She then signed into her e-mail and composed a quick note to Professor Turner, asking him to change at least a little of his talk on Hemingway to add writing the short story. She layered on thick the part about him being such an expert and how one of the writers wanted to expand his studies in the genre. Being appreciative of someone's skills wasn't totally sucking up, right?

After she was done with that chore, she scanned the rest of her e-mails. Nothing from her agent. Nothing from her publisher. But a lot of spam asking if she wanted to learn how to write or if she needed some extra inches in the bedroom. Cat wondered if a human was even behind scanning the e-mail addresses since she didn't think many Catherines would be interested in that kind of marketing.

Closing the laptop, she tucked it away and headed back to the kitchen to fill Shauna in. By the time she got there, she was too late. Seth sat at the table, talking about Chance and his second death.

Shauna's eyes widened as Cat walked into the room. "Wow, I can't let the two of you go anywhere without getting involved in a murder. What did Pete say? How did Seth's friend die?"

"He didn't say." Cat went over and poured herself a cup of coffee. "In fact, he didn't even mention that part. It was more a notification to Seth. Uncle Pete kept everything else really close to his chest."

"Come to think of it, he didn't even say if it was murder or an accident. If Chance's death was an accident, wouldn't he have said that?" Seth stood and paced the kitchen. Then he sank into a chair. "Man, I just realized, I'm going to have to tell the guys about Chance."

"I think they'll just be confused. I mean, they all thought the guy was dead anyway." Cat sat at the table next to Seth.

"You're kidding, right? People are going to be mad. They'll question why we were told he was dead. And in the end, they're going to blame the government. Just another secret that 'they' kept from us." Seth made the air quote marks in the air. "Which means the reunion will turn into a conspiracy theory discussion and not a true reunion. Maybe I'll just wait until they leave and send a group message. That way I don't have to hear about how everything in the freaking world is a lie."

"Does the entire group feel this way?" Cat stared at Seth as he sank his head into his hands.

"Enough of them do. And fear breeds fear, so the discussion will always run back to this." He looked at Cat, hopeful. "What's the chance that Pete will solve the case and find the killer by Wednesday evening? At least if they have someone to blame, it might slow down the chants."

Cat shrugged. "Undetermined. I know he wants to solve it quickly because Shirley's coming in tomorrow. You have on your plan to pick her up at the airport, right?"

Seth nodded. "I might have to do some airport runs on Thursday too, in case some of the guys don't have transportation."

"Ugh, I told the writers that you'd take them hiking on Thursday. Do I need to move that to Saturday?"

He stood and started pacing again. "No, leave it. I'm not the official driver for the group just because I moved back here. They should be able to find a driver."

"Are you sure? Because I can just move it to Saturday."

"I said it was fine!" His voice echoed in the kitchen.

Cat glanced at Shauna, who met her gaze. She didn't remember the last time Seth had raised his voice. Even when they fought, it was more of a discussion. This was a side of him she'd never seen. "Okaaaaay then. Sorry for pushing."

He walked over and rubbed her shoulders. "I'm the one who should apologize. I'm letting this whole thing get to me."

The kitchen door opened and Uncle Pete walked inside. Feeling the tension, he paused in the middle. "Is this a bad time? Should I come back later?"

"No, we're just talking." Seth left Cat's side and plopped into a chair at the table. "I've got Shirley's ride scheduled in my book for tomorrow. So don't worry about that."

"Actually, that wasn't want I came to talk about." He poured a cup of coffee. "Do you have some time? I hate to ask, but I'd like your opinion on a few things."

"Like?"

Cat didn't like where the conversation was going. Seth's name had come up as a possible murder suspect before. She didn't want him put through that again. "Maybe he should just sit this one out?"

"You're not the boss of me." Seth's smile told her he was kidding with her. At least a little. "What do you need, Pete?"

"Come up to Chance's cabin with me. The guy's place looks more like he's the perpetrator rather than the victim." Uncle Pete glanced at Cat. "Don't take this the wrong way, but I'd like you to come as well."

"Why?" Now Cat felt shock running through her system, as well as being nervous about Seth. "You're always telling me to keep my nose out of things."

"I need a layman's viewpoint. To me, the cabin looks just like it should for a bachelor living off the grid. Except for one area. That's where I need your help because you're good at these puzzle things. Maybe you can figure out what he was watching." He shook a finger at her. "Now, don't you be thinking I'm going to invite you on these types of investigations all the time. This is a special circumstance, so I hope I'm not going to regret it."

Cat smiled but instead of responding, turned to Shauna. "The group is out touring the town and you know where Brodie is, so you should be guest-free until we get back."

"I've got to stock the dining room with treats and then finish dinner. Should I expect you back by six? Or later?"

"Better make it seven. I suppose you're not making your Sunday fried chicken." Uncle Pete looked like a puppy who was begging for a treat.

"Sorry, no, it's shepherd's pie. I can put one in for you, though, if you want." Shauna tapped her laptop. "I've been a little drawn into these edits today. Next Sunday, I promise I'll make you your favorite dinner."

"That would be great. Shirley's staying over to next Wednesday so she'll be here as well. I've been bragging on your chicken for a while, I think she'll feel left out if she doesn't get to try it before she leaves for home."

Cat started to say that dinners weren't included in the bed-and-breakfast rate they'd charged Shirley, but she swallowed the words. She was going to have to get used to the fact that her uncle had a new woman in his life and, therefore, in her world as well. And all things considered, she liked Shirley. "Let me grab my notebook and a backpack. I'll be right down."

"We're not doing an overnight," her uncle called after her. But Cat didn't even pause. She ran upstairs, grabbed some tennis shoes and a jacket, then went to her office for supplies. She pulled out a fresh notebook and a couple of pens. Then she tucked her phone in her pants pocket so she could take several pictures. Sometimes you could miss the important thing just because your attention was drawn to something else. Having the pictures to look at later would give her a better understanding of the victim and of the scene of the crime. Uncle Pete didn't like to share the official photos.

Seth and Uncle Pete were ready by the time she got downstairs. They continued their conversation about some football team as they got into Uncle Pete's Charger and headed out of town. Cat rode shotgun and she wanted to change the music, but he had so many attachments around the radio, she didn't want to touch anything.

Finally, Uncle Pete pulled the car over and they were at a trailhead. "We have to walk from here. I need to get this closed before the snow falls, or I won't know what's in the cabin until spring thaw."

Glad she'd grabbed a heavier jacket, Cat pulled it on as she got out of the car. The air smelled like snow. Cold, icy, and heavy. Seth always laughed when she told him this, but she'd been right every time she'd declared that snow was on its way. She didn't know if she had a special sense about these things, but in high school, she'd been called the weather girl by Seth's friends. "We better hurry then," she mumbled.

Seth glanced her way and smiled. He'd remembered her special power, even if he hadn't believed in it. They'd been hiking for ten minutes when they'd turned the corner and came out on a clearing. In the middle of the clearing, a small cabin stood. No electric lines ran to the house, and Cat wondered if they could even get cell service since they were on the opposite side of the mountain from town.

"He had an old hound that we'd found on the porch. He'd helped himself to his bag of dog food in the barn, but it was almost empty when we got here." Uncle Pete glanced around the cabin, which had an abandoned feeling. "Poor dog, if you all hadn't found Chance, he probably would have starved to death up here."

"Where is he now?" Cat asked as she snapped pictures of the area.

"We took him down to the shelter." Uncle Pete shook his head. "Tom, who runs the place, wasn't too hopeful that they'd be able to find a home for him before his time ran out. Senior dogs are really hard to place."

Seth stood near the step to the cabin. Cat could tell he was hesitating and reached out her hand to him. He grabbed it like a lifeline and they went to the front door, where Uncle Pete had just cut the police tape and unlocked the door.

He handed each of them a flashlight that he'd grabbed out of his backpack. "It's kind of dark in there."

Cat walked through the door, shining her light over the well-kept rooms. There weren't even any dishes in the sink. Chance had kept his place neat and clean. Cat wondered if it was the military training. Seth was that way too. For a bachelor, his apartment was cleaner than Cat's room ever was. She opened a door and shined her light on the walls. They were covered with paper and lines made of yarn. "I think I just found the party room."

"Seth, come see this. This is what I wanted to show you." Uncle Pete squeezed Cat's shoulder. "Leave it to you to find the needle in the haystack."

"All I did was open a door." Cat handed her flashlight to her uncle. "Shine that over on the first wall, please."

She started taking pictures and by the time she was done, Seth stood looking at the papers that Chance had taped on the walls.

"This doesn't make any sense. Some of it is from the little town in Germany where we were stationed. But there weren't any terrorists or radical groups there then." He pointed to a page a few feet away. "And this is a list of the professors at Covington. Michael's name is circled, but then again, so is Jessica Blair's."

Cat frowned. Why had Chance been interested in her ex-husband and one of her former friends? It didn't make any sense at all. She left the crazy paper room, as she now thought of it, and wandered through the rest of the house. She snapped pictures, one after another, until she heard her uncle call her name. "I'm coming."

She met them at the doorway to outside. "It's just so sad. One day you're living life and the next, you've fallen off the edge of the world and no one is there to feed your dog."

"The medical examiner hasn't told me this officially, but I'm thinking cause of death wasn't an accident. Chance McAllister was murdered."

Chapter 5

Cat spent the evening going through her pictures, trying to make sense of the room of pages. If she hadn't known Chance had been murdered, she would have put this all aside as the ramblings of a crazy man. But Seth didn't think his friend was crazy. He hadn't said much on the way home, but she could see it in his eyes. Seth thought someone had targeted Chance for something specific. Which could be on the walls. Or could be the money in his pocket. Finally, she pushed the laptop away and went to bed.

Her sleep had been disturbed with vivid dreams of an old hound dog standing at the door to her house. A handwritten sign was on the dog: PLEASE FEED AND LOVE ME. Cat knew one thing, she didn't need any more pets. They already had five barn cats and a horse. A big dog like the one that had visited her dreams wouldn't fit in the house. Not with monthly paying guests.

She pulled herself out of bed and into the shower

before the dream dog could look at her again with those big, sad eyes. She was a sucker for the underdog. And this dog certainly fit the bill. Someone would adopt him, she knew they would.

Dragging herself downstairs, she found Shauna already up and baking. If she hadn't met her friend in her prior job, bartending, she would have thought Shauna was some type of house fairy who lived in the kitchen. The truth was that Shauna had found her passion.

"Good morning. I swear, when the retreat isn't in session, you're always so bright and chipper in the morning. What is it about running the writers' group that gets you so down?" Shauna handed her a cup of coffee.

Cat sank into a chair and sipped the warm, lovely liquid. "I don't know, maybe it's the fact we keep running into dead bodies? What's going on with that? You know the Covington kids have started calling this place the Dead Body Retreat?"

"Hasn't seemed to stop them from applying to attend. Last month the dean told me we had more applications come in than any other month since we opened." Shauna nodded toward the ceiling. "Speaking of Covington, our favorite student is back in the house. He came in about nine when I was in the dining room cleaning up for the evening."

"I do hope he's going to at least try to be part of the group. The retreat has been a great learning process for the students if they bond and work with the other writers." Cat held on to her cup like it was a lifeline. "Anyway, today should be pretty busy, what with our first trip to the library and Shirley coming in this afternoon."

"I should have her here by one," Seth said as he came in through the hallway door. "I'll stop at a drive-in and get lunch for the two of us, but you may want to expect her for most of the meals. I think your uncle is going to be busy this week."

"Yeah, I got the message last night." Cat stood to refill her cup and gave Seth a kiss. "How did you sleep?"

"Badly. Chance just didn't seem like the type of guy to fake his own death and disappear. Why didn't I ever see him? I would have recognized him, I'm pretty sure." Seth poured his own coffee.

"You're saying you never ran into him. Not since you've been back from the service?" Cat studied Seth's face. She could see the pain etched around his eyes for his old friend.

Seth shook his head. "And that's weird too. Pete said he'd stayed off the grid and out of town except for emergencies, but to not see the guy in over ten years? That's just odd. I'm going over to visit his dog and see if I recognize him."

"You are friends with a lot of the local pets," Cat teased.

"Maybe we should think about taking the old guy in?" Shauna took one look at Cat's face, then laughed. "Or maybe not. I take it you're at the pet limit?"

"I just don't know how he'd deal with so many people around all the time. The insurance agent is already making noises about increasing our umbrella policy in case someone jumps on Snow and gets hurt." Cat grabbed a muffin and cut it in half.

"If someone gets on my horse without my permission, I'm going to be the one to hurt them."

Shauna stood at the stove cooking bacon. "And that's a promise."

"I'll make a sign for the barn. Something like, YOU CAN VISIT THE ANIMALS, BUT DON'T GET IN THEIR PENS. That way, if we expand at any time, I don't have to update the sign." Seth started to write down the task in his notebook. "What? A little too direct?"

"Maybe not direct enough. I'd prefer DON'T RIDE THE HORSE." Shauna lifted the crispy bacon onto a plate covered with a paper towel. "Who wants eggs and how?"

"I'll have two over easy." Seth took a plate out of the cupboard. "I can make my own toast. Do you have anything else going?"

"I've got two hash brown casseroles warming in the oven. The smaller one's for us. I'll take it out as soon as your eggs are ready." Shauna took out another pan and put some butter in the bottom.

The three of them worked on getting breakfast done so they would be ready for the writers who would be getting up soon for their first retreat day. Shauna had already set out coffee, juice, and several choices of breakfast treats to hold them over until eight when she put out the main course. Like the hash brown casserole in the oven. Today they would also have scrambled eggs and bacon.

Cat watched the other two as they moved around the kitchen. The retreat had been going for just over a year now and the days had a routine to them. Or they did if someone wasn't found dead during the first few days. Cat thought back to her first retreat, when the dead guy had been one of her writer guests. Tom Cook had already been a famous and successful author when he'd arrived, and it had been that fame that had put him in the killer's sights. Now, Seth had lost a friend. Again. It really didn't seem fair.

The door to the kitchen opened and Brodie walked in. "Sorry to bother you, but the coffee carafe is empty. Could I get a cup from here?"

"Of course." Shauna hurried over to take the carafe from him. "Let me fill this and I'll run it back out. But first, I'll pour you a cup. Do you want a travel mug or a ceramic one?"

Brodie blinked, confusion on his face, but didn't answer.

Shauna held up the two options and his face relaxed.

He pointed to the travel mug. "That one. My mom always said I was a klutz. I'd hate to spill on your carpet or something."

"Where are you from, Brodie?" Cat asked as she watched him move from one foot to another.

"Idaho. It's a really small town outside Boise. But when I got a full ride to Covington, I accepted right away. Mom said it was because of our last name. She said it made people nervous so they gave us what we asked for." Brodie took the cup from Shauna. "Look, I don't think I got off on the right foot with the other guests, so if you want me to leave, I will."

"Why on earth would we want you to leave?" Cat smiled at the obviously nervous student. "You're here for the retreat, so just enjoy it. They'll accept you if you just be yourself."

He smiled and held up his cup. "From your mouth to God's ear. Another one of my mom's favorite sayings."

He left the kitchen and the three of them looked at one another.

"That was weird." Cat was the first to break the silence.

"So what is his last name?" Seth asked.

Shauna laughed. "Capone. You don't think the college thought he was connected, do you?"

"Maybe he is and doesn't know it. He never said anything about his father." Cat pondered the question. Dante would know, but she'd promised both Seth and Uncle Pete that she'd stay away from the suspected mobster who had been her husband's best friend. Lines blurred in Aspen Hills, but even she knew the guy was trouble. The fact he was drop-dead gorgeous as well was beside the point. Especially since she and Seth had just gotten back together.

"Well, at least he's a little calmed down from yesterday. Maybe the guy has mood swings. What do you think, Shauna?" Seth set his empty plate in the sink.

"Are you asking because you think I have mood swings?" Shauna eyed him from the counter, where she was chopping fruit for the guests. She held up the knife, looking at it, then at Seth. "Seriously?"

"I would never insinuate something like that." He looked at Cat. "Shauna wasn't a knife thrower in a circus when you found her, was she?"

"Almost. The place where she bartended didn't

even bother to hire a bouncer for her shifts. She did all the work." Cat smiled as she scanned her schedule. "Okay, I'm heading upstairs to work, but I'll take the group to the library, so have everyone meet downstairs at eight forty-five. I don't want Miss Applebome giving me the evil eye because we're late."

"I could take them," Seth offered. "Miss Applebome likes me because I replaced the roof on her porch last year."

"Sure, suck up to the one woman in town who thinks I'm a thief." Cat refilled her coffee cup.

"You did take a book from the library without checking it out." Shauna pointed out without looking up from her chopping.

"It couldn't be checked out, or I would have. And besides, that book helped solve Tom Cook's murder." Cat held up a hand. "Fine, you're right. I took a book. But I brought it back. It's not my fault she has cameras all over the library."

"And that's what all the criminals say when confronted with their crimes." Seth moved to the back door. "Face it, Cat, you were saved by your uncle. Otherwise, you'd be doing hard time."

Cat put a lid on the cup. "For stealing a college yearbook? Besides, Miss Applebome wouldn't have pressed charges. This way she gets to make me feel guilty every time I walk into the library. I think it's her evil plan. To kill with kindness."

"See you all later. I'm heading to the barn to work on the loft. I'm worried about that roof. Especially if we get a foot or more of snow. I don't want the horse and cats to have to move into the house with us." He left through the back door.

"Do you need help with anything before I leave too?" Cat looked at her friend.

Shauna reached up and turned on the stereo. Country music poured out of the speakers. "I'm good. I'll come upstairs and get you a few minutes before you have to leave."

When Cat reached her third-floor office, she booted up her computer and turned on her own stereo. Her writing music was more classical than Shauna's tastes, but she needed to listen to only instrumentals, otherwise, she'd start singing along to the music. She glanced at her notebook, where she'd kept her timeline and notes on the book she was writing, but instead of opening her latest draft, she went to Google.

Keying in Chance's name, she added Aspen Hills just to see what would come up on the dead, then alive, and now dead again soldier. And as a habit, Cat leaned down and opened a drawer in her desk, pulling out a new notebook.

Absently she started writing down everything she knew about the man, including the fact he was in Seth's unit in the army. Then she added everything she'd found online, which wasn't much. She leaned back in her chair and looked at the notes. Then she returned to the pages and built a timeline.

Once that was done, she started searching for the town near the army base in Germany. Maybe there was something in the news about Chance, or something weird happened around when he supposedly died. She got a listing for a local newspaper, but it didn't have any online archives. She tucked the notebook in her tote and closed out Google. But instead of writing, she went to her e-mail program and cleaned it out, answering the last of the important missives just before Shauna knocked on her door.

"I'm ready." Cat shut down her computer and grabbed her notebook. She met Shauna at the door. "I'm going to hang around a bit at the library after I drop off the writers. I have some research to do for this new book."

"Research on army boot camps?" Shauna guessed as they walked down the stairs.

Cat nodded. It wasn't much of a lie. She was researching the army, just not for the fictional one she was writing in her book.

Cat was surprised to see Brodie standing with the group at the front door. "Are you coming as well? You probably could give Ms. Applebome's lecture by now."

"I want to come. Besides, we're going to Reno's for pizza afterward and I can lead everyone back here after lunch." Brodie beamed as the others nodded.

"Okay then, let's go." Cat let Brodie lead the way and she closed the door behind them. Jocelyn stood waiting for her on the porch.

She nodded to Brodie. "He came into the dining room at breakfast and apologized for yesterday. He said he wanted to help and be part of the group. I don't know what happened, but he seems to be a different guy. So, we haven't told him we actually know our way around."

"I like this new Brodie, so don't tell him." Cat smiled as they walked through the neighborhood and toward the college. They'd just come up on

Dante's place, but from the deserted look of the house, he must be out of town. When he or any member of his family was here, the driveway was filled with cars and people milling about.

"The houses here are so beautiful. They must have cost a fortune." Jocelyn glanced at Cat. "What did you get yours for? Do you mind telling me? Or is that a totally rude question?"

"Actually, we got it cheap because it was in horrible shape when my ex and I bought it. The college had used it as a frat house after the president had built a new home. There was a lot of remodeling that needed to be done. I think the college might have given Michael a bit of a deal on it because he was their star economics professor. I probably wouldn't have been able to put together the retreat without getting the house free and clear after my ex died a couple of years ago. Of course, now I have a remodel loan."

"Archer and I are looking at buying a house, but the area is just so expensive. We've started looking out in the suburbs. We could commute to our jobs easily enough with the mass transit system there." Jocelyn pointed to Dante's house. "Of course, it's not going to be anything like that one. What is that house, five thousand square feet?"

"Probably. I've only been inside once. But I don't think any of the old houses on the street are for sale right now. They go fast when they come up now."

"Well, at least you have a place where you can live and make a living." Jocelyn studied Cat as they paused at a corner, waiting for the light to change so they could walk across. "Are you making a living from the author gig? Or is it the writers' retreat that keeps food on your table?"

Uncomfortable with the question, Cat gave her standard line. "I make a good living from the books. I'm lucky that I get sizable advances to enable me to write. But I have to say, the retreat brings in enough money to keep the house going. A big house has a lot of expenses."

"Hopefully we'll be able to talk more about the business side of being an author?" She dropped her voice as they crossed the street. "I haven't told the others, but my agent called last week with an offer on a series. I'm not really sure if I should take it or hold out or just self-publish. There's so many things to think about."

"First off, congrats! That's amazing. But you are the only one who can make the decision on how you want to be published. I take it you were looking for a traditional deal when you got your agent. Maybe she can help guide you?"

"Maybe, but I want to know my options. Before I jump into something I might regret. I think we're all smarter if we talk to each other and share the information. Is that naïve? Archer says I'm just asking for trouble if I try to compare offers." She paused as the library came into view. "That place just takes my breath away."

"You're not naïve, you're smart. And we can talk about this on Wednesday without telling your secret to the rest of the group. Unless you decide to share. It's totally up to you. Most of my retreats do want to talk about the reality of publishing. Even though sometimes it's a depressing discussion."

"Then it's a good thing Shauna bakes us all

those amazing treats so we can drown our sorrows in chocolate and sugar." She paused at the bottom of the stairs. "Thanks for talking with me. I'd love to chat more just the two of us if you have some time this week."

"I'll make time." Cat grabbed the railing. "But for now, I need to get you inside for your Library 101 session. Your instructor doesn't like being kept waiting."

As Cat had predicted, Miss Applebome stood at the door to the library conference room watching as the group came into the lobby area. She waved the writers over and sniffed at Brodie. "I believe you could skip the class if you wanted to, Mr. Capone. But with your lack of study skills, it might do you some good to have a refresher."

Man, Miss Applebome *really* didn't like Brodie. Even more, Cat thought, than she disliked Cat.

Brodie smiled as he walked into the room. "I've been looking forward to getting a refresher. I'm pretty sure there's a lot of things about the library that I don't know."

As the rest filed into the room, Miss Applebome crooked a finger at Cat. Surprised, Cat moved closer to the older woman. "What's going on?"

"I wanted to let you know I'm sorry about Seth's friend, Chance. He would come into the library often, especially at night to research. He was obsessed with military strategy books." Miss Applebome looked into the room where the writers sat. "I can't believe anyone would want to hurt such a gentle soul."

Chapter 6

Knowing that Chance had been seen in the library researching before he died, Cat wondered how she could figure out what precisely he'd been studying. Miss Applebome had closed the subject and the door on her when she went into the classroom to give the writers a library tutorial. But, she'd given her an idea. Miss Applebome had referred to Chance as Seth's friend. The only time he'd probably used the library before enlisting was during high school. All the local kids got full access to Covington's library starting their freshman year. If he had been researching lately, he could have still used that access card. Cat crossed to where a bored student stood checking in books.

"Good morning. I was wondering if Chance McAllister had any books on reserve." Cat glanced at her watch, trying to imply a sense of urgency to her question.

"Let me look." The student flipped back her

long, straight blond hair and keyed into the computer. "Do you know his ID card number?"

"No, sorry. I didn't get that from him. Can you just look up by name?"

The girl shrugged. "Sure. Hold on a minute." She went back to the screen. "Yeah, he has four on hold. None of them have become available yet."

"Can you print me off a list of those books and the ones he's checked out in the last six months, no, make that the last year." Cat tried looking as bored as the other girl appeared. "I'm helping him document his thesis."

"If you don't do it while you're researching, it can be a beast to complete the listing afterward. I don't envy you." The girl hit a key and pages started coming out of the printer. "Especially this guy. I hope he's paying a bunch of money, since there are pages of books."

"Thanks. I'm probably getting way less than he should be paying." Add in the fact the guy was dead and couldn't pay anything, Cat figured the lie wasn't that much of a stretch. She took the pages from the girl and went to sit at a table away from the registration desk. Glancing through the books, it looked like Chance was doing a study of early Colorado history and gold mining techniques. Cat knew there were still some gold miners who lived by themselves in the mountains. Had this guy been one of them? Maybe that was what had gotten him killed. He'd found a little bit of gold in a creek and hadn't been as secret about it as he should have? But then again, whom would he have talked to? She put the book lists into her notebook, then went over to the computer to start looking up newspapers that might have online archives from around that time. Two hours later, she was out of ideas and hadn't found even a mention of Chance McAllister except for his high school football stats.

She tucked her notebook into her tote and left the library. The bright sun had warmed the day so she took her puffer jacket off and stuffed that into the tote as well. Heading home, she decided to stop at the Written Word, Tammy Jones's bookstore on Main Street. The bell rang above the door as she walked into a smell of paper and coffee. No one was at the checkout desk, so she moved through the displays to the back of the store, where Tammy had an office.

"I'll be right out," Tammy called from the back.

"No worries. I'm just looking for military books," Cat said.

"Go to the left under the windows. I don't have many, but there's some good ones there." Tammy was used to Cat's strange research requests. She didn't always buy books from the store, not if they were available at the library and she wouldn't use them again and again. But if she was going to dog-ear a book due to her need to keep referencing it, she purchased a copy. Like her book of spells she'd bought for Tori's education at her new school. Cat didn't want to drown the books in witchcraft knowledge, but she needed some to be able to craft the story and make it feel real.

The thought always made her smile since she was trying to make a book about a teenage witch feel real. The same thing would occur with the new boot camp book. Even if Seth wouldn't give her information about the real-life experience, she'd find it somewhere.

She squatted next to the shelf and touched each book as she looked at the topic. Nothing that would have the information she was needing. She stood back up and, turning, almost ran into Tammy with a pile of books in her arms.

"Hey, Cat. I didn't realize it was you. What are you doing here?" Tammy set the books on the table.

Cat reached out and took the first one off the pile. It was a new release from a famous thriller author. She'd never met the guy, but she'd heard rumors he wrote one book a year and always started writing on September first. She sat it back on the pile. "I'm looking for a book that describes the boot camp experience. Preferably in the army, but right now, I'd take anything. Even fiction."

"Hmmm, let me think. If I remember right there's a choose your career book about joining the army. I don't have one in stock, but I could order it for you. I'll look around and see if there is anything else that might help too. Boot camp, huh? Doing some research?" Tammy grinned. She was a true fan of Cat's series, and they'd started meeting over coffee to talk about writing. Tammy wanted to write a novel and thought picking Cat's brain might help her get started.

"Yep. You ready for your seminar on Friday? The guests are travel bloggers and historical writers, both general and romance." Cat realized she still didn't know what Brodie was writing, but he could stop into Tammy's shop anytime.

"I wanted to tell you how much I'm loving these

sessions. I learn so much just talking to other writers. It's been amazing for my writing." Tammy grinned. "And they've been good about buying books, so it's been profitable too."

"Best of both worlds." Cat glanced at her watch. "I better get back. Shauna's probably got lunch on the table. "Thanks for looking for me. I'm just trying to get a feel for the time even if what I'm writing doesn't have to match up exactly."

"I would hope not. You have such a lovely paranormal and young adult voice. I'd hate to see you go into a genre that didn't match your style."

Leave it to Tammy to be blunt and direct. Cat didn't take offense. "See you Friday!"

"Looking forward to it," Tammy called after her.

Cat wandered home, thinking about the new book and the scene she wanted to write as a reaction to the scene she'd written a couple of days ago. The writer's mind. It stayed focused on a story until it was finished. The author may not be able to tell you what day it was, but they could tell you when a plot point happened and what they decided to do about it.

When she opened the door, Shauna was on the phone, her back to the door.

"Look, I told you I'd think about it. That means more than one day. Sorry if I'm not meeting your timetable, but I'm not rushing into this. I have to be certain on the investment before I decide to spend that much money." Shauna turned and saw Cat in the doorway. "I've got to go. I'll call you later this week."

Cat closed the door. "Sorry if I interrupted."

"Cat, it's your house. You don't have to apologize." Shauna tossed the phone onto the table. "I haven't wanted to bother you with this, but I'm a little fed up with my brother."

"Jake? Uh-oh, didn't the trip go well?" Cat walked over and sat at the table.

Shauna shrugged, then joined her. "I should have realized that my parents had told him about the money Kevin gave me. He was all about me getting it set up in a portfolio that would be making twenty percent."

"What? He told you he could make that much? That sounds either impossible or really risky." Cat shook her head. "My financial planner doesn't even like mentioning double digits."

"Yeah, he's promising way too much. Either he's delusional or he's in some really risky investments. Either way, I don't want my funds to be invested with family. It makes bad bedfellows." Shauna tapped her fingers on her laptop. "I'm going to send him an e-mail directly stating that, because when I tell him no on the phone or in person, he doesn't seem to understand the word."

"I'm sorry. I know you were hoping for a better outcome." Cat didn't have siblings, but she knew Jake's pushing would have kicked Shauna in the gut.

"Well, it is what it is." She leaned back in her chair. "I'm surprised you didn't ask for a chunk to buy into the retreat."

"You're already a full partner. How much more money do you want to put in? I guess we could build a pool out near the barn, but it would cut down Snow's pasture." Cat stood and grabbed her a soda.

"I didn't put money in. You had the house. You should get something," Shauna protested. "I've been thinking about this for a while. I could pay off the remodel loan."

"Let's think about that." Cat held a hand out. "You need to hold off and not do anything with that money for a year. Let it sit while you're dealing with the grief. Then, after a year, if you want to put some skin in the game, I won't fight you."

Shauna nodded. "I guess that's fair. Just don't let me slip and give it all to Jake. I have a feeling I'd be poor by Christmas if I did."

"You're smarter than that, even if he is family." Cat glanced at the clock. "Do you want help with lunch?"

"Actually, I've already made sandwiches for French dip. All we need to do is heat up the au jus and make French fries. We still have about thirty minutes before noon. Unless you're hungry now. Seth and Shirley are eating on the way back from the airport." Shauna paused as she was lifting the cover on her laptop.

"No, thirty minutes will be fine. I'm going to run upstairs and check my e-mail. I'll be down to help as soon as I'm done." Cat stood, but Shauna held up a hand.

"Look, thank you for being a good friend. You could have just taken my offer of money and run."

"I might still. Let's see how our profit and loss statement holds up through the winter months." Cat grinned as she left the room. The house was quiet with the guests all at the library. Since a couple of them were writing history, she'd bet that they would be spending as much time as possible combing the stacks while they were here. But evenings, she bet the living room would be filled with chatting writers.

The house felt happy when the retreat was in session. Like even the house enjoyed the warmth and comfort of a lot of people living inside. Maybe it was the yummy smells that came out of the kitchen all day and half the night while Shauna baked for the group, but mostly, she thought it was the people who made the retreat feel homey.

She powered up the stairs and worked at her computer until her timer went off. Then she signed off for the day. If the writers did word sprints, she'd use the laptop in the study. During retreat weeks, she saved her manuscript in the cloud so she could work anywhere in the house. On non-retreat weeks, she worked only in her office. That way she could close the door and call it a day rather than thinking she needed to work longer and longer hours—one of the bad habits she'd picked up when she'd been trying to teach and write at the same time. She'd had no life. Now that she was back in Colorado, she'd decided she would have a life as well as a career. Which made her work harder, and be more focused during the times she did write.

Going downstairs, she was met by her uncle. "Hey, what are you doing here?"

"Actually, I was looking for Seth, but Shauna already told me he was on his way back from Denver with Shirley. So I was sent to get you for lunch." He followed her down the one flight of stairs.

"Why did you need to talk to Seth?" Cat had a bad feeling it was about Chance's death. And when her uncle shook his head, she knew she'd been right. "You can't just pop in and not tell me what's going on. Frankly, you have to expect it's the price of the meal."

"You're saying there's no such thing as a free lunch?" He chuckled as he held open the kitchen door for her. "I guess I could give you a teaser."

"After we eat." Shauna set the last plate on the table.

Cat took in a big breath. The kitchen smelled like a roast had been slowly cooking all day long. Her stomach growled in response. "That works for me. I'm starving."

They ate in silence for a few minutes; then Uncle Pete stood. "Anyone else need some iced tea?"

He refilled the three glasses when both Shauna and Cat held up their hands. Then he sat back down. Dipping a fry into Shauna's special French fry sauce of ketchup and horseradish, he focused on her. "You haven't told us about your trip. What did you get to see? Any shows?"

As Shauna listed off the shows and tourist spots she visited, Cat noticed she never said we, just I. Apparently Jake had been too busy to show his now-wealthy sister around the sights. And yet he'd just assumed she would invest in his projects. Cat saw a worried look cross Uncle Pete's face and wondered if he'd figured out the same thing. Of course, he had. The guy was a trained investigator. Not an amateur like her.

But to his credit, he just nodded and then went into a story about how he'd seen *The King and I* with Yul Brynner on his one and only trip to New York City. "My wife always kidded me that it was that experience that made me love live theater. And she probably wasn't wrong. I could feel the dance scene and wanted to learn to waltz, just like the king had."

She smiled as her uncle told his story. He had a natural gift of storytelling, bringing you into the scene. To make you feel like you were sitting beside him in the darkened theater and watching the play with him back in the day. She knew where she got her love of story.

As they cleaned up the plates and Shauna put a brownie with a scoop of ice cream in front of each of them, Cat focused on her uncle. "Okay, tell us what's going on with the case. Did you already find out who killed Chance?"

"You must think I'm a miracle worker. Or maybe the guy scribbled a note and put it in his pocket just before he died. Like 'if you find me dead, look at Jim.'" Uncle Pete took a bite of the brownie. "Shauna, I don't know how you do it. Your desserts are like heaven."

"Just time and practice. Probably a lot like what you do when you're investigating." She slyly moved the conversation back to the subject.

"Well played." He sipped his coffee, then leaned back in his chair. "I don't know how much you've figured out already but . . ."

"I . . ." Cat started to tell him she wasn't investigating, but from the look in his eyes, she stopped. He'd known she'd at least try to figure out more about Chance McAllister. Especially since he'd known Seth. "Sorry, go on."

"Chance apparently had bought that gold mine

claim and cabin before he enlisted. His folks didn't know about it, so nothing happened to change ownership when the estate was settled. He was young, there wasn't much of an estate except the insurance money." He took another bite of the brownie. "So, after he apparently died in Germany, he came home, got into the country, and started living in the woods. From the people I've talked to in town, they've said Chance had been there for years. They couldn't pinpoint a beginning."

"He was that far off the grid? But what about bank accounts? Did he have a car?" Cat couldn't imagine living so close to town, but so out of touch with reality.

"From what we found in his cabin, he had paper accounting on one bank account. It got a deposit once a month and he lived on a portion of that. Two thousand dollars on the first. At least that's what we can see from his records. We're trying to track the deposits down. The problem is the bank doesn't have a record of Chance having an account. So we're trying to figure out what the name on the account is. That's why I wanted to talk to Seth. The grocery store had several charge slips from the last day he came in. I want him to look at them and see if the names mean anything."

The room got quiet and Uncle Pete finished his brownie. "I guess I better go back to work and see if anything else came up from the computer scans."

"That's it? That's all you have?" Cat was floored.

"Until we know who he was and why he was

killed, yep, that's all we got. A man living under an assumed name and being paid a nice chunk of change to stay under the radar."

"It's got to be the military or maybe the CIA," Cat murmured.

Uncle Pete put on his hat and kissed both her and Shauna on the cheek. "Thanks for lunch. And keep your conspiracy theories down to a dull roar, okay? We work in fact here, not maybes."

After he left, Cat and Shauna looked at each other. Then they said at the same time, "Definitely CIA."

Chapter 7

Seth arrived home at two p.m. Alone. He grabbed a couple of cookies and sat at the table, where Cat and Shauna were sitting discussing the next few retreats. They turned and stared at him.

"What?" he mumbled through a mouthful of cookie.

"Did you forget why you went to Denver?" Cat asked.

He laughed and finished the cookie. "No, my charge had me drop her off at the police station to see Pete. Her bags are in the back of the car. I thought I'd see what room you wanted her in before I hauled them inside."

"Did you talk to Pete when you dropped Shirley off?" Shauna asked.

"Yeah, we talked. You guys are starting to scare me." Seth stood to pour a cup of coffee. "Why are you asking so many questions?"

"Just tell us." Cat leaned back in her chair. "You know what we want to know."

"Oh, you're wondering if I knew any of the names from the charge slips." He grinned as he set down.

"Yes, that's what we're wondering." Cat looked at Shauna. "It's always a waiting game with him."

"And you love it." He sipped his coffee. "Anyway, I found a name that I thought looked suspicious. Dwight Washington. Two of Chance's favorite presidents."

"Why would you purposely call yourself Dwight?" Shauna closed her laptop. "It's been a long day. I'm going upstairs and reading for a bit before I have to start dinner. Let me know if you need anything."

Cat watched her friend leave. "I'm worried about her."

"I take it the family reunion wasn't all she thought it should be?"

"Yeah." Cat left the subject where it was. If Shauna wanted to tell Seth about her brother, it was her story to tell, not Cat's. "So how's Shirley?"

"She's good. All tanned from Alaska's summer is what she said, but I think she's been hitting the tanning beds. And her hair is different. Highlights, I think." He winked. "I guess she's getting ready for visiting Pete."

"If I can think of her as a writer, I'm okay. Thinking of her and Uncle Pete, I wig out just a little." She remembered something she'd found that morning. "Did you know that Chance was studying local history and gold mines?"

"Part of being a good panner is knowing where the big hits were in the past. If I was trying to find gold, I'd be reading all the old texts written during the gold rush. Then I'd study the maps and see if I could land a perfect mining claim." Seth grabbed a third cookie and broke it in half. "It would be hard, especially without GPS finders and the fact that streams don't flow the same way as they did back then."

"So you'd have to take into consideration things like mudslides and maybe even forest fires." Cat pondered the idea.

"Exactly. Because your text may reference something that's not even there anymore." He finished his cookie and stood to take his cup to the sink. "So, where do you want Shirley?"

"I think Shauna set up room 210. The key is on the desk out in the lobby. Put it back there after you drop off her bags, and I'll check her in when she decides to show up." Cat glanced at the clock. She had a while before she had to play hostess to the writers. "I'm grabbing a book and heading to the living room to wait for the writers to come back from the library. Although they may not come back since it's so close to dinnertime."

"Well, after I drop off the bags, I'm going back to my apartment. Pete wants me to go through my stuff and see if I have anything of Chance's. Or anything about his death. I'm sure I stuck the news report into my trunk."

"You have a trunk filled with things from your time in the army? Don't tell me you have a gun in there too."

"If I had a gun, it would be perfectly legal and registered." He let his lips curve into a smile that portrayed a lot more than humor. "You could come over and search me."

Cat felt her body heat and she shook her head.

"No time, the retreat is in session. And I'm sure you meant search *your house.*"

His eyes danced with humor. "Did I?"

"I'm going to go read. We can talk about what you really meant next week, when we don't have five extra people in the house." Cat met his gaze. "I love you, Seth Howard."

"I love you too, Cat."

He left the kitchen through one door and Cat left through the other. She'd left the mystery she'd been reading in the study so she went to grab it off the desk. Michael's desk. She smiled as she brushed her fingertips over the antique wood. Some people only got to love one man. She'd loved two, but had come back to her high school sweetheart. The world felt right.

Pushing away thoughts of both men, she settled onto a living room couch and got lost in a futuristic world where good did conquer evil, even if it took three hundred pages.

The guests came in right as she'd finished the book. She was sitting in the living room, in what she liked to call a good book coma or hangover. Where her mind didn't want to leave the magic of the world she'd just created as she read the story.

Sydney found her first. "There you are. We're just popping in to get ready for dinner. Although it feels like all I've been doing today is reading and eating. Do you want to join us?"

"No, go ahead. Shauna's making us dinner here." Cat patted the couch next to her. "Come sit down for a minute and tell me about your time at the library. What did you work on?"

"Well, I spent the afternoon soaking in travel

books. I love looking at the pictures and imagining ourselves on that trail or in that swimming hole." She grinned and Cat thought she was imagining something else too. "But my dear husband, he was working on a project up in the literary section. I do believe he's kicking the dust off his fiction-writing muse."

"He mentioned he enjoyed writing short stories." Cat knew the third floor of the library had an amazing assortment of how to write books, including a few dedicated to the art of the short.

"Well, he's got the bug again." Sydney glanced at her watch and then jumped off the couch. "And I'm going to have to hurry if I'm going to be ready to leave soon. We'll talk later."

"Sounds good." Cat listened to the chatter of the writers as they made their way upstairs to their rooms. She loved this part of the retreat, where everyone was super excited about their plan. She'd have to make sure that Professor Turner had gotten her message about changing up his seminar tomorrow. Tonight, after they came back, she'd offer to sit and talk business or craft, or they could watch a movie. In her year of experience, groups typically chose the movie, being a little too shy at the beginning of the retreat to open up about their careers.

She stood and stretched. Shauna should be in the kitchen by now; she'd go see if she could help finish with dinner. But when she got to the kitchen, it was empty. She glanced at the clock. It was fifteen till and her friend liked to eat early so they were done by the time the writers came back from dinner.

Cat wandered upstairs to the third floor and
knocked on Shauna's door. When no one answered,
she tried the knob. It was unlocked. Cat peeked inside, but Shauna wasn't asleep on the bed. Instead,
two photos lay on the bed. One was a picture of
two dark-headed kids. Probably still in elementary
school, grinning at the camera like they were clowns.
The second was a more recent shot. Shauna and a
man who looked like the boy in the other picture,
but grown up, looked solemnly into the camera. No
joy on either face, the picture contrasted the other
like night and day. Shauna had been trying to reconnect with the brother of her memories. Instead, she got the financial planner from hell.

Life wasn't fair.

She shut the door. If Shauna wasn't in her room
or the kitchen, there was one more place to look.
The barn.

As she reached the lobby, she saw her uncle and
Shirley coming in the front door. "You're here."

Shirley threw herself into Cat's arms and
squeezed. "It's so good to see you."

Cat, a little surprised at the over-the-top emotion,
patted the woman on her back. Finally, Shirley released her. "You too. Did you have a good flight?"

"I had to change planes twice. Who goes to Seat-
tle and then Los Angeles just to get to Denver?"
She glanced around the lobby. "This place hasn't
changed a bit. Maybe I'll do some writing in my
room since Pete has told me I've made the trip for
nothing."

"That's not quite what I said. I just have to solve
the murder of this gold miner and then we can go
to Denver this weekend, like we planned." He fo-

cused on Cat. "Tell me you're going to keep her busy this week so I don't have to feel guilty."

"I'm kind of busy with the retreat," Cat reminded him. "Of course, as a graduate, Shirley's welcome to attend any of our sessions, but I'm not going to be able to play tour guide."

Shirley patted her hand. "And no one expects you to babysit me. I know my way around. I'll attend some of the seminars, wander through the campus, and maybe even do some writing. I haven't picked up the manuscript for a few weeks. This could be a good thing for me."

"I'm so sorry about the change in my schedule. At least when I go to Alaska, they don't call me back to work a case." He pulled her into a hug. "We should just meet up there instead of me trying to save a few vacation days."

"Yet. They haven't called you back yet. And it's fine. I'll be fine. I'm pretty sure I've said that a few times now." She focused on Cat. "How many times does it take for your uncle to get the point?"

"I'm not sure I've even reached it." Cat handed Shirley a key. "Shauna said she already charged your card for the week, so if you feel abandoned and decide to leave early, we'll refund you the days."

"Cat! That's a horrible thing to say." Uncle Pete looked at her like she had a third head when she and Shirley started laughing. "Oh, I get it, play with the old guy's emotions. See if you can get a rise out of him."

"She's a chip off the old block." Shirley took the key. "Did Seth get my luggage upstairs?"

"Yes, ma'am." Cat closed the desk where they kept the keys and locked it. "We'll be having dinner as soon as I find Shauna. You're welcome to stay."

"Your uncle is taking me to that Mexican restaurant we went the last day of the retreat. But I'm sure I'll see you all soon." She turned and smiled at Uncle Pete. "Talk to your niece for a few minutes. I'll run upstairs and get ready."

Uncle Pete followed Cat into the kitchen, where Shauna was working at the stove. "I thought she was lost."

"She was." Cat paused by her friend. "Where were you? I went upstairs to find you, but you weren't in your room."

When Shauna turned toward her, Cat could see she'd been crying. "I was blowing off some steam with Snow. Jake called because he didn't like my e-mail answer, so the conversation got a little heated."

Uncle Pete poured himself a cup of coffee. "Shauna, there's some things you should know about your brother."

"Like he's a jerk and a crook and was trying to steal my money? Those kind of things?" Shauna brushed a stray tear off her cheek. "Your newsflash is a little late. I'm already quite aware of what he can do."

"I'm sorry, Shauna." Cat put a hand on her friend's shoulder. She didn't deserve this, not while she was still grieving the loss of her boyfriend. It wasn't fair. Family should be there for one another, not just to make money.

Shauna turned back to the stove. "It is what it is, Cat. You can't expect a leopard to change its spots. I'd just hoped for more."

"If you need backup, you let me know. I don't want him pressuring you." Uncle Pete watched Shauna's ladder-straight back. "You deserve a lot more."

She turned and walked over to where he sat. Then she kissed him on the cheek. "I have everything I need. A group of friends who love and respect me. And a horse in the barn."

"Don't forget the cats. You have cats to play with," Cat added to the thankful list.

The door opened and Shirley came in. She paused at the edge of the room. "I've interrupted something."

Cat stepped toward her, trying to give Shauna some time to compose herself. "Not at all, you're right on time. I'm jealous of your dinner tonight. That should be lovely. I only get to the restaurant on retreat weeks now."

"I love the food there. Especially the margaritas." Shirley came and sat next to Uncle Pete. "But I'm not positive this is the best time for you to take off from the case. Are you sure you have time?"

"I have to eat. And if I get to eat with such pleasant company, it's a bonus in my eyes." He patted her hand. "The case will keep. I've run into a dead end and need to let the clues settle in my head."

"I'm an excellent listener if you need to bounce off some theories." Shirley squeezed his hand.

"I wish that line worked on him when I said it." Cat met Shauna's gaze. "He tends to get grumpy when I try and help. Doesn't he, Shauna?"

"Don't drag your friend into this. Besides, I get grumpy because you're not a professional. One of these days you're going to get hurt or wind up in the wrong place." Uncle Pete put a finger to his lips. "Oh, wait, that already happened last month."

"I was just looking for Shauna, honest." Cat held up her hand. "And I wasn't hurt."

"You're lucky. That's all. You always have been walking under a heavenly star. Your mom said she was going to make you a pillow with *Where Angels Fear to Tread* embroidered on the front." He stood and held his hand out to Shirley. "We need to get going if we're going to make our reservation."

"Have a great night," Cat called after them.

But they were lost in each other. They waved, distractedly; then Cat heard Uncle Pete whisper to Shirley, "You look lovely."

After they left the room, Cat shook her head. "Man, they're so sweet I feel like I'm going to get diabetes."

"I think they're cute together. And such a perfect match. Maybe you should write a crime mystery about two retired police officers who solve crimes together while falling in love." Shauna stirred something on the stove.

"That's an idea, but I'm not much on the cozy mystery type of story." Although Cat had to admit, the idea had legs. And maybe would touch a chord with the readers. It could be something she should look at . . .

"Cat? Where's Seth?" Shauna asked, and broke Cat's train of thought.

"He ran to the apartment. Do you know he has a trunk with his army stuff in it?" Cat went to the counter and grabbed plates and silverware. "It's kind of creepy, keeping all that stuff, don't you think?"

"I think it's lovely. It's a way for him to reconnect when things get mixed up, and memory is a funny thing. Sometimes it plays tricks on you. Better to have documented proof of what actually happened. That's why I journal every day. I want my life to matter."

Cat wasn't sure what journaling had to do with having a life purpose, but since this was the most words her friend had said since getting home from New York City, she let the comparison go.

The door flew open and Seth stepped inside. "Where's Pete? I need to show him something."

"What did you find?"

Seth held up a leather journal. "I wrote notes about my time in the army. I thought maybe you would—well, never mind. But when I went back to read about Chance's death, I'd forgotten one piece. They never found a body."

Chapter 8

"Well, that makes sense now, but why did they think he was dead?" Cat watched as Seth paced the room. "Didn't you say they'd brought back a body?"

"They did. It just wasn't Chance's. After reading my notes, I realized there were a couple of guys who were on the same mission. They found one guy, but the other two, the commander told us they'd died in a fire. I assumed they'd found the body later, especially since the base held a memorial for all three. It was a crazy time and I was assigned on a different project and working ten- to twelve-hour shifts when this all went down. Security on the base went up and we were locked in for several weeks after the incident."

"So he might have just disappeared." Cat reached for the journal. Seth tucked it under his arm. "Where is Pete again? The station said he checked out to come here."

"To come here and pick up Shirley for dinner.

You missed him by about fifteen minutes." Shauna nodded to the table. "Sit down and we'll eat and you can tell us what's in the journal."

"I'm going to run up to my room for a minute and I'll be right down." Seth left the kitchen before either woman could speak.

"What's in the journal he didn't want you to see?" Shauna set a plate of pan-fried pork chops on the table.

"You got that feeling too?" Cat shook her head. "No clue, but he's being pretty closemouthed about the time he was in Germany. Maybe he was on a top-secret project?"

"Could be true, but he said he was keeping the journal for you." Shauna returned to the table with a baking dish with bubbly macaroni and cheese right out of the oven.

Cat nodded to the fridge. "I'm not going to ask because obviously he wants to keep me out of it. Do you want something to drink?"

The rest of dinner, a steaming bowl of green beans cooked with a few bacon crumbles, was placed on the table, and Seth arrived seconds after that. He always was good at showing up right on time for meals. Even when they were dating in high school, Seth ate with her family on most nights.

The conversation turned to things not murder as they enjoyed dinner. When a door shut in the front, Cat hurried and put her plate in the sink. "Sorry, I've got to run and play hostess. Do you need me to take anything out to the dining room?"

"Already set up for the night." Shauna waved her off. "Go play with your writer friends."

"I'm going up to my room to watch the game."

Seth cut a piece of chocolate cake and put it on a plate. "Let me know when Pete comes in. I've texted him, but he might not check his phone before he leaves."

"With an active investigation? I'm sure he's at least monitoring it." Cat paused at the door. She thought about pushing Seth on the journal, but then dismissed the idea. She had guests in the house. If she and Seth needed a talk, it would have to wait until after they got on the plane on Sunday.

She moved through the hallway and saw Brodie in the dining room. He was refilling his coffee and had a plate filled with treats sitting on the table waiting. "Hey, are you the only one back?"

He nodded, carefully checking the seal on his travel mug. "They were all still chatting about houses and married life, so I came back to write."

"What are you working on?" Cat took a brownie and broke it in two. She sat down on one of the chairs and watched him.

He glanced around, checking to see if anyone was in the room. Even though the room was empty, he dropped his voice. "I'd appreciate it if you kept this between us, but I'm writing a young adult fantasy book."

"Really? I didn't peg you for a fantasy guy." Cat studied Brodie. His blond hair and too-straight teeth could have gotten him elected to any office on campus. Fantasy geeks were usually less Brooks Brothers than Brodie portrayed. She guessed he hadn't had a lesson in branding yet, and she mentally added it to the list of things to talk about. Readers liked it when their favorite authors were a lot like them. And Brodie looked prelaw, not swords and sorcery.

He sank into his chair. "I haven't told anyone, not even my professors. They think I'm writing some crime thriller and they always want to read it. I've tried, but when I sat down to start this, the words just flowed. And I'm fighting for every sentence with the other book. Do you think I'm making a mistake?"

"You have to go where your muse is taking you. Writing should be fun. Your first reader is you. And if you're not having fun, neither will your readers." She leaned back in her chair and broke the rest of the brownie in half again. "So what do you love to read?"

"Tolkien, Robert Jordan, Katherine Kurtz." He sighed. "My folks didn't approve of me wanting to write for a living. They said I needed a real job to fall back on when I failed with writing."

That was less than supporting. Cat didn't say the thought aloud. Instead, she nodded. "I get that they are worried about you. Being an author is a hard road to go down. You have to be at the right place at the right time to break out. But writing something that's not authentic to your voice, that's a guaranteed way to fail. Your readers will feel the conflict in your story. And not in a good way."

"So you think it's okay? That the book will sell?" Hope seeped into his eyes.

Cat took another brownie and repeated the process, breaking it in half. "All I can say is if you don't try, you'll never know. Let your professors read your stuff. Write as much as possible. Then make a decision. Right now, you're failing without even trying to succeed."

"I already told the group I was working on a crime fiction book." He shook his head. "I feel like such a liar."

"Sometimes it's hard to admit to anyone when you're doing something that is so close to your heart. Be open with the group. They'll understand." Cat smiled and thought of her past retreat writers. "And if they don't, well, you'll probably never have to see or talk to them again. They are a great critique group for you because you're not invested in what they think."

"You're brilliant." He jumped up from his chair. "I'm going to go write and tomorrow, when we're having breakfast, I'm going to let them know what I'm writing and apologize for lying. Do you mind if I use the study on this floor?"

"Not a problem at all. And it sounds like you've got a solid plan for the week." Cat stood and followed him to the study. "I just need to grab my laptop off the desk."

She left him there and settled into the living room to play with her new story. It was good to write something different. Some people never found their true voice because they want to write what they think will sell or worse, what they think they should write. People needed to realize that writing is all about telling the story. And if you don't like the story you're writing, write something different. She opened her word processing document and got lost in the world she was building.

About ten, she realized the writers hadn't come

back. Shutting down her laptop, she took it into the kitchen. Shauna had already cleaned up and shut everything down. She sat her computer on Shauna's desk and checked the back door. It was locked. She hadn't seen Uncle Pete or Shirley come in either, so they must be at Bernie's with the writers. Bernie's was the local watering hole where townies and college kids mixed on most nights.

Cat didn't like drinking on nights before she had to write, and she wrote most days, so for the last couple of years, she'd been cutting back on her alcohol consumption. But with the writers for this session being couples, maybe there was the idea of date night pulled into the retreat. Either way, she felt this session was going to feel different from the last few. She couldn't decide if that was a good or bad thing, but it definitely was a thing.

She turned the lights off in the kitchen, then mirrored the action with the lights in the hallway and foyer. The lights over the stairs stayed on constantly to keep guests from missing a stair on the way down for a midnight snack or bottle of water. Each guest had a key and she had her cell number on the door sign, just in case someone had left the house without their key cards. She glanced around the foyer, then made her way upstairs and settled into bed to read.

The next morning, she woke early and got downstairs to find Shauna setting up the dining room for brunch. "I don't think your writers have much of a sweet tooth this session. A lot of the treat plates were untouched."

"I think they were at Bernie's last night." Cat glanced at the cookie plate. "Do you need any help?"

"No, I've got everything set up for the early risers, but we may not have many of them." She put a cover over the just-from-the-oven cinnamon rolls.

As if to prove her wrong, Brodie strode into the room. "Hey, I guess I'm the first one awake."

"I guess so. Do you need some breakfast now, or will you wait for the group?" Shauna turned to face him.

"I'll wait." He smiled at Cat. "I've got some things to say anyway. But I'll have one of those rolls. My mom used to make these on Christmas morning to hold us over until breakfast."

"Most of my best memories surround food." Shauna plated up a cinnamon roll. "The coffee's fresh and there's orange juice in the pitcher there."

Cat followed her out and into the kitchen. "Brodie's writing fantasy. That's his big secret."

"Well now, I would have only been more surprised if you'd said romance." Shauna set the tray she'd brought back in from dropping off supplies back in its place on the counter. "He doesn't look the part."

"That's exactly what I thought." Cat poured herself a cup of coffee. "We had a long chat last night since he came home to work while the others went out to play."

"Did Seth catch Pete?" Shauna glanced at her watch, then poured a cup of coffee too and sat at the table.

"Not that I know of. I went to bed about ten and

they hadn't come home yet." Cat didn't want to think about Seth's journal. "Today Professor Turner is talking at ten as normal. I've asked him to speak on writing the short story."

"Instead of Hemingway? How on earth did you get him to agree with that?"

Cat shrugged. "He didn't actually agree. I sent a message via e-mail. But I'll check with him this morning when he gets here to explain it to him."

"Sounds like a fun job. The man does love his Hemingway." Shauna sipped her coffee. "Oh, by the way, do me a favor and pick up the phone this week."

Typically, that was Shauna's role since she could schedule someone a lot faster than Cat could even hope to open the software. Cat slipped into a chair by her friend. "Sure, but can I ask why?"

"I think you know." Shauna leaned forward, putting her elbows on the table and hiding her face in her hands. "Seriously, I should know better than even to think things in my family could be normal. I was so hopeful that Jake had grown up finally. Did I tell you that when I was bartending in LA he came to stay with me for a week and stole my rent money?"

"You have to be kidding." Now, Cat felt thankful that she didn't have siblings.

"He showed up in town, spent one night, and when I woke the next day, he'd written me a note saying he needed to 'borrow' the money and I'd have it back in a week." She rubbed her face. "He just didn't say what week. I asked him about it when I was in New York, after he'd hit me up to be my money manager for Kevin's inheritance. He sat there and lied, saying he'd sent me the money and I must have forgotten."

"Harsh."

Shauna nodded and sipped her coffee. "The guy's a loser and now he knows where I'm living, it will take a while for him to get the message that I'm not supporting him in his wild schemes anymore."

"Well, I'll pick up the phone, but if I get him on the line, I'm going to speak my mind," Cat warned her friend.

Shauna laughed and stood, taking ingredients out of the fridge to start a breakfast casserole. "I wouldn't expect anything different."

Cat finished her roll and refilled her coffee. She headed upstairs to work in her office for the next few hours. She'd sent a chapter to her agent last week and hoped to see a response before she got too far into this book. Especially if Alexa didn't think she could sell it. Cat knew it wasn't always about the quality of the writing or the story that made the difference in a possible sale. A lot of times it was about the market and what publishing houses were buying. If the idea didn't ring for her agent, she'd put the story away and start something new. But she really, really wanted to write this story and a few more books afterward.

That's why she loved working in series. The story was never totally complete, and the world she'd built stayed alive as long as she was writing in it. Details fell away, but she'd be walking in town or in a new part of Denver she'd never seen and think, this would be a great place for a character to live. Or work. Or have grown up. The stories were always with her.

She wondered if Seth and Uncle Pete had talked. Would Seth's journal have insight into why Chance had disappeared in Germany, only to resurface back here, hiding in the woods under another name?

She read through her e-mails and deleted most of them. Then she checked the date on when she'd sent Alexa the chapter. Had it really only been four days? *Stop watching the water boil in the pot.* As she opened her Word document, a knock on her door brought her out of her musing.

Every time she'd tried to sit down and work, a distraction happened. At least it did when she let it. Expecting one of the writers, she closed the window on her computer before calling out, "Come in."

"Don't hate me for disturbing you." Uncle Pete came into the room, a plate of cinnamon rolls in one hand and a carafe of coffee in the other. "I come bearing gifts."

"I've already eaten one." The smell of sugar and cinnamon and coffee filled the room. She stood and crossed the room, taking a pile of papers off the small coffee table and putting them on a side table. Then she grabbed her cup and refilled it from the carafe. "But I'll run on the treadmill later."

"Smart planning." Uncle Pete handed her a napkin and held out the plate. "You pick."

Cat didn't hesitate. She grabbed the closest roll and took a bite before setting it on the napkin. "Shauna is a food goddess. That's all I have to say."

"You're not alone in your assessment." He nodded to the computer on the desk. "Did I interrupt
your writing?"

"I was just getting started, so this is a good time."
She sipped her coffee. "What's going on?"

"I wanted to thank you for taking in Shirley this
week. I know my absence will be less of an issue
since she can do all that writing stuff." He stared at
her. "You two are a lot alike. You both live in your
heads a lot."

"Thanks, I think?" Cat set her cup down. "But
you already thanked me for letting Shirley stay
here. And besides, she is paying for her room. I'm
sure Shauna gave her a deal on it, but she's a paying guest, not just a drop-in, so no worries."

"Well, there's another favor I have to ask you."
He leaned back and pulled a notebook out of his
pocket. "I would ask Seth, but he's a little out of
sorts right now, trying to deal with Chance's
death."

"Did he tell you about the body?"

Uncle Pete nodded. "I'm trying unofficial chan-
nels to see if I can get any confirmation of that, but
officially? The army is standing by their statement
that Chance McAllister died in Germany."

"Okay, so how do they explain who is in your
morgue?" Cat broke off a piece of the roll. She
wasn't hungry, but it was so good.

"They say the testing must have been wrong."
He sat the book on the table and tapped it. "I
found this in the cabin. It's filled with a lot of conspiracy stuff, but I wondered if you could see the
man behind the words. Tell me what you think."

"I'm not a profiler." Cat stared at the book, part

of her not wanting to touch it. The other part ached to know his story.

"You're smart. You have good instincts about people. And I think your writing mind sees things differently. I'd ask Shirley, but then she'd fall down the rabbit hole and want to work the case with me. I'd like to keep her out of it if possible. This is supposed to be a vacation, not a consultation." He focused on his cinnamon roll.

The room was quiet for a few minutes while they ate. Uncle Pete wiped his hands on his napkin and put the fork on the plate. He looked at the journal that Cat hadn't touched. "Are you interested? I don't ask you to be part of the investigation often. In fact, usually I'm trying to keep you out of these things. I need you this time."

She sipped her coffee. "I'll see what I can do."

Uncle Pete rose. "Then I'll let you get back to your writing. I'm walking Shirley to the library this morning. She's got some research to do."

"Ask Shauna for the extra library card we keep on hand. That way if she finds something she wants to check out, she can bring it back to the house." Cat stood and followed him to the door. She touched his arm. "Thank you."

"For what?" He looked down at her and smiled the way he always had, no matter if it was first day of school or just before the senior prom. He'd always been there for her.

"Thanks for letting me in on this investigation." She hugged him.

He ran his hand down her hair and patted her back, just like he had so many times before. "I hope I don't regret this."

Chapter 9

Cat forced herself to write, to get her allotment of words done before she'd allow herself to get lost in the project Uncle Pete had given her. But the mere presence of the journal sitting on the coffee table kept distracting her from the task at hand, so by the time she was at her daily word count, it was time to go downstairs and talk to Professor Turner. She'd start reading Chance's journal after lunch. She closed down her computer and as an afterthought, locked the journal in her desk, then locked the door to her office. Normally, it was open, but on retreat weeks, she made sure to lock it just in case a writer would try to wander in and claim her spot. She didn't mind sharing the house, but her office was her sanctuary and off-limits.

She got downstairs just as Professor Turner was coming in the front door. She glanced at her watch. He was twenty minutes early. Just enough time for some treats in the dining room and for him to totally rearrange her living room. She hurried down the last few steps and crossed the foyer to greet him. "Professor Turner, I'm so glad to see you. It seems like we haven't run into each other for ages. Come into the dining room and let's get some coffee. Shauna made your favorite muffins for today."

"Oh, my, well, isn't that lovely." He glanced in the direction of the living room. "Maybe I should set up first."

She took his arm and led him to the dining room. "No need. I've got the chairs all arranged. All we have to do is get out the white board and move the lectern so you have somewhere to talk from. Or, you really should consider just sitting down and doing a fireside chat type of lecture. I'm sure you'd feel better not being on your feet so much."

"Oh, I like standing and talking. It makes me feel like I'm in my classroom." He chuckled. "I guess you can't teach an old dog new tricks, can you, Catherine?"

You mean like getting you to call me Cat? "You are definitely not an old dog." She nodded to a chair. "Now, you just sit there and I'll get you your coffee. Do you want anything in it?"

"Black's fine." He set his briefcase on the chair next to him. "I got your message about the lecture last night and although I'd love to help . . ."

"Great! Tristin is so looking forward to it. He looked you up on the college's website and your short story class is all he can talk about." She rolled over his objection, setting down the cup of coffee and a plate with a muffin and two cookies on it. "I wasn't sure if you liked chocolate chip or peanut butter, so I got you both."

"You're spoiling me, Catherine." He took a bite of the muffin. "I guess I could shorten the Hemingway section just a tad. You know your guests are always welcome to come and chat with me during office hours. I'm not sure I've mentioned that before."

Only every time you speak. Cat smiled. "I'll be sure to send them your way when they have a question. Sometimes I just feel like I'm guessing on some questions. I mean, I only taught first years during the time I was at Covington. Well, and the journal students. That was always fun."

"The journal work is very important to the status in the academic community of our English Department at Covington. You should never say 'only.' You were a valued member of the faculty when you taught with us. I'm surprised the dean hasn't invited you back. At least on a temporary measure."

Cat shrugged. The dean had offered her a creative writing class for next year's schedule. She just hadn't decided if she was going to take it. Teaching took up a lot of writing time and frankly, with the retreat going better than she'd imagined, she didn't need to teach. But without a new contract, she needed to do something with her time. No use blurting all this out to Turner so he could pass her hesitancy back to the dean. "Maybe someday."

"Professor Turner, I didn't know you'd be here." Brodie stood in the doorway between the dining room and the hallway. He stepped inside and held out a hand. "I took your short story class two years ago? Brodie Capone?"

"Yes, of course. You were writing those very literary shorts. I was very impressed." Professor Turner shook his hand.

"I'm thinking about switching up to young adult fantasy for my genre." Brodie grinned at Cat. "I've had some interesting discussions with the others in the group, and they all agreed I should write what I love."

"Well, sometimes writing isn't just about what you love, Brodie. It's an art and you need to treat it with the respect it deserves. I wasn't being polite when I said I loved your stories. You should try to send some to the literary journals to see if you can get published. It will do wonders for your career." He picked up his cookies. "Sorry to hurry out, but I need to get set up for the seminar. I'll see you inside."

Brodie looked crestfallen. Cat put a hand on his arm. "Don't listen to him. Journals are great for those of us who want to teach. But if you really want to write fantasy, no one should be able to stop you. Not even a well-liked professor."

He nodded, then looked across the hall, where Professor Turner had just entered the living room. "To be honest, I didn't *really* like his course."

Cat grinned and grabbed a bottle of water. "I better get in there before he starts moving couches. See you in a few minutes?"

"Definitely. I'm bringing my computer so I can write while he talks. That way he thinks I'm paying attention."

"A man with a plan. I like it." Cat turned and followed Professor Turner into the living room. She'd returned her own laptop there and after setting him up and letting him have time to go over his notes, she sat in the back of the room and checked her e-mail. Still nothing. An instant message came over her screen and she opened the bubble.

Want to do lunch at The Diner when you're done with the seminar? Seth's message asked.

She typed her response: *Sure, but what about Shauna?*

The answer came too quickly. *She can cook her own lunch. I'll tell her we'll be out so she doesn't overprepare.*

Sounds good. Cat smiled as she typed the response. Kind of like playing hooky. She and Seth had escaped from classes a few times in high school and once when she'd been a freshman at Covington. He'd brought a picnic lunch and they'd gone to the park to sit and talk. It was the week before he'd been deployed. After he'd left, she'd gone to that park to sit and read a lot. Until they'd broken up.

As she sat, listening to Professor Turner wax poetically about Hemingway, she started planning her next month. She could have this new book finished and a proposal done. Then she'd send it to Alexa. And then she'd start on a new Tori book. If her publisher wanted it, that would get her ahead of the game. And if she sold the new book and got an extension on Tori, then she'd need the prep work to enable her to keep commitments for two series.

And if they didn't want it? She took a deep breath. Well, she'd just cross that bridge when it happened. She finished up her planning, putting everything on her calendar. Weekly word count goals. Tentative deadlines. Retreat weeks. By the time Professor Turner asked for questions, she had planned out the rest of her year. And she'd even set aside time for date nights and girls' time. She smiled at the finished product. The most exciting part of the plan was she didn't have anything planned for the week between Christmas and New Year's. Maybe she could talk to Seth today about scheduling a trip to somewhere warm and tropical. Rolling her shoulders, she closed the computer, happy with the work she got done.

"Professor Turner, thank you again for an excellent seminar." She walked up to the lectern, where he was putting his note pages into his briefcase.

He glanced up at her, a surprised smile on his face. "Well, thank you, Catherine. I'm always impressed with a student who is as attentive on their notes as you and Mr. Capone are. I'm always suspicious of students who take notes by hand. Who knows what they're writing in those notebooks of theirs."

"Well, you know I love a good seminar." She put a hand on his shoulder and started to walk him to the door. "Thank you again, and I'll be sure to let the guests know you are available for additional consults on Hemingway if they need you."

He stopped short and looked at her. "Also short stories. I *would* enjoy working with your students on short stories. I'd forgotten how much I love the format."

"Yes, definitely. Short stories as well. Maybe you could keep that part of the lecture available for next month. We can try it out with a few groups and see if it's well received." She handed him his jacket.

"That sounds perfect. You always have such good ideas." He tipped his head. "Thank you again, Catherine. Lovely to see you as always."

When he'd left, she turned and found Seth standing in the foyer, watching her. "I can't believe how good you are at the political BS."

"BS 'r' Us." She walked over and put an arm around him. "Turner's a nice guy. Just a little obsessed for my tastes."

"Yeah, I hear you're dating a guy who doesn't even have a degree." He smiled down at her. "And you being a full professor and all."

"I was a full professor. Now I'm just an author with a side hustle." She glanced around. "Maybe we should leave now before anyone collars me for something."

"Too late for that," a male voice said behind them.

Archer and Jocelyn stood on the stairs behind them.

"Oh, don't listen to him. You two are such a cute couple. Go ahead and escape. We're fine. The group of us are going to Reno's for lunch." She held a finger up. "And before you ask, yes, Brodie's coming. The boy can be a charmer when he wants to be."

Archer glanced down at his wife. "Do I have something to worry about?"

She slapped his arm. "I'm old enough to be his mother."

"Oh, surely not, maybe his older sister?" Seth corrected her.

Jocelyn giggled. "Now aren't you a smooth

talker? No wonder you convinced our Cat to run away for a lunch date."

As we walked toward town, Seth took Cat's hand in his. "The writers this month are funny people."

"Funny? As in humorous or weird?" She hadn't spent a lot of time with any of them this retreat, which was unusual. She wondered about the dynamics of having two sets of couples at the sessions. Was that what was throwing it off?

"Funny as in different. The group feels different this time," he said.

"I feel it too. I think it's because they're married. They talk to each other more. There's not an opening for others to get in there. And since the other people are a couple too, they don't see the difference. Except poor Brodie. He's the outsider in the group."

"Maybe that will change and they'll accept him."

Cat shrugged. She had to accept that this session was just going to be different. And everyone would enjoy it, except Brodie. "I don't know. He's a good kid, but I'm not sure the week is going to completely work for him. He needs approval and contact. If he was a loner, he'd be fine. I guess I'm going to have to work with him more than the others."

"You're good at changing up your style to what others need."

Since he'd opened the door, she decided to jump into the water. Or go through it? She was mixing her metaphors. "Seth? What's going on?"

He turned his head toward her, not missing a beat, and continued to walk. "We're going to lunch."

"I know that, but why?" Cat pressed the question. Seth didn't just spring impromptu dates on her. Never had. Not even in high school. The guy liked his day, week, and freaking life planned out in advance.

"With going through all my old stuff, I've been thinking a lot about the time I was in the army." Seth wasn't looking at her, but he didn't let go of her hand. "It's got me a little clingy, I guess."

"You worried about us? We just had a great vacation together. We work together one week a month. And you like working with the writers. What can you be worried about?" Cat stopped walking and turned Seth to face her. "You know I love you, right?"

He nodded. "It's just that, well, I thought we'd always be together. I know, I was young and idealistic back then, but I didn't think you'd fall in love with someone else. Ever."

"I can't change what's happened in the past. And I can't predict what's going to happen in the future." Cat squeezed Seth's hand as he started to pull away. "But I can tell you that I do see a future for us. I loved Michael. But he was never quite honest with me. He wanted me to see the man he wanted to be, not the man he was. You've always been completely honest and open. And I love that."

"The day you got married, I'd convinced myself if I walked into that church, you'd pull a runaway bride moment and we'd go off and live our life. That the whole thing would be a blip." He smiled at her. "I guess I was watching too many soap operas at the time."

"I've always loved your romantic side." Cat

reached up on her toes and kissed him. "If I'd known how that marriage would turn out, maybe I would have. But all I can do now is be with you. Every day. Even on days you're not here, my thoughts are with you. We have a second chance. Let's take it."

Seth pulled her close and hugged her. "We broke up just after Germany. I was probably a little touchy when I got home because of Chance's death. Or, I guess, his disappearance. I needed some stability in my life."

"And I threw it out the window by trying to change the plan on you." They started walking toward town again, still holding hands.

"I sound like a kid who didn't get what he wanted for Christmas." Seth chuckled, but his laughter sounded forced.

Cat shook her head. "No, you sound like someone who had his heart broken. I'm sorry I did that to you. I got paid back in spades when I divorced Michael, believe me."

"I don't want to compare pain. I just want you to know how much you mean to me." He blew out a breath. "Those journals of mine, they were all about what I saw our lives together to be like. How many kids, where we'd raise them, what their names would be, I had everything planned. I just didn't realize that those were decisions that we should make together, not me alone."

"Well, we have a second chance." She paused at the door to the restaurant. "And I'm starving. I hope you brought your wallet."

"I thought you bought meals during retreat week." He held the door open for her. "Just kidding. This one's on me because I needed some Cat time."

When they were seated and their orders taken by their waitress, Seth slumped in his chair. "Thanks for letting me vent. I needed to get that out. Man, reading those journals are like stepping back in time. I don't even want to read the ones after we broke up. I'm sure I sounded like a teenager with his first breakup."

"It might have *been* your first breakup." Cat sipped her iced tea. "We started dating before we were sixteen, well, if you call hanging out on my porch dating. We were the 'it couple' in high school. Everyone expected us to be married and have a bunch of kids by now."

"I hadn't thought of it that way. No wonder I was in such a dark place." He put his hand on his chest. "You ripped my heart out."

"Now your drama club experience is coming out." Cat laughed as the waitress put a basket of bread and fresh butter on the table. "Remember when we did *Our Town*? Man, was that depressing or what? Who gives that play to angsty teenagers to act out?"

Instead of answering, Seth stood and was enveloped in a bear hug by a man who actually looked like a bear. They did a few back slaps and bro hugs before he held the guy out to look at his face. "Terry Planter. When did you get in town?"

"Joey and I have been here for a few days. We took the opportunity to get some hiking in before the reunion. I'm staying at the Holiday Inn next to the freeway. I'm looking forward to Wednesday."

He kept his eyes on Seth. "I can't believe how good you look. The last time I saw you, man, you were a mess."

Seth smiled at Cat. "I was. But I'm not anymore. Terry, I'd like you to meet my girlfriend, Cat Latimer."

Terry reached out his hand, but then paused. "Wait, *the* Cat? Your high school sweetheart?"

Cat stood and took Terry's hand. "One and the same. I'm glad to meet you. Seth doesn't talk about his friends from the army much."

"I can see why. We're kind of a shady bunch." He smiled at her. "It's nice to finally meet you, Cat. I can see why my buddy here was so hung up on you."

"Thanks." She could feel the heat come to her cheeks.

"Anyway, I've disturbed your lunch." He handed Seth a card. "Give me a call if you can get away for some drinks tonight. I'd like to catch up before the reunion. You know it's going to be crazy loud there."

"Sounds good." Seth tucked the card in the back pocket of his jeans. "I'll try to carve out some time. We're pretty busy with the retreat this week."

"Well, if you can squeeze out some time, I'll buy the beer." He slapped Seth on the back and nodded to Cat. "Again, nice to meet you."

Seth and Cat sat down as their food arrived. Terry weaved through the tables and out of the restaurant. "Sorry about that. I didn't realize he was coming in early."

"No worries. It was good to meet him." Cat

picked up a French fry. "You should go out with him tonight."

"Should I?" He grinned as he picked up his burger.

She handed him a napkin to wipe the ketchup off his chin. "Of course, you should. One, he's a friend. And two, he might remember more about Chance's first death."

Chapter 10

Uncle Pete's Challenger sat in front of the house when they returned after lunch. Seth wasn't happy about pumping his old friend for information about Chance, but finally, he'd agreed to ask him a few questions. If only to make sure they remembered the time the same.

He pointed out the car. "Do you think Pete's here to see Shirley?"

Or to tell us about Chance? The second question stayed unspoken, but Cat knew it was there for both of them. "My guess is Shirley."

When they walked into the kitchen, Shauna, Shirley, and Uncle Pete were at the table. They each had coffee and a slice of apple pie in front of them. Even after eating apple treats for over a month due to a generous gift of fresh apples from the local orchard, Cat's mouth still watered when she smelled the cinnamon and apple pastry warmed from the oven.

"Just in time for dessert." Shauna popped up and plated two more slices. "Cheddar cheese or vanilla ice cream?"

"Vanilla ice cream," they both responded at the same time.

Cat laughed and pointed to a chair. "Sit and I'll get the coffee."

"So, Pete, what brings you to the house today?" Seth looked at Shirley and raised his eyebrows in an implied question.

Shirley, sitting next to him, slapped his arm. "No, it wasn't to see me. Pete had a break in the case."

"Really?" Cat set the coffee cups down and then sat on the other side of Seth. "Did you find the killer?"

"Don't go putting the cart in front of the horse now." Uncle Pete shook a fork at her. "All we know is that someone used Chance's credit card at the store. He's a miner, so I sent a couple of guys out to pick him up for questioning."

"I can't believe people make a living panning for gold in today's world." Shauna sat the pie and a fork in front of Cat and Seth. "It seems so Old West."

"Believe me, it happens in Alaska too. People live off the land in places so remote, they are only accessible with a plane." Shirley looked at Cat. "I've been working on a closed room mystery where everyone is snowed in with the killer in an inn near Fairbanks. I'm just not sure if I should go totally realistic and keep them locked in together until April or May, or if I have the snow melt just enough to get a police crew in there to solve the murder and rescue them. Think *The Shining*, but with more people and no ghosts."

"Sounds interesting." But Cat didn't want to talk books. She wanted to hear about the guy using Chance's card. "He had to kill him if he had the card, right?"

"Maybe. It's going to take some explaining to convince me he didn't have a part in the guy's death. But while we wait for the suspect to be escorted back to town, I thought I'd come and spend some time with Shirley." He frowned, looking at the two of them. "Where have you been? I don't think I've seen you on a date during retreat week before."

"It was impromptu," Cat explained.

"You must have come up with that. Seth doesn't do anything on the spur of the moment." Uncle Pete took a bite of his pie. Looking at the two of them glance back and forth at each other, he shook his head. "Seriously? It was Seth? What's wrong with you lately?"

"Can't a guy want to spend time with his girl?" Seth patted Shirley's hand. "I seem to see you here and not at the station, working a case."

"Now, boys, stop arguing. Let's talk about something less controversial. Shauna, I heard you went to New York. How was the New York City trip?" Shirley took a sip of her coffee.

Shauna started laughing and the rest joined in. Shirley looked around. "What did I say?"

Cat sat in the living room that evening, waiting for the writers to get back from dinner. Seth had left to meet up with Terry. And Shauna was in her room, watching cooking shows. This was the strangest retreat she'd had and she felt disconnected with all of the writers, except for Brodie. He was out with the group for dinner as well. She picked up the journal that Uncle Pete had left for her and started reading.

A noise at the doorway brought her out of the story. Shirley stood there, laptop in hand, looking at the almost-empty room. Cat sat the book down and waved her inside. "Come on in."

"Where is everyone?" Shirley crossed the room and set her laptop on the coffee table. "If I didn't know better, I'd swear you were on a non-retreat week."

"I know. Everyone is always out of the house. Tristin and Sydney went photo shooting this afternoon, and the rest were at the library either researching or, in Brodie's case, writing. They hooked up for dinner and from what they told me, they should be back here afterward." She curled her feet up underneath her. "I'm glad they're working on their stuff, but honestly, the house feels a little empty. I love having a full house—well, I do once a month."

"You've taught your introvert side to be a good hostess." Shirley smiled. "That's not a bad thing. I guess different retreats feel different. When I was here, we spent a lot of time together, talking and reading and writing. But this group, they're usually gone, unless there's a seminar."

"Maybe tomorrow will be better. We're having the 'ask the author' session. That usually brings people together." Cat rolled her shoulders. "And

Thursday, Seth's taking the group hiking again as long as the weather cooperates. Do you want to come?"

"I'd love to if you don't mind. I think with this new lead, Pete's going to be busy with the case. I swear, the paperwork it takes to close a case is crazy. Even after the suspect is charged." Shirley glanced at her watch. "Do you mind if I write while we wait? I've been working on that story I mentioned this morning and I'm really involved in the plot."

"No worries. I'll be here if you want to talk. I already got my words in for the day, so I'm taking advantage of the time to get some reading in. I never get to read during a retreat." She picked up the book. "And you know where the refreshments are."

"I sure do. Shauna's baking has gotten better since the last time I was here. And it was crazy good then." Shirley patted her stomach. "I've been spending some quality time with your treadmill in the mornings."

"I should."

The room grew quiet as Cat leaned back in her chair and read. Two chapters later, she heard the front door open and close. She stretched and set the book down. "I'll go grab some hot chocolate and more cookies and let them know that we're in the living room."

Shirley nodded, not looking up from her keying. "Can you bring me back a cup of coffee?"

Reaching the dining room, Cat was surprised to see Brodie alone in the room, filling up a travel mug. "Hey, are you the first one back?"

He turned and grinned at her. "Yeah, the others are going to the bar for karaoke night. I wanted to come back and work on my story. I got some great ideas while I was researching mythology at the library today."

"Shirley and I are in the living room. She's writing, I'm reading, if you want to join us, you can."

He shook his head. "Actually, do you mind if I use that study again? I love being in the solitude and quiet while I'm working. I guess some people like the noise and clutter. Sydney told us at dinner that when she was working on her MFA, she used to stop at a bar after class to do her homework."

"I'm more like you. I like my quiet time." Which was why her office had been set up on the third floor, away from all the distractions of the house. "Of course, you can work there. But if you get lonely, you know where we are."

He paused as he was filling a plate with cookies. "Actually, for the first time since I've left home to attend Covington, I don't feel lonely here. You have a very welcoming house. It's like it has an old soul attached to it."

"Houses with souls, you're definitely a fantasy or paranormal writer." Cat smiled and poured a cup of coffee for Shirley and a hot chocolate for herself. Then she made a plate of two of each of the different types of cookies. "You have a productive session tonight. Tomorrow we're getting together to talk about the author life at ten. Are you coming?"

"I wouldn't miss it." His eyes sparkled and for a minute, Cat felt like the room brightened just a bit too. She shook her head. Now he had her doing it.

"The dining room is open all night, but Shauna won't restock anything until the morning. So what you see is what's available." She picked up the tray. "It's nice to have you here this week."

"Thanks." He shouldered his backpack that held his laptop and moved past her into the hallway.

Cat took a minute to look over the food offering. The other writers would probably want munchies when they got back to the bar. *Just because the retreat is different, doesn't mean they aren't getting what they need out of the week.* She let the thought comfort her, but as she went back to the living room, she had to admit, she missed the evening get-togethers where the group would talk about their daily progress. Maybe she'd gently mention the idea tomorrow.

She sat the tray down on the table, and Shirley grabbed her coffee and looked around. "I thought they came back?"

"Karaoke." Cat settled onto the couch with her hot chocolate. "Brodie's working in the study, so it's just us."

"I can go work in the attic or my room if you want to be alone." Shirley glanced around the cozy living room. Cat had turned on the gas fireplace and the room just sang home. At least that's what Brodie would say.

"I'm reading. You're not disturbing me. Besides, I get three weeks a month of just me and Shauna in the house. It's nice to have company." She took a cookie and broke it in half. "How's the writing going?"

"I'm trying to pants this one. Not outline it to death. Writing this way has been hard. I keep thinking I don't know where it's going, but then I sit down and start typing and the characters take over. It's weird." Shirley picked up a cookie and took a bite of it. "But I like it. The characters are surprising me."

"Sounds like you're enjoying the process." Cat took out a notebook and started an outline of what she'd read so far. Mostly it was all about the weather and the research he'd done on the old mines and the history of panning in the area. No names of anyone alive, at least not yet. She set the notebook down and started reading again.

Several pages later, she'd found a name. Walter. No last name, just Walter. She glanced up at Shirley. "Did Uncle Pete mention the name of the miner who had Chance's credit card?"

Shirley frowned, typed a couple of words, then stopped and looked up at her. "Actually, no. He said it was a local miner, but he didn't tell me a name. Why?"

"I'm going to give Uncle Pete a call." Cat stood and took her phone out into the lobby. The lights on the fence posts on the driveway and the walkway to the house glowed warm in the darkness. Brodie was right, the house did feel welcoming. She dialed her uncle's number.

"What?" The one-word greeting told her all she needed to know. The questioning wasn't going well.

"Is your suspect named Walter?" She glanced at the page where Chance had mentioned the guy.

"No, it's Harvey. Harvey Nelson Hood. Why?" She could hear a smidge of interest in her uncle's tone.

"Nothing. Chance's journal mentions meeting up with a Walter in town to talk about the mining history of the area. Just wondering if we'd found more to attach him to the victim."

She heard her uncle's slow breath. "No, but according to Harvey, he got the credit card from Chance's body when he found him in the tree. That and two hundred dollars that he quickly spent over at Bernie's bar."

"You believe him." Cat could hear the resignation in her uncle's voice.

"Maybe. We still have to verify his alibi, but according to him, he was sixty miles north of here when the coroner estimates Chance was killed."

"What was he doing?" Cat saw Shirley approach and hold up Cat's coffee cup. She knew the ex-cop was really just trying to find out what was happening, but she let her pretend that the woman just needed more coffee.

"Selling his gold flakes. There's a pawn shop in Collinsville that deals with raw materials." He paused. "Look, I've got to go. Tell Shirley I'm sorry, but I'm going to be tied up here for the rest of the night."

"She's busy writing so she probably doesn't even miss you." Cat smiled at Shirley, who was standing by her with two steaming cups in her hands.

"Now, you're going to get me in trouble." Shirley laughed.

"Later." Uncle Pete disconnected the call, and Cat put her phone in her jeans before taking the cup from Shirley.

"So, did you find a clue?" she asked as they walked back to the living room.

Cat shrugged, looking at the time. Almost ten and the other writers were still out. "Maybe. But it's not the guy Uncle Pete has at the station. He says he'll be tied up the rest of the night."

"I figured." Shirley settled back on the couch and sipped her coffee. "The only thing I can control is what I do with my spare time. If I get a good chunk of this draft done, the trip will still be productive, even if we don't get to spend time together. Besides, he'll owe me on our next adventure. It's a win-win."

"You're a calculating woman." Cat smiled at her. "I don't think Uncle Pete knows what he's got himself into."

"Well, let's just keep it that way, okay?" Shirley set her cup down and picked up the laptop. "I'm enjoying spending time with your uncle."

Cat went back to reading the journal and making notes every time this Walter was mentioned. By the time she was ready to go to bed, she had seven separate days that they intersected, but still no other identifying information. Like a last name.

Shirley stood and stretched. "I'm beat. I'll see you in the morning. Thanks for being my writing buddy tonight."

"But I wasn't writing." Cat tucked the book under her arm and put the empty cups and plates on a tray.

"Company is company. At home, I have to rely on my dog Buck to talk out plot points. He's a great listener but never has any brainstorming ideas." Shirley headed upstairs. "See you in the morning."

Cat took the tray into the kitchen and loaded the dishes into the dishwasher. Then she checked the locks on the back door and turned off the lights. The other guests were adults and she shouldn't worry about them. But as she glanced at the clock, she still hoped they would be safe on the walk home.

Taking one last glance outside, she made her way upstairs with the journal and her notebook in hand. Maybe she'd just read a few more pages before she went to bed.

Chapter 11

Wednesday morning's sun woke Cat. She'd fallen asleep reading. It wasn't the first time that happened or the last. She picked up the journal from where it had fallen during the night. Tucking in a bookmark, she headed into her bathroom to get ready for the day. Today was her "ask the author" seminar, and although she'd given the session multiple times by now, it still made her nervous to open up her process to her guests.

She let the warm water ease away the doubts and by the time she entered the kitchen, she could at least fake a happy attitude. Shauna was already busy at the counter, mixing a batter. "Good morning. Whatever you're making smells wonderful."

"I've got a batch of cookies in the oven. The treats I left out last night were all gone by the time I checked the dining room this morning." Shauna poured blueberries into the bowl, then picked up a muffin pan. She sprayed it with oil and then filled the cups with the batter.

"Brodie came back after dinner and wrote for a while. Shirley and I were in the living room until eleven. But I don't know when the rest of the group came back." Cat filled her cup with coffee and grabbed a slice of banana bread already on a plate ready to be taken to the dining room spread.

"I thought I heard someone downstairs around one." Shauna shrugged when Cat narrowed her eyes at her. "Sue me, I'm still not sleeping well. I was walking the hallway on the third floor. I'm surprised I didn't wake you and Seth up too."

"When Seth falls asleep, nothing wakes him." Cat glanced around the kitchen. "Anything else I should take out?"

"I'll follow you out with the juices." Shauna opened the fridge and took out two pitchers. "Orange and cranberry this morning."

"Sounds like fall to me." Cat backed into the door and held it open, waiting for her. "I'm surprised *I* didn't hear you. I don't think I fell asleep until after midnight myself."

Shauna followed her into the dining room. "We should just expect not to sleep well during retreat weeks. I'm always concerned if they're out late. I know they're adults, but I still worry."

With what had happened during some of the retreats, Cat didn't fault her the feeling. In fact, she felt the same way. She set the muffin baskets on the sideboard and took in the dining room. Shauna must have cleared it from last night's munchie group. The table was clean and shining under her partner's watchful eye. "Looks like we're ready in here."

"Yeah, I'll take out more for breakfast later on

in the morning, but for now, this will get them going." Shauna glanced at the clock. "I'm surprised Shirley isn't up yet."

Frowning, she glanced around. "Maybe she's working in the study?"

Shauna shook her head. "She would have shown up for coffee. She didn't come into the kitchen, and the coffee out here was cold this morning."

A door slammed in the foyer and Cat heard voices. She stepped out of the dining room and saw Shirley kissing Uncle Pete. She quickly moved back into the dining room.

"Who is it?" Shauna moved to go around to see, but Cat held her back, grabbing her arm. She whispered, "Don't go out there."

"Why not?" Now Shauna was curious and tried to look around the doorway.

"Because my niece doesn't want to disturb us." Uncle Pete, with his arm around Shirley, walked into the dining room. "Tell me you have coffee. I need to get to the station, but I'm the one who starts the first pot, so I'd love to take a cup to go."

"Of course, we have coffee." Shauna moved to the sideboard and filled a travel mug for Uncle Pete. She grabbed a muffin and put it in a paper bag she kept in the sideboard. "And a bit of breakfast to get you going."

He smiled as he took the cup and bag. "You're the best, Shauna."

After he left, Cat tilted her head at Shirley.

"Don't ask, I won't tell." Shirley poured her own coffee. "Besides, we're both consenting adults here."

"I don't know why you're paying for a room."
Cat watched as Shirley's face pinked with emotion.

She grabbed a muffin and headed to the door.
"Let's just say your uncle and I are old-fashioned."

Cat watched Shirley almost sprint up the stairs
to the second floor. When Shauna came back into
the dining room, she started giggling.

"It's not funny," Cat said.

"It kind of is. I mean, how many times has your
uncle made comments about you and Seth sneaking out when you were kids. Or finding you parked
at the lookout. This is so payback for his teasing."
Shauna took one last look at the dining room and
moved to the hallway. "Besides, they're cute together."

"I know. And I know he needs someone in his
life, but she lives in Alaska. That's long-distance romance to the max." Cat followed her friend into
the kitchen.

"I don't know, it could be worse. She could be
from Europe."

Cat filled a travel mug so she could take coffee
to her office. "I guess. Anyway, I guess we know
who you heard moving around last night. It must
have been Shirley leaving."

"Yeah." Shauna glanced at the clock. "I better
get moving or no one's going to have breakfast
this morning."

"I'll be in the office if anyone needs me." Cat
left the kitchen and started up the stairs. She ran a
hand over the polished wood. The house had
years of lives lived in it. She always loved thinking
about who else had touched this staircase. What

had they been thinking when they did? Who had made love in the bedrooms upstairs?

She shook her head; that idea had taken her right back to Uncle Pete and Shirley. And that was one visual she didn't need in her head. Not now, not ever.

Escaping to the sanctity of her office, she booted her computer and brought up her work in progress. It was time to get words down on the page.

She hit her word count and had time to pull the file on the notes and questions she'd kept over the year or so she'd been doing the seminar. Most groups asked the same questions, but once in a while, a new one would pop up and she'd add it to the list. That way she never had to think about what she was going to say, she always had a jumping-off point.

Seth was in the kitchen eating an omelet when she finally made her way back downstairs. She walked over and kissed him quickly. "Did you sleep well?"

"Better than Shauna, I hear." He grinned at her. "How did you take finding out your uncle's not a saint?"

"I already knew that, so get real. Besides, just because they spent the night together, you don't know if they did anything. They might have been talking until it was too late to drive her back to the house. Or they'd been drinking." Cat put her travel cup in the sink and grabbed a bottle of water.

"You keep thinking that; maybe you'll even convince yourself it's true." He focused on his plate. "Did Pete mention anything about Old Harvey? I heard one of the deputies found him late last night drunk out by his mine."

"Was that the guy who had Chance's credit card?" Shauna asked as she set a plate in front of Cat.

"Yeah, I guess he slept through the ride and they put him in the drunk tank." Seth sipped his coffee. "It was all the discussion down at Bernie's when I popped in yesterday. Terry said he was going to be there to meet for a few beers, but he never showed up. I guess I have something to give him grief over tonight."

"That's right. You've got your reunion this evening. What time are you heading over?" Cat took a bite of the fluffy omelet and almost sighed when the cheddar cheese hit her taste buds.

"Four. We're doing pictures early, then talking to the press. And after the buffet, the drinking and lying portion of the evening starts."

"Lying portion?" Cat narrowed her eyes.

Seth shrugged. "You know, stories seem to expand with age. What was just a shot in the distance becomes a narrow escape from death. And I'm going to talk to Terry and the gang about Chance. Maybe one of the guys knows something that I've forgotten."

"Maybe I should come and ask a few questions of my own." Cat pointed a fork at him. "You never want to talk about your time in the military. Maybe I could get a few ideas for the book I'm writing."

He shook his head. "Sorry, this session is by invite only and you're not invited."

"That's rude," Cat complained, but Shauna laughed.

"Sorry, honey, but not even the wives were invited to this reunion. If you want, I can set up a breakfast meeting tomorrow so you can meet some of the guys." His gaze met hers and she felt the love and attention he was projecting. "Maybe they can help you more with this boot camp book."

"I would love to meet some of your friends. But it can't be tomorrow. You're taking the group on a hiking trip, remember?"

Seth slapped his forehead. "I forgot. I'll get the backpacks and hiking stuff ready today and set out in the foyer. That way all we have to do in the morning is load up the SUV. Are you coming with us?"

Cat nodded. "I wouldn't miss it." She didn't add that she wanted to get some pictures of the area where Chance's cabin had been just in case she could see any clues. She'd have to reach out to her uncle later and see if this old miner was the killer. Having the murder wrapped up with a bow would mean that Uncle Pete could take some time off and actually be with Shirley. "I think Shirley wants to come along too."

"Sounds like a plan." He finished his breakfast and went to the sink to rinse off his plate. "My day's just become pretty full, but I'll have my phone if you need me."

"Talk to you soon." Cat called after him as he disappeared into the basement. She played with her food, then set down her fork, watching Shauna. "You think I'm pushing too hard about Seth's time in the military, don't you?"

"I think Seth will tell you what he wants to tell you on his time frame. You need to let him come to you."

"But there's a murder to solve . . ."

Shauna turned from the stove. "And that's your problem how?"

Cat shifted uncomfortably in her chair. Not making eye contact, she shrugged, then brightened as she thought of an answer. "I'm worried about Uncle Pete spending enough time with Shirley while she's here?"

Shauna shook her head, laughing. "From what I saw this morning, they are making time to be together just fine."

Cat hid her face in her hands and groaned. "Fine, fine, stop. You're right, it's not any of my business. I've got a seminar to give in ten minutes. I better go set up."

Grabbing her folder, she left the kitchen and the now-laughing Shauna. Cat realized her friends were the first to tease her. But she knew their hearts were in the right place. She ran into Brodie coming down the stairs with his laptop.

"Great, I thought I was going to be late." He beamed at her. "I've got lots of questions for you."

"I'm glad. Did you get a lot of words in this morning?"

Brodie nodded, his head bouncing like one of those dog statues on the back of a car. "I'm almost through with the book. That's one of the questions I have. When I finish the book, what's next?"

Tristin came out of the dining room. "From what I hear, the best answer to that question is to write the next book."

Cat laughed. "You've been studying your publishing business."

Sydney followed him into the living room. "He's

obsessed with the idea of being an actual author, as he says. Of course, I'd be happy with just being known as a travel writer. I love getting to visit other places and encouraging others to travel there."

"I'm sure being an author of fiction is a little different from nonfiction, but I can give you my impressions for both." Cat frowned as she glanced at her notebook. Maybe she hadn't prepared quite as well as she should have for this group.

"I'm sure we'll have an insightful discussion." Archer sat on the couch with his wife, watching the rest of the group come into the room. "Besides, what good does knowing it all do for anyone? There has to be surprises in life to keep us on our toes."

"You're exactly right, Archer. So, are we ready to talk? I've got some notes from prior sessions to work from, but are there any questions you all want to make sure I cover?"

Cat listed off the questions onto a flipchart. As she finished the list, she smiled. All of these questions had been in her presentation already, so she was prepared. As she took a sip of her coffee, she relaxed and started talking.

Two hours later, the group was out of the house, walking toward town and Reno's for lunch. Shirley had joined them. Apparently, Uncle Pete hadn't solved the case with the stealing miner. Cat took her file to the kitchen, where Shauna was folding laundry. She'd stripped beds and cleaned the rooms while Cat had the work session downstairs. Their system was working well. Or at least had for most of the retreats. Shauna changed sheets only once in the middle of the week, freshening the bedrooms and baths daily with fresh towels. When they opened the other wing, Cat thought they might have to hire some extra help to clean the rooms since Shauna had so much on her plate now.

"Let me help fold." Cat took a towel out of the basket. The clean smell and feel of the fluffy towel almost made her sigh. There was nothing like a clean towel in her mind.

"So your uncle called. He's taking Shirley out to dinner tonight and we're not supposed to wait up for them."

"Got it." Cat folded a second towel. "I guess the miner dude didn't kill Chance?"

"Not according to your uncle. Witnesses have him drunk in a Collinsville bar at the time Chance was murdered. Then he came into Bernie's with a lot of cash the next day. It was only when he ran out of the money that he pulled out the credit card. Once Bernie saw the charge the next morning, he called Pete."

"So we still don't know who killed this guy? I was hoping that Seth could go to his reunion without looking at his friends as suspects." Cat grabbed the last towel. "Many hands make light work" was her mom's favorite saying. And Shauna didn't let her help much, so she felt good when she could.

"You don't think any of the guys who served with Seth could be involved, do you?" Shauna set the basket on the floor, then grabbed a bottle of water.

Cat laid the folded towel on top of the basket, then went to the fridge to get her own bottle of water. She hadn't meant to say that aloud, but she had. Finally, she sat next to Shauna and stared at her unopened water.

"Cat?" Shauna's voice held kindness, concern, and a touch of worry.

Cat looked up and met her friend's gaze. "I do think this is something to do with the platoon or the group or whatever you call it. I'm afraid Seth doesn't know everything about his old friends."

Chapter 12

Before they sat down to lunch, Cat made a trip out to the barn to visit the kittens. Shauna had scheduled appointments for the brood and their mother, Angelica, to get fixed so five kittens wouldn't turn into twenty more in less than a year. She should have let Shauna give some of the litter away, but Cat liked each one of them for a different reason. One was feisty. One cuddly. And one, Ali, was a fighter. He'd pick a fight with the straw bale if he thought he could get it to react. His determination made Cat smile.

She filled the bowls with food and checked their automatic water dish that Seth had set up to the barn's water system. When it was cold, she'd have to remember to come outside and check it daily since it didn't have the automatic warmer, like the water trough that Shauna's horse, Snow's, did.

Once she sat down on a straw bale, the kittens came running for attention. Angelica, the mother, ignored her and went straight to the food dish.

The cat had been on her own, after her prior owner had died, so she had solid priorities. Cat wondered if she'd ever trust that food would always be there for her after scrapping by for months. She'd brought the cat down from Outlaw, the local Old West tourist town nearby, when she'd realized Angelica had been living on her own in the ghost town. She wouldn't have survived the winter up there, especially with the four babies that came right after she'd made Snow's barn her home too.

Maybe people were the same way. Maybe their past lives and adventures put a mark on them like Angelica. Had Chance just checked out of society because he didn't trust the world anymore? Or had something else happened in Germany? Would one of Seth's buddies be involved? Or was his disappearance higher up on the power grid? They may never know. Uncle Pete hadn't ruled out the fact that this might have been an unfortunate accident, but if so, what had happened to the gun? She wondered what the autopsy report had said, but she knew asking her uncle was hopeless.

All she could do was keep her eyes open and finish reading the journal to see if there were any clues to why Chance had disappeared.

Or, she thought as she scratched an orange belly as the kitten purred under her hand, maybe there was someone she could ask. The ex-fiancé. Cat could see if she was still in town. If she'd gone to school with them, she might be able to find contact info on the high school's alumni site. She almost remembered the name, but maybe they'd had a class together that would solidify the relationship. She'd like to think the girl might remember her, even if it had been years since graduation.

Happy that she had a plan, she gave all the kittens one last cuddle, then headed back to the house. If Seth was there, maybe he'd remember some of the other kids whom Chance had hung around with. It was a long shot, but someone had to know something about Chance. Especially if his death had more to do with his past before the military than his current hermit lifestyle.

The sun warmed her face as she left the chilly barn. The smell of fall, crisp and tart, hung on the air. Someone had been burning leaves nearby because she could smell the burnt oak in the distance. Colorado was on the edge of winter, and she could feel the chill and thought of snow as she walked into the house. Tomorrow's hike could be their last chance to get outside and enjoy the mountains she loved.

Life in California had been nice. Sunny, sea-kissed wind had kept her from missing the snow and freeze of her home in Colorado. But now that she was back, she was hyperaware of the change of seasons. Especially when it brought the holiday season along with it. She hadn't even started thinking of gifts for Seth or Uncle Pete, but Shauna? She'd had too many ideas of what the budding cookbook author might want. And she also wanted to tuck in a personal item so she knew Cat didn't just see her as the retreat's cook.

Holidays were a land mine of emotions. But she loved getting just the right gift. From a special hat or scarf for Uncle Pete, to a just-right tool or sports item for Seth. She agonized over every decision. Better to focus on Chance and finding his murderer than go down that perfect rabbit hole too soon.

Seth wasn't in the kitchen when she came back. Shauna caught her looking around and shook her head. "You just missed him. He has all the hiking stuff ready to go and told me he was meeting a friend for lunch."

"Oh? Who?" Cat tried to make the question sound conversational, but when Shauna laughed, she knew she'd failed.

"Jerry, I think. He said he was one of the guys from the army. I made soup and sandwiches for lunch. Will that work?"

"Tomato basil?" Cat didn't really have to guess. She could smell the sweet tomato as soon as she walked in the door. "One of my favorites. Maybe it was Terry?"

"Good." Shauna poured the soup in bowls and sat them next to the plate piled with sandwiches. "I didn't know Seth was leaving or I wouldn't have made so many. Typically, he eats a couple in the afternoon for snacks."

"My mom always called him a growing boy. But I think he just had a super-high metabolism. Keep them in the fridge. He might need a midnight snack when he gets back from the reunion. Or we can take them on our hike too."

"Don't get me wrong, but I'm kind of excited to have a full day to myself. I'm going to make meatloaf and scalloped potatoes for dinner, so after I get the rooms refreshed, all I have to do is get the dining room set up for evening snacks." Shauna took a sip of her soup. Then looked at Cat with concern. "You are going with them on the hike, right?"

"Nice to know I'm missed around here," Cat said with a laugh, "but yeah, I'm going. I think it might be the last time we get to explore this year." Cat took a ham sandwich off the pile. "You could come with us, if you wanted."

"No, I'm going to put the finishing touches on this proposal, I hope, then start sending it out to agents. I finalized my list last week and I'm anxious to get started submitting. I'm hoping that they like it."

"It only takes one yes." Cat had held back offering to send it to her agent as she wanted Shauna to understand the business, not just have an easy insider track. She didn't know much about the cookbook world of publishing, but she didn't think Shauna should have a problem getting someone to take on the project. "I'm going to see if Chance's ex-girlfriend is around and pay my condolences. Do we have enough cookies for a small box?"

"We do. Sherry lives in town with her new husband. She's a teacher, and he works out at the lumber mill. I guess she likes men who work with their hands."

Cat's heart fell. If she was a teacher, she'd be in the classroom and not available this afternoon. "Wait, how do you know this?"

"Roger, the manager at the store, knows her. I guess he went to high school with all of you. He was a little put out that you didn't recognize him the last time you were in looking for me."

"Wait, that was Roger from high school? Man, he's changed. He used to be scrawny and dorky looking. Now, he's kind of handsome."

Shauna shook her head. "Don't tell me you were one of those girls who were all about appearance."

"No, not one bit. Besides, I was already dating Seth at the time." Cat focused on her soup. Maybe she'd go over after dinner. With Seth out of the house, he wouldn't rat her out to Uncle Pete.

"And just because I know you don't know this, I'll tell you that the elementary school is out for parent-teacher conferences this week. So if you go over to the school, you might be able to catch her in between appointments."

"I don't understand how you keep track of all of this stuff." Cat pondered her friend as Shauna finished her soup.

"I really love living in this small town. And some of my friends have kids in grade school. We talk about almost everything, not just how the apples look this week." Shauna stood and grabbed a box off the shelves near the door. "Give me a minute and I'll pack some cookies. I'm assuming you don't want me to mention this to Pete if he shows up this afternoon."

Cat took her dishes to the sink and rinsed them before putting them in the dishwasher. "He's already talked to Sherry, so it's not like I'm stepping on his toes. I just want to know if she knows anything about when Chance died the first time."

"And if something comes up about Seth during his army time, you're going to not pursue that, right?" Shauna closed the filled box and sat it on the table.

"I don't see what the big deal is. I mean, why won't he talk to me about that time?" Cat shrugged into her coat and picked up the box. "I'll be back in a few. I have a feeling this is just a dead end."

"Be careful." Shauna followed her to the door. "I know you've investigated murders before, but this one feels different. Like it was personal."

"Yeah, but which person was targeted? The reclusive miner who had lived off the grid for years? Or the army guy who'd disappeared during his tour?" Cat asked, not expecting an answer.

"Could be both." Shauna held the door for her, but Cat could feel her friend's gaze on her long after she'd reached the sidewalk.

This was a fool's errand. Asking a woman about a man who had basically dumped her and had set up a new life. She felt cruel even bringing the subject up, but she really wanted this murder to be solved and her life back to normal.

"Cat, wait up," a woman called from behind her.

Cat glanced at Mrs. Rice's house next to her. If it was her neighbor, Cat wouldn't get away with just a quick hello and a bit of conversation. She considered ignoring it, but then her mom's voice broke through her thoughts. She had promised she'd be nicer to Mrs. Rice last week when she'd called and talked to her parents. Guilt made her stop and turn around.

To her delight, it wasn't Mrs. Rice hurrying toward her, but Shirley, pulling on her parka as she walked.

"Shirley, what are you doing?" Cat reached out to grab the end of a purple scarf that was just about to fall on the ground. She held it out as Shirley adjusted and zipped up the coat.

She took the scarf. "I'm coming with you to interview this Sherry woman. I'm at a dead spot on my book and I'm tired of waiting for Pete to wrap this case up so we could spend some time together."

"You're coming with me?" Cat watched as Shirley pulled gloves out of her coat pocket and slipped them on. "How did you know I was even going to talk to Sherry?"

"I have a bad habit of eavesdropping." She nodded to the sidewalk. "Are you ready?"

Cat wasn't quite sure how she felt about Shirley listening in on all their conversations this week. Had she heard Cat's concerns about her relationship with Uncle Pete? Or was she just kidding her. "You really don't eavesdrop, do you?"

"Sorry, I did this morning. I try not to, mostly because it's not my job anymore." Shirley fell in step with Cat as they started toward the elementary school. "I was in the hallway when you told Shauna you were going. I ran to the foyer, grabbed my coat, and ran outside to head you off. But you're a pretty fast walker."

"Habit." Cat wasn't sure how she felt about Shirley tagging along, but at least she'd have someone to verify her story if Uncle Pete asked what she thought she was doing. Many hands share the blame as well as the work. Cat smiled as she thought about her adjustment of one of her mom's favorite sayings.

Shirley glanced at the remodeled Victorian

they were passing. "Isn't that your friend Dante's house? It's really lovely. For a bachelor, he's done a fantastic job of taking care of the house and the landscaping."

Cat was pretty sure that Dante had a group of people he paid to keep the house and all of the surrounding lands in tip-top shape. Some days, she wished she could ask to borrow his staff to get the lawn in shape or clean the house, but Seth didn't even like her talking to the guy. Seth didn't get jealous much, but Dante pushed all of his buttons. So Cat tried to stay away. A fact that Cat figured Shirley knew from Uncle Pete.

"I don't really talk to Dante. And he's really not my friend. He and my ex-husband were close." Cat pointed at the next cross street. "We'll turn there and the school is a few blocks south."

Shirley must have gotten the hint to change the subject because she was quiet for a few minutes. Finally, she turned to Cat. "So what are you going to ask her?"

Cat shrugged. "I kind of wing it when I talk to people. I'm going to give her the cookies and tell her how sorry I am for her loss. Then, depending on where the subject goes, I might add some additional questions as a space for them comes up in conversation."

"You know that's not the way investigators come at an interview. They have a list of questions that are carefully constructed to elicit the correct response from a witness. You have to be careful you don't lead a witness to say something compromising that may lead you down a path that just wastes time." Shirley pulled a small notebook out of her purse. "I've written down a few opening questions you might want to use."

Cat didn't even look at the notebook, although every fiber of her being wanted to snatch it from Shirley's hand. "I'm not an investigator. All I'm doing is trying to figure out if this has anything to do with Seth or me. I want to feel safe in my house."

"Do you seriously expect me to believe that line of bull pucky?" Shirley sighed as they came up on the school. The playground was empty, and the parking lot had only a smattering of cars parked near the entrances. "I swear, small towns really need to rethink their school buildings. A shooter could come in at one of three entrances I can see right now from this vantage point. It's really not safe."

"It's sad that they have to think that way now. A school should be a sanctuary for kids to learn and grow. Not a place for them to be afraid." Cat headed down the sidewalk to the main entrance.

"The school in my neighborhood banned home-baked cookies due to the high number of kids having a peanut allergy." Shirley matched Cat's stride as they walked.

Pausing at the door, Cat turned toward her. "I don't understand. What's that got to do with anything?"

"Some people are afraid of things we don't consider threats. You have to know you're in danger to feel fear. If you haven't experienced a real threat, you won't be afraid of a random issue that happened across the country." Shirley pulled the other door open and walked through toward the office.

Cat followed. She understood what Shirley was

saying, but she wasn't quite sure how the conversation had turned. Her uncle's girlfriend was a bit of a mystery. And one that Cat needed to figure out before she became her aunt. She hurried to meet Shirley at the front reception area, all enclosed in glass.

A young woman lifted her head from a computer and smiled. "Good morning, how can I help you today? Are you here to meet with your child's teacher?"

"Actually, no, but I do need to talk with Sherry Flood. Does she have a minute?" Cat held up the cookie box. "We have a delivery for her."

"Oh, my, she will be ecstatic. I swear, she's had such a bad week, she deserves a truckload of cookies." The receptionist reached for her phone.

"Oh, no. What's been going on?" Cat asked as the woman looked for a number on a sheet.

"An ex-fiancé died recently. The police were here to talk to her on Monday to break the news. The principal substituted in for her class for the rest of the day. She was distraught." The receptionist held up a finger. "Sherry? Are you with parents? No? Great. I'm sending a delivery down to your classroom."

She hung up the phone and stood, smiling. "She has ten minutes before her next appointment. You have plenty of time."

As the woman gave them directions to the classroom, Cat thought about Sherry's reaction to hearing about Chance's death. She guessed finding out a guy was dead a second time couldn't have been easy. But then again, it had been over ten years.

They walked down the wide hallway, decorated

with fall foliage handmade by the students from each class. As they walked away from the office, the class level must have increased as the projects were more detailed and more attractive.

Mrs. Flood's name was over a door in big letters made of construction paper. Cat glanced at Shirley as she opened the door. "Ready for this?"

"As much as possible. You have the lead. I'm just here to see what she says." Shirley grinned.

"And to keep me out of trouble with Uncle Pete."

Shirley shrugged. "It's a side benefit."

A dark-haired woman stood from her desk when they entered. A laptop sat on the desk, along with a large cup that probably held coffee. Cat could smell the rich goodness.

A smile creased the woman's face as she walked toward them. She reached out a hand. "Good afternoon. I'm Sherry Flood. Are you related to one of my children?"

Cat shook her head. "No, I run the writers' retreat over by the college."

Sherry's face showed her confusion. "I'm sorry, do you have me confused with someone else?"

"No, I'm not explaining well, sorry. I'm Seth Howard's girlfriend. I understand your ex-fiancé was a friend of his."

"You're Cat." Relief showed on Sherry's face. "I was a couple years younger than you and Seth. You probably wouldn't remember me. We ran in different circles. No one from that time would think I'd ever have become a teacher. Most of my teachers wouldn't have thought I'd even finish high school."

"I'm not sure they expected me to succeed either. I was told that if I went to college I could be a nurse, a teacher, or a secretary. When I told my guidance counselor I wanted to be a police officer, he almost swallowed his tongue." Shirley was glancing at the bookshelf near the door. She held up a well-used copy of *A Wrinkle in Time*. "One of my favorite books."

Sherry relaxed and eased a hip on the desk. "Mine too. I love reading it aloud to the class. What can I help you all with today?"

"I wanted to say I was sorry for your loss." Cat held out the box. "I guess I should be more specific. I'm sorry for your recent loss. It must have been hard finding out that Chance was alive all these years and then find out he was dead."

"Actually, I knew he was alive." Sherry took the cookies and opened the box. "These smell heavenly."

Chapter 13

Cat stood staring at the woman in stunned silence. She glanced over at Shirley, whose face was as impassive as stone. Finally, she decided to go with her gut. "Wait, you knew Chance was alive? When did you find out?"

Sherry picked a cookie out of the box, then offered one to Cat and Shirley. Both women took a cookie, but let their hands drop down to their sides. Sherry went back to her desk and pulled out her chair. She nodded to the two folding chairs set up for parents by the side of the desk. "Grab a seat. It's going to take a while to explain. But really, you have to leave as soon as the next set of parents arrives."

Cat and Shirley followed her directions and sat. When Sherry didn't say anything else, Cat repeated her question. "So you knew that Chance was alive? The whole time?"

"Oh, no." Sherry shook her head and sat the cookie on a napkin she'd taken out of her desk. "I mourned him when they told me he was dead. I buried him; then I went on with my life. I met my husband while I was going to school. After graduation, we got married and I got pregnant. So we moved back here from California so I could be closer to my family. Nate doesn't have family."

Cat bit at the cookie, reminding herself that Sherry needed to tell the story her way.

Shirley must have felt the same way because she just nodded as Sherry hesitated.

"Anyway, it was about five years ago. I was in the grocery store late one night. Nate volunteered to put Tricia down for me so I could go shopping. I turned the corner and ran my cart into his. When he looked up, I knew." Sherry bit her lip. "He was older, of course, and had that awful beard, but I knew. He saw I recognized him and, well, I saw the tears in his eyes."

Sherry wiped at her own cheeks. "I finished my shopping and checked out, and he was there in the parking lot, waiting for me. He offered to buy me a coffee and then he told me everything."

The hair on the back of Cat's neck rose. "What did he tell you?"

"He said he'd been tired of the army. So when an opportunity arrived, he faked his death and moved home. Of course, if anyone knew, he'd go to prison, so I couldn't tell anyone." Sherry sipped her coffee. "Like I would have told anyone. He asked about my life, told me he was happy for me, and then we left. I tried to pay for the coffee, but he said he could afford a cup of coffee for an old friend."

"You're sure he said he faked his own death?" I

pressed the point. "That was the only reason he left Germany?"

"That's what he told me." Sherry sighed. "Of course, I felt like he was holding something back. I thought it was about us. You know, since I was married and had a family and all. I thought he didn't want to tell me how much he loved me still."

Cat felt Sherry's gaze on her.

"I heard you married some college professor. Chance thought if any couple would make it, it would be you and Seth."

The statement felt like an accusation. Cat tried not to be defensive, but she shifted in the metal chair. "We broke up between his assignments. I thought I was in love with Michael and married him. People make mistakes."

Sherry nodded slowly. "They do. Did you know Seth bought a ring while they were in Germany? Chance went with him to introduce him to a local jeweler. I guess he must have jumped the gun on the happily ever after."

A knock came at the door and Sherry held up a finger. The door closed again as Danny's parents realized Sherry was talking to another family. One that maybe had more problems than their own.

"That's my cue. I've got to go back to my real world." Sherry stood. "I know I probably didn't give you what you wanted, but really, it's all I have."

"I appreciate you talking with us." Cat felt shell-shocked. She'd seen Seth in the back of the church when she'd pledged her love to another man, but she thought he was just there to make sure she was settled with the decision. At least, that's what she'd told herself at the time.

Tears shimmered in Sherry's eyes and she opened a drawer to grab tissues. Cat wanted to reach out and pat the woman on the back, or give her a hug or something to let her know it was going to be okay. But she held back on the urge.

"He lied to me, didn't he?" Sherry watched their faces for a reaction. "Do you know why he left Germany?"

Cat shook her head. "I don't. But if I find out, I'll let you know. Again, I'm sorry for your loss."

"Somehow, the loss this time was more for what could have been. I grieved losing the man oh so many years ago. This time, I had to let go of the fantasy relationship I could hold in my mind as a just in case. Which makes me sound like a real witch. But he was my first love." Sherry walked them to the door. "Thanks again for the cookies. Although I think they're going to be gone long before my conferences are completed today."

Shirley didn't say anything until they were back on the sidewalk on the way home. "Well, that wasn't what I expected to hear."

"I didn't know what I expected, but you're right. She knew he was alive five years ago. Which puts her and her husband back on the suspect list, doesn't it?" Cat looked over at Shirley as they walked.

"Maybe. Pete probably eliminated them by checking out their alibi when he first talked to them." She nodded when she saw Cat's dubious expression. "It saves time. Especially when you have no idea where an investigation is taking you. Crossing people off the list is just as important as finding the one who did it."

Shirley paused at the corner of Warm Springs. "I'm going to go to the station and give Pete this new information. It might not change who and what he's looking at now, but I think it might cross some t's for the investigation."

"I'll see you back at the house." Cat turned left to go to the house, leaving Shirley standing at the corner.

"Cat?" Shirley called after her.

Cat spun around and walked back toward Shirley for a few steps. "Yes?"

"It was fun playing detective with you. You're good at the interviewing thing because you put people at ease."

Cat waved and turned around. She'd thought Shirley was going to ask her how she'd felt about the ring. About Seth. Which, of course, Cat wouldn't have been able to answer. When she got back to the house, Shauna was out of the kitchen, so Cat grabbed a soda and went upstairs to her office to work.

There, she put down all the things she knew about the reclusive Chance and tried to set up a timeline. She still believed that there was a connection between what happened in Germany and Chance's death. Proving it or even going down the right path at this point was going to be the problem.

A knock came at the door and Cat realized it was dinnertime. "Come in," she called out to probably the waiting Shauna. Instead, Brodie entered the room.

"Cool office. I bet I could write the great American novel in a room like this." He leaned on the doorway. "Shauna asked if I'd come up and let you know there's soup on the stove. She had an appointment in town tonight."

Shauna's grief group met on Wednesdays, so that was probably where she'd gone. Cat turned off her computer and stood. "Thanks. Are you going into town with the group?"

He shook his head. "Actually, I'm going to let them go by themselves tonight. Any chance I could get some of that soup? If not, I can go back to the dorm and grab something at the cafeteria. I'm trying to get this chapter done tonight. If I plan it right, I might have the first draft done before I leave here on Sunday."

"Then come grab some soup and bread." Cat walked out into the hallway, then locked her office. "You can eat with me in the kitchen."

"Cool." He followed her downstairs, chatting about his book and how much he'd gotten done this week. When they reached the kitchen and settled at the table, he dug into his meal like he hadn't eaten in a week. He must have sensed her watching because he got a sheepish grin on his face. "You all put out really good food. My mom cooks like this and I haven't been home in a few years. It's hard to get the money scraped up for the travel, and the car I brought died a year ago."

"What do you do when the dorms close for the session?" Now Cat was concerned. Brodie definitely was a scholarship kid, not one of the moneyed families who typically attended Covington.

He shrugged, not meeting her eyes. "I work for Bernie on the weekends, so he lets me flop in the back room. It gets quiet around three. But I get a lot of writing done on those nights."

The kid was always looking for the silver lining. Cat shook her head. Brodie's financial worries weren't her problem. But her concern stayed with her long after he'd eaten a third bowl of soup and left to go to the study to write.

Michael had always kidded her about wanting to bring all the strays home. And she'd kind of done that when the house had been her own. Shauna had moved from California to help her set up the retreat. And Seth stayed here so much that she wondered why he even kept his apartment. She wondered if bringing Brodie in, just when the dorms were closed, was just a wild idea or if she was being led to a decision. She decided to talk to Shauna about it tomorrow. Maybe there was another option than the kid sleeping on a cot in a bar storeroom.

Cat cleaned up their plates, left the soup warming on the stove for Shauna's return, and moved into the living room to see if any of the other writers came back to the retreat after dinner. She didn't have a good hold on how the writing was going, if at all. These four kept their writing, if they were doing any at all, secret and completed away from the house. Tomorrow when they were hiking, she'd try to get a feel for how close each person was to their weekly goal. It was her responsibility as the retreat leader.

By the time she'd finished the book she'd been reading, the house was still mostly empty. Shauna had come in, ate her dinner in the kitchen, then went straight up to bed. Brodie had emerged from the study, bleary-eyed and tired, and had gone upstairs just after Shauna. Seth and the couples were still out at their respective outings.

She went upstairs, leaving the role of retreat wrangler on the main floor. After getting ready for bed, she curled up with Chance's journal. She'd been so caught up with the day-to-day stuff for the retreat, she'd forgotten to finish reading. So far, she hadn't found anything to report to Uncle Pete. Mostly it was an accounting of his days. Things that had happened at the claim that day. Deer he'd seen wandering through the trees. What he'd eaten and an ongoing shopping list. She figured the stream of consciousness style was part of not seeing anyone for days. And even when he came into town, he hadn't really made any social connections. Had he been afraid of being found out? Then why had he told Sherry? That was an easy answer. Sherry had recognized him. So he'd had to talk to her to keep her quiet about his location. What had he gotten into so long ago in Germany that it was still following him years later?

Or, the more likely answer had he not wound up dead and in the morgue, was the guy bat guano crazy?

She tucked a pillow under her head, turned on the television for a little white noise, and started reading, not noticing when she drifted off to sleep.

She dreamed of walking through jewelry stores with Seth and Michael. Neither of the men seemed to notice the other. Cat kept running from one to another, looking at the perfect ring, when they turned on her and circled around, chanting over and over, *Which one, Cat? Which one will you choose? Which one, Cat?*

She woke up in a cold sweat on top of the covers. The journal lay open beside her. Sometime during the night she must have fallen asleep and into that crazy dream. She could still hear the question. *Which one will you choose, Cat?*

She wanted to banish the questions and the memories. She'd chosen once. And it hadn't been a bad choice. Michael had just been complicated and unwilling to let her into his life. Seth was different. And, according to Sherry, he'd bought her a ring, once upon a time. Which made sense of why he didn't like to talk about his army days. Then she'd been lured into the professor life . . . and the professor's bed. And that had been that.

Rubbing the dream away from her chilled arms, she glanced at the clock. Three a.m. Too early to get up and start the day, but she didn't think she'd get back to sleep. Maybe if she made some hot cocoa and read for a while, she might start feeling sleepy again. Or at least she'd get the journal read and be able to report her lack of any findings back to Uncle Pete.

She grabbed the journal and quietly headed downstairs. She didn't meet anyone on the stairs, not that she expected to. No, normal people were asleep in bed at this time, not sneaking downstairs for a late-night snack.

Letting the water heat for hot chocolate, Cat curled up on one of the chairs and started reading the journal again.

According to the rumors flying over at the post office this morning and again at the grocery store, the guy Seth's girl married instead of him has done the dirty with some-

one else. She's taken off to greener pastures, California, I hear. It's funny what people will chat about in a public place. I'm almost invisible to these college types. At least as long as I shower before coming into town. Most everyone in town treats me like those homeless guys with a bucket out for money and a sign declaring their disabled vet status. But I do hear a lot of gossip. More than I heard when I was a clean-cut army type. Or maybe I just listen better now that I'm forced to be out of the world. I'm going to have to keep an eye on this Michael guy. Maybe Seth can reclaim that girl if she ever moves back home.

The whistle went off on the tea kettle and Cat set the book down. Was this why Chance had Michael's name circled on the paper in his cabin? Chance had turned himself into an observer of Aspen Hills. A habit that could have been the reason he had been killed. She'd let her uncle deal with that possibility, but she decided to write it down with the page number so he could look at the original document.

She made her cocoa and, as an afterthought, grabbed the whipped cream from the fridge. She glanced at the Kahlua in the liquor cabinet, but decided adding alcohol may not have the effect she wanted, and layered the whipped cream tall on top of the hot drink.

Sipping the cocoa, she continued reading. A noise at the back door made her jump. Wildly, she looked for something, anything to defend herself with. She grabbed the basket of cookies off the table and stood by the counter.

Seth pushed open the door and squinted at her. "Why are you up still?"

"I couldn't sleep." She set down the basket. "You're out late."

"That's the thing about reunions, everyone had a story. About where they are now, and remember when, and of course, Chance was on everyone's mind. No one seems to know anything about his life after his death. They all told the same story, how he died in a bombing in town. I knew that store had been hit, but I didn't realize that's where Chance died. Or didn't die, I guess."

Cat frowned. "I thought he was shot during some assignment."

Seth came over and took a cookie. "Honestly, that's what I remember. Guess I was wrong."

"Did you catch up with Terry? What did he want to tell you?" Cat pulled the basket closer and looked at the cookies. Deciding not to indulge, she pushed it back toward Seth.

He took two more and used the back of his hands to hide a yawn. He stared at her, thoughtful. "You know what? He never said. I guess it wasn't as important as he made it sound in the e-mail. We just talked about Chance and the old days. Then we grabbed some dinner before heading over to the hall."

Cat thought about mentioning what Sherry had said and decided this wasn't the time. Instead, she glanced at the clock. "We still hiking at nine?"

Seth groaned a little. "Yep, which means I need to crash or you'll be leading the hiking group and I'll be passed out in the SUV."

Cat smiled as he stopped by her chair to kiss her on the top of her head. "See you in the morning."

"You should get some sleep too. You're grumpy when you're tired. Oh, yeah, Terry did keep asking me if I'd been up to Chance's mining claim. I guess he didn't listen when I'd told him I didn't know he was even alive. Much less living here in Aspen Hills." He paused at the kitchen door. "Want to walk up with me?"

"Go ahead. I'm going to finish my cocoa and then I'll head to bed." She turned back to the journal and started reading as Seth disappeared into the hallway. Cat wondered where this Terry fellow was staying and if she could carve out some time to go visit him. Maybe he'd be more upfront with her than he had been with Seth. From how Seth had described him, it sounded like Terry was more interested in finding out if Seth had known that Chance was alive. And what he'd known about the claim. Maybe they should change their hiking path tomorrow and check out Chance's cabin and the mining claim. Cat found it hard to believe that this was all about something that happened over ten years ago.

She could feel sleep start to take over. She glanced at the journal; she still had about a quarter more to finish. She'd just tuck it in her backpack tomorrow and steal reading time wherever she could find it.

As she was heading upstairs, she thought about Seth and the ring. It definitely was a conversation they were going to have sooner or later. And if she had anything to say about it, the talk would happen as soon as he got back from dropping the guests off at the airport on Sunday.

Chapter 14

The next morning, Cat and Shauna sat together at the kitchen table going over the plan for the next few days.

"You know, it almost feels like we're not in session. The two couples are either at the library or the bar at night. Brodie holes up in the study, writing. If we didn't have sessions during the day, I wouldn't see any of them," Cat grumbled as she glanced at her planner. "Tomorrow is Tammy's bookseller talk in the morning and then I'll do a 'What did you get done?' session after dinner, if the group comes back. I feel bad for Brodie, he's missing out on all the good stuff the other students get from the retreat."

"Don't feel bad. Brodie has learned a lot. And from what he told me this morning when he came for coffee, he finally feels comfortable writing in the genre he loves. He thought since he was going to school on scholarship, he needed to be the next

Hemingway or something." Shauna scribbled in her planner.

"We really need to sit down and have a talk about money and genres. He'd realize that his best shot to make a living in this career isn't to focus on literary works, but to find a hot genre and just keep publishing." Cat tapped her pen on her planner. "Maybe next month, I'll add a 'planning for the year' session. I can add it to Thursday or Saturday, and hold it the last two months of the year and January."

"Add in June. Sometimes that's a great place to reconnect with your goals or resolutions and still have time to get things done," Shauna added. She opened her laptop. "We aren't full for June, so I'll add it to the marketing for the session."

"Did you move up the hiking adventure sessions? Maybe we can do three—with the last one scheduled for September." Cat studied her year-at-a-glance notes. "What's the last month we're fully booked?"

"March." Shauna flipped through a few pages on her paper calendar. "Should I do some advertising for the Christmas gift-giving season?"

"Yeah, we have a balloon payment due in July this year and I'd really like to be a little flusher in the business account before summer."

Shauna set down her pen. "You know I told you I'd add in money if we needed it."

"When are you going to see your investment guy? I think you need to get that money set aside before I become weak and take you up on one of your multiple offers." Cat stood and refilled her coffee cup. "And I don't mean your brother as your investment guy. There's a local guy who works with the college who I'm pretty sure isn't involved with the families. You could check him out with Uncle Pete first, he'd know."

"That's a great idea. Even if I put it into a long-term CD at this point, at least it would be out of my hands. Then maybe Jake would stop calling me and trying to convince me that now he could turn me a fifty percent profit." Shauna made some notes in her to-do list. "I'll reach out to Pete next week after Shirley's gone and get this money locked up."

"Uh-oh. I heard my name. Am I interrupting you girls?" Shirley stood at the doorway to the kitchen. She was dressed in a soft blue blouse and dark blue pants. She typically wore darker clothes that looked more like the police uniforms she'd worn her entire career. Cat liked this look on her. Shirley looked softer, more feminine.

"Come on in. We're just planning for next year's sessions. As a graduate, maybe you could give us some insight."

Shirley made her way into the room. "I loved our session. I felt like I was part of a group that grew together. But this one . . ."

Cat saw the unease cross the woman's face. "Go ahead, say it, we've been saying the same thing."

"So it's not my imagination, it's different, right?" Shirley went to pour a cup of coffee. "During my session there was always people in the living room, talking or writing. And the dining room was more of a break room. This time, I know people are here, but it seems like a ghost town."

"But if they're getting work done, maybe it's okay," Shauna added.

Cat shrugged. On one hand, she agreed with Shauna. Writing was a personal process. Where one person loved the interaction and writing together as a group, another wanted privacy and total quiet while he or she wrote or created. On the other hand, she missed interacting with the group like she usually did. "I guess we'll find out tomorrow when we do the writers' review. This group just might be different. Although we may want to know coming in that a group is filled with couples. It changes the retreat's dynamics. Maybe we should be offering different things to couples?"

"It's a thought. I checked February's group and it's all individuals, so if you wanted to do a couples-only session, we'd have to push it out a few months. And maybe not invite a Covington student." Shauna stood and checked the muffins in the oven.

"Or invite a couple." Cat shrugged. "I knew a lot of married couples when I was getting my advanced degree. Finding a couple who are both in some type of English degree might be challenging, but I could throw it out to the dean next week."

"Maybe your uncle and I could come to this session. That way he could see what you're doing here firsthand." Shirley took a muffin off the table and put it on a napkin in front of her. "He's always saying he's going to work on his book. This way, he'd have to actually do it."

"Uncle Pete's working on a book?" Cat stared at Shirley, who was smearing butter on her muffin.

"You didn't know?" Shauna asked from where she stood at the fridge, where she'd pulled out a carton of milk. "It's some kind of mystery, right, Shirley?"

"Technically, it's more of a thriller. At least from what he's let me read." Shirley glanced at Cat. "It's really good. Maybe he was nervous to tell you, since you're a real author and all."

Before Cat could respond, Seth walked in the room. "Good morning, ladies. How did you all sleep last night?"

As everyone settled in to eat a quick breakfast, the chatter around the table turned to today's hike. Cat felt like she'd been punched in the stomach by Shirley's revelation. Why hadn't her uncle told her that he wanted to write a book? It had never even come up in conversation, yet both Shirley *and* Shauna had known. She wanted to ask Seth if he'd known too, but she couldn't handle the fact that if he did, she would be the only person her uncle hadn't confided in. Was it because she was too busy with her own work? Had he approached her about it and she'd shut him down somehow?

She was thinking about their conversations for the last few months when she heard Shirley's question.

"You don't mind if I tag along on the hike today, do you?" Shirley was finishing up the last of her fruit bowl as she asked Seth the question. "After Cat and I went to visit Sherry yesterday, I realized I hadn't been doing any of my workouts this week. I'm a little sore just from walking a few blocks. I need to get off my butt at least a few times this week before I fly back home."

"Sure." Seth took a bite of the wheat bread that

Shauna had made yesterday and sliced for toasting today. "I already made you a backpack, but Brodie's coming too, so I have to make one for him."

"Well, he can be my hiking buddy." Shirley picked up her empty plates and silverware, and took them to the sink. "Thanks for breakfast. I'm running upstairs to get my laptop and I'll grab a quiet place and start writing. I'm getting a lot done here. Especially since Pete's working so much. I might just finish this book before I leave."

"Be at the front by nine thirty ready to go," Seth called after her. Then he finished his omelet and repeated Shirley's actions. "I'll be downstairs. Let me know if you need anything."

"See you soon," Cat responded.

He paused at the basement door. "Cat? Would you like to meet some of my army buddies? You could ask them what they thought about boot camp. We're getting together tonight after dinner around seven for a drink at Bernie's. I'd like them to meet you."

Cat's eyes stung, but she wasn't going to cry. She swallowed the tears down and nodded. "Of course. I'd love to go."

"It's a date then." The crooked grin he flashed at her reminded her of graduation night, when he'd been across the gym, talking to his folks, when she walked inside. He turned, waved, and shot her that grin. And her heart had flip-flopped. She'd forgotten about that, well, until now. Seth had been her high school sweetheart and, as she should have realized back then, her soul mate. Then she'd been too intrigued by the older man with a library bigger than hers who was in love with her. Now, this felt right again. Better than she'd felt in the years since their breakup.

"I've got to finish setting up the dining room." Shauna went to the sink and rinsed her dishes before washing her hands. Cat stood, but Shauna waved her back. "I've got this. I'll do the rooms while you're gone. Then I'm going to meet up with my beta reader again."

"Who is your beta reader? Tammy?" Cat rinsed her plate and refilled her coffee cup.

The blush on Shauna's face told her she'd missed the mark. But if not Tammy, who else in town would be helping. Probably someone at the college. Or maybe it was a virtual meeting? Cat left it alone. Everyone seemed to be holding on to some sort of secret lately. Even her with Sherry's revelation yesterday.

"Whatever, don't tell me." Cat grabbed a banana and headed out of the kitchen. "I'm writing in my office. Tell Seth to come get me if I lose track of time."

"It's not that I don't want to tell you . . ." Shauna stopped talking and turned back to the oven, where she took out the last batch of muffins.

"But you're not going to," Cat added, and left the kitchen. If she wasn't a stronger person, she could get a complex around here. Thinking of a house of secrets, she went upstairs and poured the angst she was feeling into her new story.

She was just reading over the few pages she'd completed that morning when a buzz from an incoming text came from her phone. She picked it up and read it aloud. *"You have ten minutes before we leave without you. Make sure you wear your hiking boots and layer up. It's probably going to be chilly for a few hours. Love you, Seth."*

The last three words made her smile. She did love the guy. And what did the past matter. It was how their relationship was going now. And this time, she wasn't going to mess it up.

She turned off the computer after saving her document and left the office to get ready in her room. She took only half the time given her and was downstairs waiting in the foyer before Seth arrived. Brodie was sitting on the bench in the foyer, looking at his phone. He stuffed it in his pocket when he heard her footsteps.

"Hey, how's the writing going today?" She smiled and sat next to him, her down vest in her hands.

"I can't believe how fast this story is pouring out of me. If I forget a name or what happened before, I just put in a few Xs and go on." He glanced around the empty foyer. "Jocelyn told me that's what she does with a book. She says she picks it up during edits and cleans the document up then, rather than slow herself down while she's writing. She's right, it makes you feel okay about not knowing something specific."

"I do that, especially since I'm writing a series. I had a character I introduced in book one, but I was telling his story in book three. Instead of going back and grabbing his name and description, I made notes in the document on what I needed. He was called XXX for two chapters before I had time to go back and get his real name." She'd liked that character. He became one of the stronger side characters in that book and had earned his way into her heart.

Seth came into the house through the front door. "I can't believe you're already down here. When I sent the text, I thought you'd be at least a little late. She gets tied up in her books sometimes."

Brodie laughed. "Well, I guess I'm a real author then, because I get lost in the story too. I've been late for dates with my girl and I'm not sure she believes me when I tell her it's because I was writing."

"Well, if you need me to talk to her, I'm an expert in the field of dating a creative." Seth smiled at Cat. "The bunch of you are an interesting type."

"That's why I just gave in and started writing. I knew I'd never be number one in her eyes so I might as well have my own project going." Archer crossed the foyer with his wife by his side.

"So not true. You are definitely number one . . . as long as I'm not in the middle of a scene. I swear, he waits until he hears my fingers flying across the keyboard before he asks some stupid question, like where's the paprika." Jocelyn laid her head on her husband's shoulder. "He doesn't like it when I say right where you left it."

"If it was truly where I left it, it would be out on the counter." Archer kissed the top of his wife's head. "Although I shouldn't complain. I cook, she cleans up. Her storage system with the groceries and the spices is just a little challenging at times."

"Guilty as charged." Jocelyn focused on Cat. "You're lucky you have a built-in chef. My mind is so distracted by the story I'm working on, there's times I'm pretty sure I forgot to either bring in everything, or I've left stuff on the floor in a box instead of putting it in the freezer."

"That's why we do everything together," Sydney

said as she and Tristin entered the foyer area, hand in hand. "That way if one of us has writer brain and is off in la-la land thinking about the next blog, the other can pick up the slack."

Tristin shrugged on his light jacket. "It's usually her that's zoned out. I have to admit, she does a lot of our brainstorming. Anyway, enough about writing. Where are we going today? Same hike?"

Cat turned to Seth, realizing she hadn't suggested moving the hike, but she was surprised when he jumped in.

"We're going on a different trail today. Archer had said he wanted to see a miner's claim and there's one that just opened up, so we're going to check it out."

"Is it the one that belonged to the dead guy? Won't law enforcement want us to stay out of the area?" Brodie's eyes widened and Cat could tell he was reconsidering his decision to come on the hike.

"Actually, you're right, Brodie. It does belong to Chance McAllister, but I've cleared our trip already with the chief of police." Shirley pulled on a beanie as she walked over to the group. "And, as ex-law enforcement myself, I'll handle any discoveries we might make that affect the case."

"You're saying we're on an official police adventure?" Archer's eyes went bright. "I know it's not the same process as the time period I write about, but I'm going to pretend we're a deputized posse out to find the bad guy."

"Now who's going to be lost in his head?" Jocelyn smiled lovingly at her husband. "He gets to play cops and robbers."

"Actually, it's cowboys and Indians, but without the Indians. At least in the time period I'm writing about. But I'm so excited to get to see a real mining claim. I hear a lot of the current miners use old techniques and tools."

"I guess we'll see then." Seth looked around the foyer. "Everyone's here. Are we ready to jet?"

"Let me refill my coffee container and I'll be out the door." Sydney held a hand up when Tristin started to say something. "You and I both know that I need at least two cups before I'm even a tad sociable in the morning."

"We've got a few minutes. Everyone, go stock up on refreshments. Use the bathrooms if you need to because the first one to say they need to stop gets dropped off on the side of the road to walk back."

The group chuckled and moved into the dining room. Archer handed his cup to his wife and took off for the restroom on the bottom floor. Seth glanced at Cat. "What?"

"I'm not kidding. Go get some food. Some coffee." He glanced toward the stairs. "Do you need to run to your room?"

"No." She grabbed his arm and leaned into him. "Is this the way you're going to run kids around? Like a drill sergeant?"

"Seems to work." He leaned down and kissed her. "And exactly who's kids are we talking about me running around?"

"Let's talk about that later. Like maybe in a few years?" She giggled as he let go of her, then went into the dining room and put a few cookies into a paper bag and filled up his cup, chatting with the guests.

She went into the kitchen to say goodbye to Shauna, but she wasn't there. A note on the white board said, *Gone shopping.* Cat checked the back door to make sure it was locked, then left to meet up with the group.

Time to go exploring. And with Shirley on hand, her uncle wouldn't be griping about her getting involved in his investigation. At least she hoped he wouldn't.

Chapter 15

The ride out to the trailhead was filled with chatter. Archer told stories about miners in the gold rush days and how other miners would jump claims. "A lot of people died, just over a rumor of gold being found."

"Well, you know 'money is the root of all evil,'" Jocelyn added.

Sydney laughed as she watched out the window. "I'm sure I could avoid the pitfalls if someone would just give me the chance of being rich. I'd be a very good girl."

Tristin tousled his wife's hair. "You'd be living the good life out of an all-exclusive resort."

"Yeah, but you could be writing the Great American Novel while I laid by the pool and worked on my tan." Sydney rested her head on Tristin's chest. "I totally have a plan for the situation."

"Well, let's just hope the money holds out until I get the book written, find a publisher, and get on the *NYT*'s list."

"We'll only need, what? Two three months for that?" Sydney lifted her head, gazing at him hopefully.

"How about two or three decades?" Archer corrected. "I hear the book business is rough, right, Cat?"

"It's not as easy as some people think, but at least you all are doing the right things. It's a write, revise, submit, repeat type of business. The more you finish and get out there, the closer you'll be to winning." Cat pondered the question. "If you want to talk more about this, we could have a fireside chat tonight after dinner?"

"That sounds lovely. As much as I've enjoyed playing at Bernie's this week, I think I've hit my limit of dark bars and White Russians. And, since we're hiking today, maybe we could do at least one sprint tonight to get some words in? I have to admit, writing at the library every day has been heaven. I've gotten more done on this book in a few days than I did the last couple of months." Jocelyn poked Archer in the belly. "Maybe you should win the lottery so I could stay home and write full time. Then I could get this level of word count done every day."

"I'll get right on that. Right after I capture a real, live unicorn for the backyard." Archer glanced out the window. "Honestly, Cat, I don't know how you write here. I'd be out every day seeking out new historic places to catalog and photograph."

"Now, hold on, Archer, travel logs are our business, not yours," Tristin complained.

"You could go in together with a historic tour business. Archer could find the places, Jocelyn write about the history, and then Tristin and Sydney would lead the tours." Brodie grinned at the couple. "And I could drive the bus and write my books on the off season. Of course, you'd have to pay me a living wage to drive so I could take the winter off."

"Everyone wants a piece of the action," Archer said. "So what about you, Cat? Do you and Seth want a piece of this? We could use the retreat house as our preferred housing provider."

"Then I'd have to work as a hostess more than one week a month." Cat shook her head. "I mean, I like you guys, but you should see the house when it's not retreat week. It's so quiet, I can write all the words."

"Well, our evil plan has been thwarted," Jocelyn said. "I guess I better call my boss and tell him I will be at work on Monday."

"It's not Monday yet," Seth announced as he pulled into the parking lot for the trailhead. "And today's a perfect day for a hike. Let's get going and not wish our time together away."

As they unloaded the SUV, Cat pointed to a small sedan at the far end of the parking lot. "Looks like we're not the only ones taking advantage of the good weather."

Seth glanced over at the car. "Looks like a rental."

Cat peered at the vehicle. "It has Colorado plates."

"Yeah, but it's new and has a sticker in the front driver window. I'm pretty sure that's the logo for the local rental car agency." Seth moved to the back of the car and started handing out back-packs. "Come get your supplies."

As he handed out the packs, Cat crossed the lot and looked at the car more closely. Seth had been right, it did have a scannable sticker on the front window. She pulled out her phone and took a picture of the plates, as well as the car. Just in case. She didn't want someone messing with her vehicle while they were gone. And if they did, at least she had a clue to one person who might have seen the activity go down.

When she got back, Seth handed her a bag. "The car's going to be fine here. Your uncle sends out patrols to check out the lots on every shift. Just in case."

"I know, but now I feel a little better leaving it here alone." She pulled on her pack. "Did you lock the doors yet?"

"Get used to the constant reminders." Archer elbowed Seth. "It's just what women do."

Seth took out the keys from his pocket and double-clicked the remote locking the car and let Cat hear the beep. "Locked up. Again."

"Thanks." She glanced at the trailhead. The last time they had been here was to help Uncle Pete go through Chance's cabin. She made eye contact with Seth and imagined he was thinking the same thing. "Are we ready then?"

Shirley came and stood next to her. "I just wanted to remind people that there has been a crime committed somewhere here in this section of the woods. So if you see something out of the ordinary, please let me know. And don't touch it or pick it up."

"You mean like this gun in the bushes here?" Brodie asked, pointing to a spot near the parking lot. When Shirley's eyes widened and she started to move toward him, he laughed. "Sorry, just kidding. There's nothing there."

"Kid, you're going to find out you don't mess with a law enforcement officer, retired or not." Shirley pointed a finger at him. "I'm pretty good at finding dirt in anyone's background. Do you want me to start digging and let your new friends know what I found?"

"No, please, I'll be good." Brodie fell to his knees in an exaggerated begging motion.

The group laughed at his antics.

"If we're done playing"—Seth pointed to Brodie—"can we get this hike started?"

Brodie jumped up and saluted Seth. "I'm ready to go."

"I kind of liked him better when he didn't talk so much," Seth fake-whispered to Cat, who broke out in laughter.

Archer slapped Brodie on the back. "Son, you need to temper your moods. You're up, then down, then up again. Have you talked to a doctor about this problem?"

His eyes widened as they moved to the trail. "No, do you think I need to?"

"It couldn't hurt." Archer and Brodie disappeared into the tree line.

Seth shook his head. "I better get up there or they might take the path going to Thunder Mountain instead and we'll be knee-deep in snow before you know it."

Cat watched as he took off to get ahead of the

men. Cat pointed to Tristin and Sydney. "You guys go next."

"Mind if I walk with you?" Jocelyn asked Cat.

Shirley nodded. "Go ahead. You guys follow Sydney and Tristin, and I'll bring up the rear. That way I can keep an eye out for any uninvited visitors joining our group."

Jocelyn put her hands over her ears. "If you're talking about hairy animals, I really don't want to know. I could end my vacation without seeing one bear and I'd be perfectly content."

Cat started walking to the trails. "Typically, they stay away from the trails, especially if they think hikers are going to be out and about. They'd rather not be seen."

"That works for me." Jocelyn matched Cat's pace. "So tell me about how you published your book. Did you get an agent with the first book?"

Back on more solid ground with the conversation, Cat fell into her "bought" story. She had one that she told most retreats and surprisingly at several reader events when she had a Q&A session. There was always a writer in the group who wanted to know the magic handshake to getting published. But they always seemed a little disappointed when Cat explained there wasn't one. She always finished with a caveat. "Networking is all good and fine. But if I hadn't written a great book, Michael introducing me to Alexa at a party would have just been small talk. Write the best book you can. Then write another one. Didn't someone say you needed to write one million words before you became a master at your craft?"

"I'm pretty sure I've written more than that over

the last five years, but it's nice to hear that you feel like the work is how you got your agent. I know life is all about who you know, but there has to be a chance for the rest of us, right?"

The group was gathering around what Cat knew as Chance's cabin. When she got to the front, she realized the front door had been kicked in. She looked at Seth. "Call Uncle Pete and let him know there's been a break-in."

Shirley shook her head. "We need to clear the area and make sure no one's still in there. Take the guests over next to the outhouse. Keep Pete on the line while I'm going in, just in case I need backup.

Seth handed Cat the phone. "You call your uncle. I'm going in with Shirley."

"Hold on a second." Tristin pulled what looked like a club out of his backpack. "Take this. I always carry one just in case we get attacked during a hike."

"Tristin can use mine and protect the group while we wait." Sydney pulled a matching club out of her bag, but this one had a bedazzled star on the front. Sydney started moving the others to the edge of the trail.

Cat hung behind. She dialed Uncle Pete, then hugged Seth as she waited for him to answer. "You be careful."

When her uncle picked up, she walked toward the others and explained the situation.

"What do you mean Shirley and Seth are going into the cabin?! You all need to get out of there and back down the hill." Uncle Pete sounded like he was already on his way to the cruiser.

"I don't think anyone's here, but we wanted to make sure before we finished our hike. Just because someone broke in, doesn't mean it's the guy who killed Chance. And besides, he'd have to have a lot of bullets in his gun to get all of us." Cat watched the front of the cabin, holding her breath as Seth and Shirley disappeared inside.

"Seriously, did you have to say something like that?" Jocelyn whispered. "It's like tempting fate."

"We're fine here, honey." Archer rubbed his wife's arm. "Kids probably broke into the cabin. You know how kids are, they don't let anything that even looks abandoned be untouched for long."

Cat turned away from the group and spoke quietly into the phone. "I'm sending you a picture of the rental car that was parked on the trailhead. I'm not sure who it belongs to, but we didn't see any other hikers on the way up the mountain."

"Another reason you should turn around now." Uncle Pete sighed. "Hold on a minute."

Before her uncle had returned on the line, Seth and Shirley had emerged from the cabin. Shirley waved Cat over. "Let me talk to Pete."

She crossed the opening and handed over the phone. "I'm on hold."

As Shirley explained the situation to Uncle Pete, who came back on the line, Cat gave Seth a hug. "Everything all right?"

"Honestly, I couldn't tell any difference in the cabin from when Pete brought us up. Nothing was missing. Maybe some kid just wanted to see if he could get the door open and then lost his nerve." He scanned the forest around them. "Do you think we should take them back?"

"Depends on what Uncle Pete says, but it would be a shame to cut short a second try at this hike. Besides, Archer was really looking forward to seeing a real-life mining claim." She waved the rest of the group closer. Shirley finished her call and handed the phone back. Cat slipped it in her pocket. "What do you think? Go back or go on?"

"Pete is on his way here with a deputy, you might as well finish the hike. I'll stay here and wait for them to arrive." Shirley sank down on the porch step.

"Do you want me to stay with you?" Cat glanced at Seth, who nodded. "They can go ahead and I'll wait with you."

"Girl, I've been at worse crime scenes by myself. I'll be fine. Besides, if you remember, I'm the professional here, not you." Shirley added a smile to her words to lighten the mood. "And, if you're here, I don't get to spend some time alone with your uncle."

Cat studied her. "I thought you said he was bringing a deputy."

"He is, but the guy will probably stay with the car, waiting to see who comes down for it." Shirley's eyes twinkled. "You don't want to ruin my afternoon, do you?"

Seth took Cat's arm. "We'll pick you up on the way back down. Come on, Cat, let's get this group going."

Cat snuck a peek back at Shirley, who was now leaning back on her arms, taking in the warm autumn sunlight. "If I didn't know better, I'd say she planned this entire thing to get some time with Uncle Pete."

"You're saying she snuck up here last night, broke the door in, went back to the house, and pretended to be surprised. All to get a short date?" Seth looked skeptical.

Cat just shrugged. "I've known women to do more to get a guy's attention."

"But she already has your uncle's attention, just not his time this week," Seth reminded her.

As they were walking out of the clearing toward the guests, Seth stopped and picked up something from the ground.

Cat leaned toward him. "What's that?"

He held it out so she could see. "An American flag pin. The back's broken off, but we all got one of these last night at the reunion."

"You're saying one of your army guys was out here last night breaking into Chance's cabin? Why?"

He shook his head. "I'm not saying that. All I'm saying is this is the same type of pin they gave us last night. Heck, it could be mine." He reached up to his lapel on his coat and fingered the flag pin still attached to the coat. "Okay, then, maybe not mine. But maybe I stepped on one at the party and it stayed in my shoe until right now."

"Convenient." Cat stared at him.

"Seriously, this is not about the guys at the party." He held up a hand when Cat tried to say something else. "Sorry, the discussion is closed. For now, we're on a nice, relaxing hike. That's all. Nothing else. No talk of murder unless we find another body."

Cat rapped her knuckles on a tree. "Don't talk

like that. You know my history of being at the wrong place at the wrong time is legendary."

She followed him to the group, where everyone had to hear Seth's story for themselves. Then, finally satisfied, they fell into line and headed to the mining claim. Archer fell back to walk with Cat.

"Thank you for not just taking us back. I feel like I'm right on the edge of getting to finally see a claim and then something bad happens. Like you seeing the dead guy last time. And this time, we come across a break-in. Maybe we shouldn't go any farther. Maybe I'm bringing you all bad luck?"

"You don't really think that, do you?" Cat paused and adjusted her backpack. She glanced behind to make sure no one was following them.

"Sometimes I wonder. I mean, bad things happen when I'm around. The only good thing in my life was when Jocelyn agreed to marry me. I couldn't believe my luck that day." He smiled at the memory. "And so, I ran her up to the justice of the peace at the courthouse and we tied the knot. No way was I going to let her get away. I hadn't even bought a ring yet."

"How long have you been married?" Cat asked as they started walking up the trail again.

Archer grinned. "Twenty-three years. I have a surprise for her on lucky twenty-five. We're going to Scotland. I'm already saving all I can to pay for the trip."

"Sounds like the perfect gift." Cat put her hand on his arm. "We're going to get you to a mining claim, come heck or high water. You just keep faith in the process."

He wiped away tears off his cheeks and smiled. "Thanks. I appreciate this."

Cat watched as he made his way back up the trail to meet up with Jocelyn. It was apparent that the pair loved each other. Now all they had to do was get the group to the mining claim, take some pictures, and return to meet up with Shirley and Uncle Pete.

It should be easy.

Chapter 16

Cat swallowed down the unease she felt as they continued their climb up the trail. Going around the mountain, they found themselves in shadow, and the light dimmed even more. Cat felt her pocket to make sure she had a flashlight. Just in case. She'd stashed one in her pocket before leaving home. Along with a box of matches, a newspaper, and a pocketknife, she felt prepared for most eventualities. Including getting lost in the woods. Of course, she hadn't mentioned her over preparedness to Seth. The actions kind of felt like she didn't trust him to get them there safe and back home. Which wasn't true at all.

Yet she still had the items in her coat pocket. Maybe it was just her own paranoia of going off into the woods that had her spooked. But as they made it farther up the mountain, Cat kept looking back behind them. Just in case.

Now that they were climbing a hill, the only person Cat could see was Archer. She assumed the rest were ahead of him on the trail. It must be her writer mind that made up stories as she walked, she thought. She was always putting her characters in danger, then upping the ante just as they thought they were clear. It was kind of like they needed to earn their happy ever after. If she was one of her characters, she'd be really mad at her author, especially if something happened to them over the crest of that mountain.

Her heart pounded as she lost sight of even Archer. Cat quickened her pace. She didn't want to take a wrong turn and get herself lost. That would be embarrassing. As she crested the hill, she didn't see anyone on the trail. She pushed her walk into a little jog, then as she went around a corner, someone stepped out of the woods and into her path.

She let out a short yelp; then Seth's arms were around her. "Hey, I thought you'd gotten lost. The claim site is right through this stand of trees."

Shaking, she looked up into his face, the fear she'd felt as she came up on the empty trail seeping out of her and leaving her weak and tired. "I guess I got a little behind."

"Come on then. Archer is lecturing everyone about the history of mining in Colorado. The guy knows his stuff." He put his arm around her as they walked through the trees and into the clearing.

Cat took a couple of deep breaths; then as they rejoined the group, she took her water bottle out and took a few sips. She was almost calm again after the scare. Of course, she wouldn't tell Seth what she'd experienced. He'd just laugh at her. He was as comfortable here in the woods as he was sitting on a couch watching football.

"What's really exciting about this claim is it looks like the current miner used a lot of the original equipment." Archer pointed out a wooden sluice box and a stack of old mining pans near the creek.

"And yet, he still had a modern camp chair and a cooler." Tristin knelt by the cooler. "Should I open it?"

"This is Chance's claim so he's not around to complain." Seth walked over and squatted next to Tristin. "I say go ahead."

Tristin opened the dented cooler and held up an empty beer can. "I guess mining was a thirsty occupation. There must be thirty empty cans in here."

"At least he didn't just litter. He kept his camp clean," Jocelyn noted, glancing around the area. She pointed to the side of the mountain. "Is that a cave?"

Cat walked closer and found the small entrance. "It looks like it." She pulled out her flashlight and shone the beam inside. "It opens up after a few inches."

Seth was by her side in an instant. "Let's be careful. Sometimes miners set booby traps on their claims to keep people out."

Cat glanced around the entrance. She pointed to a broken string in the dirt. "You mean like this?"

Seth followed the string to a branch from a nearby bush. "Exactly like this. But usually, there was some sort of weapon attached. Not to kill, but to warn the trespasser."

Cat glanced around and, in the dirt next to the

cave, she found footprints, drops of blood, and a pocketknife. She stood and stepped away. She tapped Seth on the shoulder and waved him away from the entrance. "Looks like Uncle Pete has a secondary crime site to process."

By now the rest of the gang had gathered around her. She pointed to the edge of the clearing. "Everyone, go stand over there. Archer, get your photos and we're out of here. We need to hook up with my uncle before he leaves the cabin."

"Do you think it's the same guy who trashed the cabin?" Tristin asked as he pulled Sydney near him. She was videotaping the events.

"If not, it's a strange coincidence that Chance's cabin is broken into and then someone tried to get into his claim." She glanced at Seth. "I don't understand. He wasn't making enough from mining to pay even his meager expenses. Why would someone try to steal from his mining claim?"

Seth held back as the rest of the group moved to where Cat had directed them to stand. Archer was still taking pictures of everything. "Unless what the thief was looking for wasn't just Chance's gold. Maybe he had something else up here that even he didn't know about."

They made their way back to the cabin; this time the group stayed close together and Cat could tell they all felt the unease. A cloud had covered the sun and the trail looked darker, more sinister, and gloomier. When they reached the cabin, Shirley and Uncle Pete were standing in front of a resealed cabin door, talking.

"That was fast. I figured you'd be another thirty minutes at the least." Shirley stepped off the porch, then frowned. She glanced from person to person, her gaze finally landing on Cat. "Tell us what happened."

"Someone was at the claim too. They didn't trash it, like they did the cabin, but Chance had set up a sort of security system on the cave. The intruder didn't realize it was there and he got a jab with a pocketknife for his trouble." Cat looked at her uncle. "There's blood there. Maybe we can find the killer by running DNA?"

"If he's the one who actually killed Chance, then maybe." Uncle Pete glanced at the seven people grouped around the clearing. "How much of a mess did you all make? What did you touch?"

Archer raised his hand. "I touched the sluice. And one or more of the pans. And I ran my hand in the creek."

Cat bit back a smile. Archer was thorough if anything.

"I opened the cooler and touched one of the beer cans. I ran my hand through them and tried to see if there was anything else in the cooler," Tristin admitted.

The rest of the group stood silent. Uncle Pete asked again, "That's it? No one else picked up or touched anything?"

"I was watching Archer freak out about the mining stuff. It was pretty entertaining. The dude loves this old stuff." Brodie shrugged as the group glanced at him. "What? You all were doing the same thing."

Archer sighed. "He's right. I did go a little crazy when I saw the claim."

Jocelyn rubbed her husband's arm. "That's

okay. We all have things we care about. If I'd walked into a closet filled with Victorian dresses, I would have probably done the same thing. We're writers, we love the details. And when we find something that we've only just imagined before, it makes our thoughts reality."

"Well put." Uncle Pete smiled at her and Jocelyn blushed just a bit.

Or it could have been the cold air making her cheeks red, Cat thought. Either way, it was time to pull the hostess card and get them out of here and back to the house, where it was warm and there wasn't anyone trying to find a hidden treasure. She turned to her uncle. "Can we go home? You know where to find any of us if you have more questions. And it's getting cold out here."

"The sun's starting to set. I need to wait for a sweeper team to come in again. They're out of Denver, so it's going to be a while." He turned to Shirley. "You might as well go back with the group. No need you freezing out here while I wait."

"I'm staying. I flew from Alaska to spend time with you and although this might not be the experience I expected, at least we'll be together until the sweepers come. Then you can take me to dinner while you wait for any results." Shirley sat down at a picnic table, signaling that she wasn't leaving.

Uncle Pete shook his head. "Strong women. I don't understand why I'm so attracted to them. Mostly they are just a pain in the rear."

"I heard that," Shirley called out, and the group laughed.

Seth slapped Pete on the back. "You and me both, buddy."

"Hey now, don't be dragging me into this. I'm the one who suggested going home." Cat gave her uncle a hug. "Let me know if you need anything. Maybe I could warm up some of Shauna's soup and send it back up to you with one of your deputies?"

He lifted his eyebrows. "And you think it would really get here? There's not a man on my force who doesn't know how good Shauna's cooking is. I'm surprised none of them have tried to woo her to marriage."

Cat laughed. "I think Shauna falls under the strong woman category. Maybe they're just biding their time until the right moment comes along."

"Maybe, but anyone who's waiting for love to just happen is going to be disappointed." Uncle Pete waved me and the group away. "Go home. I'll text you when we're back in town so you won't worry."

Cat moved toward the group and the trail that would lead them back to the parking lot. The second hike hadn't gone much better than the first, except they hadn't found a body this time. Just evidence of a break-in or two. She thought about Uncle Pete's last words and turned back toward the cabin. Seth was bringing up the back and she pointed to the cabin. "Just what was he saying?"

Chuckling, he took her arm and turned her back downhill. With an arm around her waist, he kissed the top of her head. "I wondered when you'd respond. I think he was talking about us. How we need to make a decision about us."

"What about us? Aren't we happy?" Now Cat was completely confused. Especially since Seth had apparently understood her uncle's message and it had gone totally over her head.

"I'm happy. You're happy. But maybe we'd be happier if we took the next step." He looked down at her and they paused as he caught her gaze. "I'm in this for the long haul. Just wanted you to know that I may be coming with a question soon. I'm not asking at this minute, but, Cat, do you want me to ask?"

Emotion threatened to overwhelm her. For a not proposal, this question was a very big one. She touched his face. Seth, the guy who had always been there for her, even when she turned away from him.

He grabbed her hand and kissed the palm. "We've got to get going. You tell me when you're ready. Because I could do it today, tomorrow, or next year. I know where my future is heading. You just need to know the same thing."

"It's not that I don't love you . . ." Cat wondered if she could explain it. For someone who made her living with words, she seemed to be totally out of them right now.

"Cat, it's okay. I blindsided you with the question. I've been thinking about the past a lot lately. Mostly because of what happened to Chance, I guess. Just know that I'm ready to start our life together, anytime you are." He started to walk away, but she pulled him back to her.

"You bought me a ring." When he didn't say anything, she continued. "Sherry told me that you and Chance went to a jeweler and bought me a ring in Germany."

"I did. I was planning on asking you when we got to Fort Hood. But we never got there, together." He squeezed her. "Look, I know this isn't the right time for this. So just know, I love you."

"I love you too."

"So, can we go meet up with the rest of the group? They're probably at the car and wondering if we got attacked by a mountain lion."

She laughed as they walked forward. "No, they are probably thinking we've been taken captive by a bunch of trolls. At least that would be Brodie's answer. He's writing fantasy."

"Trolls?" Seth glanced around the darkened forest. "I could see that. Are you okay?"

Cat leaned into him as they came up on the lot. The group was standing around the car, watching the trailhead. "I'm fine. We'll have this conversation soon."

Seth held out keys and jingled them toward the group. "I'm looking forward to it."

By the time they got into town, the group asked to be dropped off at Reno's. Brodie climbed out of the car at the restaurant with the two couples. "I'll be back around six for that group event."

"As will the rest of us." Tristin slapped the kid on the back. "It's time to stop playing around and get our work done. The retreat's almost over."

Cat watched as the group walked into the restaurant and then disappeared inside. "They finally bonded."

"It's tenuous, but yes. They have brought Brodie

into their tribe. The problem is, they don't have a lot in common with a single, graduate student living on scholarship. He's barely scraping by and the other four are settled in their lives." Seth pulled the car out onto the street out of the curbside parking spot.

"I thought you might have to take someone to the airport today?"

"Actually, no. The guys decided that they're all staying in town for a few days. Did you decide about tonight at Bernie's? You should come with me if you have time."

"It depends on if the group wants to do a fireside chat. Jocelyn mentioned that she wanted to get an agent and pick my brain about my process. I don't think I can help much since I met Alexa during a faculty party at Covington. She was one of Michael's friends from his graduating class." Cat glanced at Seth to make sure she hadn't crossed a line. Sometimes, she felt that Seth didn't like to even acknowledge that time of her life had even existed.

"But she read your book and sold it. I guess she liked it then."

Cat smiled at the memory. "Michael didn't want me to send her the book. He wanted me to write something more literary, then send her a query. Instead, we got talking at the party after a few glasses of wine and she told me how much she liked urban fantasy books. They're darker than what I write, but magic is part of the world. I took a chance and told her I had a young adult manuscript and about Tori's world. She asked me to send it to her, and I did."

"And the rest is history." Seth squeezed her hand. "I don't think I've ever told you that I'm proud of you and your writing. It's something that's just yours. The retreat is kind of your and Shauna's thing, but the books? That's all you. I don't know how you do it, but I'm happy you found your thing."

"Like you and fixing old houses?" Cat glanced up at the roof as they came up to home. "How are you at roofing? We may need to look at replacing that next year."

"I've already had someone come out and take a glance at it. He says we've got another couple of winters, as long as it's not crazy weather, but yeah, a new roof needs to go on your budget." He parked the SUV in the driveway and held the kitchen door open for her.

"It's always something, right? I really hope I sell this new series." She paused inside the door, laying her hand on his chest. "Would you please read the first few chapters and tell me what you think?"

He nodded. "I can do that."

Shauna smiled as they came in. "Pete called and told me you all were back on your way. So what happened now?"

As Cat filled her in on the day, Seth excused himself to go to his room. "I've got some e-mails to answer."

Shauna stood at the stove. "Was I hearing things, or did he just agree to read your boot camp novel?"

"We had a short chat on the trails. He seems like he wants to open up about that time with me more." Cat poured a cup of coffee, holding the cup to warm her fingers.

"Well, will wonders never cease?" Shauna sat down with her own cup. "Now tell me all about what happened on the trails. Pete was a little vague about what you'd found."

Chapter 17

The trio had just finished eating when the group came back from Reno's. Sydney met Cat on the stairs. "Jocelyn said we're have a writer's meeting in the living room. I'm just running up to grab my laptop. I really need to get some words in today and having a set schedule of word sprints will definitely help."

Cat grabbed her own laptop from the study and by the time she got to the living room, everyone was there, chatting. A plate of brownies sat on one side of the coffee table and a plate of cookies on the other. Brodie grabbed a brownie and ate it in two bites.

"Hey, I thought you were off sugar this week because of cross-country." She sat her own brownie on a napkin. She didn't blame the kid. She couldn't resist Shauna's double chocolate brownies either.

"Coach is just going to have to deal with it. I'm a weak man." He picked up a cookie from the other plate. "This is my last one, I promise."

"Until when? Seven?" Archer glanced at the clock. "I'm going to totally call you out when you eat another one, you know that, right?"

"So let's get this party started. I understand you want to talk about publishing some more." Cat smiled at Brodie as he leaned back into his chair and ate the cookie.

"Actually, I think you answered my question this afternoon." Jocelyn opened her laptop. "To bring everyone up to speed, I was wondering if a normal person could get an agent nowadays."

"A normal person with a kickass project and a can-do personality," Sydney added. "I think it's all in how much you want it. Determination is as important as your ability to write, don't you think?"

The conversation went on for a couple of hours. And, as Archer had predicted, Brodie had eaten more than one cookie during that time. Archer moved the cookie tray away from where Brodie was sitting. "So who's up for some word sprints? Cat? Do you want to write with us?"

"I would, but Seth invited me to meet his army buddies for a drink this evening. If you all are done asking questions." Cat glanced around the room.

"Go, have fun. You are too tied to the retreat and us. You need some personal time, even on retreat weeks." Jocelyn made shooing movements with her hands.

"Besides, if you stay here, we can't talk about you and that handsome hunk of yours." Sydney batted her eyelashes at Cat. "And you know we love to gossip."

"You don't have to kick me out of the room."

Cat picked up her laptop. "But if you need anything, call Shauna. She'll be in the kitchen."

"Maybe you should take her too," Brodie suggested. "Then with the adults all out of the house, we could have a kegger."

Cat pointed at him. "You even try to have a party at my house and you're dog meat."

"Just kidding. Mostly." Brodie opened his laptop and glanced around the room. "But this would be an amazing place to host a party. There's so many rooms."

Cat shook her head. "I'm not sure who to leave in charge now."

Archer waved her out, mimicking the gesture his wife had used earlier. "Go and have fun. We'll keep the kid in check."

"I'm not a kid."

Cat heard Brodie's disclaimer as she was leaving the living room. She dropped her laptop off in a locked drawer in the desk in the study, then went into the kitchen. Shauna was there, working on her laptop. Cat glanced down at her jeans and T-shirt. "Do you think I should change before going to Bernie's to meet Seth?"

"How is that even a question? You're going to meet his army buddies, of course you should change. Shower and get ready and I'll set out an outfit for you. That way, all you have to do is get dressed and put on makeup and you're out of here." Shauna shut her laptop down and started to the hallway door. She paused when Cat didn't follow her. "Earth to Cat, are you coming?"

Cat wanted to say no. That she was too busy with the guests, but they had almost literally kicked her out of the living room. What was she scared of? That Seth's friends wouldn't like her? Did it even matter at this point in their relationship? She studied Shauna's unspoken challenge, then took a breath and headed to the door. What trouble could a couple of beers cause?

She got into the shower and heard Shauna come into her room, then leave. She quickly rinsed off and let her hair down. The hot water would help it curl up and she'd add a touch of product when she did her makeup.

When she walked into the bedroom, a pair of her stretch jeans lay on the bed with a pair of Shauna's cowboy boots. Not the ones she wore riding, but her line dancing ones. They had a touch of pink sparkle on the leather. She glanced at the top her friend had chosen and it was a deep V-neck tank in a sapphire blue. The only thing she was missing was a too-big belt buckle and a hat. Then she'd be cowboy'd up for the visitors. Or cowgirl'd up.

Shauna grinned when she came into the kitchen. "You clean up good."

"Especially when I have a friend doing my wardrobe selection. You don't think this is kind of trampy, do you?" Cat glanced down at the soft and flowing top.

"No way. You look classy." Shauna handed her a white fake fur bomber. "Especially with this."

Cat slipped it on. At least she'd be warm on the walk to the bar. She'd worn the bomber before and even in extreme cold, it kept the wearer nice and toasty. "Okay. I'll be home in a couple of hours, with or without Seth. And watch out for Brodie. He's in a mood."

"He's already come in to see if I wanted to join them in their writing sprints. I told him I don't tell stories. I just cook." She glanced at her laptop. "You better get going. Do you want me to call Seth and have him look out for you?"

"No, I'll text you when I get to the bar. If there's a problem, just call. I'll come right back." Cat slipped her house keys into her coat pocket. Her jeans didn't have much room for anything in the back pockets.

She stepped out into the cold night. Soon, the temperatures would drop even during the day and winter would be in full force. But she liked having all four seasons. In California, she could go to the beach and suntan in November on a good day. Here, she enjoyed snowshoeing into town to hit the library on snowy days and skiing with Seth on weekends. It made her appreciate the hot summer days when they were hiking and found a mountain lake to camp at and take a quick swim in the chilly water.

Besides, California was nice, but Colorado was home. She would have come back home sooner or later, even if Michael hadn't left her the house. She belonged here.

The lights were on at Mrs. Rice's house. Cat could see a television flickering through her neighbor's window. Another reason she liked walking on cold nights? Mrs. Rice was tucked inside with her cat. No impromptu discussions about the retreat guests or how the college kids were ruining the small town. No, Mrs. Rice wouldn't be out for long stretches until March, when the air got soft and her garden would call to her.

She tucked her hands into the coat a little deeper and cursed herself for not thinking about grabbing gloves. At least she had a beanie on to keep some of her heat from escaping. Her hair would look like a rat's nest, but it was a small price to pay for more warmth. She hurried past Dante's house even though, from the lack of lights in the front, along with no cars in the driveway, she figured he was in Boston. She didn't need the handsome mob boss coming around. He made both Seth and Uncle Pete nervous.

Thinking of Seth and his non-question question this afternoon, a smile curved Cat's lips. She wasn't ready to jump into marriage quite yet. She liked, no loved, her life now. And Seth was a lot of the reason. But settling down, having kids, doing the whole mom thing? She didn't think she was ready. Not quite yet.

She turned onto Main Street with a swirl of thoughts running through her head. A bunch of drunk college students were coming from Bernie's. As she passed, one of the group called out, "Don't go in there. There's a bunch of old guys hogging all the pool tables. It's a drag. Come drink with us."

She shook her head and kept walking.

"Do you know you're really super-hot?" the young man called after her.

"Yeah, especially for your age," another of the group added.

Cat didn't turn around but muttered, "Thanks, I think." She opened the door to Bernie's and was enveloped by the darkness. It took her eyes a few seconds to adjust to the dimly lit neon room. With the bar on her right, she scanned the pool tables for Seth. Instead, she found him sitting at a table with two other men.

She pulled out her phone, took a quick candid shot of him and his friends, and then texted Shauna with the picture. *Found our guy. See you in the morning.*

Be safe, Shauna texted back.

Cat smiled and slipped the phone into her pocket. The two of them had started the texting routine when they lived in California after Shauna had become Cat's last roommate. That way, at least one person knew where the other was at all times. The dating scene had been brutal, with several cases of women having their drinks tampered with during the few years Cat had lived there. She'd rarely gone out, but it was nice to know that she had a lifeline.

She walked up behind Seth and put her hands on his shoulders.

"Better quit that, my girlfriend is supposed to be coming down soon. She's the jealous type," he said, then turned toward her, kissing her.

She could taste the beer on his lips. "She shouldn't worry, but you should. I know where you sleep."

Seth laughed and pulled a chair up to the table next to him. "Cat, meet the guys. You met Terry before, but he's the one dressed in red. He must think he's Santa or something. Joey, here, drove in from Wisconsin for the reunion."

As they greeted each other, Cat noticed Terry's bandaged hand. "Oh, no. What happened?"

"Stupid me, I ran into a door at the hotel that I didn't know was locked. Broke the window and cut up my hand pretty good." Terry grinned. "At least, that's what I remember happening. I went to the ER this afternoon when I finally woke up. I had a bit to drink last night at the reunion."

"Well, I'm glad you're okay." Cat thought about the trap that Chance had set up at the mining camp. She really needed to talk to her uncle before her mind went racing off and blaming Terry for something he didn't do.

He picked up a pack of cigarettes and shook it. "Crap, I'm out of cigarettes and beer." He stood, gathering up the empty bottles on the table. "My turn to buy the round anyway. Cat? What can I get you?"

She called out her favorite beer and nodded when Joey excused himself to "hit the head," in his terminology. She leaned toward Seth. "I hope I didn't scare everyone away."

"Nah, they're just giving us a second to say hello. I'm really glad you came down, Cat." He rubbed her hand. "You still cold?"

"Why?" Then she saw him glance at the coat. She slipped it off and hung it on the back of the chair. "Can you tell Shauna dressed me?"

"You should let her dress you more often." Seth eyed her outfit. "The blue makes your eyes sparkle."

"You've been drinking." She laughed, then looked up as Terry got back to the table, taking the bottle he offered her. "Thanks."

"It's been nice meeting you. I can see why Seth wants to keep you a secret. You're a lovely woman." Terry sat the bottles on the table and glanced around. "Where's Joey? I'm heading out back for a smoke."

"He's around here somewhere." Seth nodded to the back of the bar. "There. It looks like he had the same idea."

"Be right back. I'm going to ask you all the embarrassing questions about why you left our boy in such a bad state the last time and make you swear to never hurt him again." Terry winked at her. "Unless you have a notion to run off with me."

"You better get out of here before you and I have words." Seth half stood, making Terry laugh. "Besides, she'd never run off with you. You're not her type."

"Now, Seth, don't you remember Germany? I'm every woman's type."

As Terry walked away to join Joey for a cigarette out back of the bar, Cat turned to Seth. "Don't you think it's weird that Terry cut his hand?"

"Not really. He's kind of a klutz. In Germany, I swear the guy was in the infirmary more times than anyone else in our unit." Seth went to take a sip of his beer, then set it down. "You're thinking he was out at the mining claim."

Cat shrugged. "Maybe. It's just weird."

"I don't know why he would be out there. He and Chance weren't that close. In fact, they argued a lot. I always thought he felt guilty about that when Chance died. I mean, he never was able to have a friendly relationship." Seth shook his head. "If Terry says that's how he got hurt, I'm inclined to believe him."

Cat didn't want to argue. Besides, Uncle Pete should be able to run DNA on the blood they found at the scene. It might not be before Terry and the others left town, but it wasn't like they were rushing off anyway. Cat put her hand on Seth's arm. "Sorry I brought up the issue. Let's just have fun tonight."

Two hours later, when Terry tried to buy another round, this time for tequila shots, Seth shook his head. "Sorry, guys, the pumpkin here has a retreat going on. We're going to have to get home at a reasonable time so we don't feel like crap tomorrow."

"It was really nice to meet you," Joey said to Cat. The man was soft-spoken, but he and Cat had talked about books and writing a lot of the night. Seth and Terry had been on a roll about the old days.

"I hope I run into you again." Cat stood and let Seth slip Shauna's coat over her shoulders. "And you too, Terry."

"Cat, did you know that your engagement ring was one of the last items of jewelry the shop ever made? That shop blew up a week after Seth picked up the ring. That's where Chance was killed." Terry frowned, rubbing his face. "I mean, where we thought Chance was killed. We got confined to base for over a month after that because they thought it wasn't safe on the streets."

Seth reached out and paused Terry's arm as he tried to take another drink. "Are you sure? I thought he was killed in some kind of a raid?"

"Sure as shit. Oops, sorry, ma'am. I'm not used to being around ladies." He grinned and Cat could see that he was feeling the alcohol. "Stay for one more round. I've missed you."

"We're going now. Keep him safe," he said to Joey. "No more running into doors."

Joey held his hands up. "I wasn't on duty last

night. I left the bar early and was already in my room, reading."

Cat and Seth were walking out of the bar when Bernie waved them down. "Don't worry about him. I'll pour him into a cab tonight like I did last night. The guy's pretty shaken up about the death of your friend."

Seth nodded. "Yeah, he is."

"You two be safe out there. The roads are slick. I take it you're walking?" Bernie glanced at the beanie Cat had just pulled on.

"Safer than driving." Seth slapped the bar. "Thanks for a fun evening."

"My pleasure." A customer called out to Bernie and he moved down the bar, leaving them alone.

"It was bone-chilling cold when I walked here earlier." Cat pushed open the door and shivered. "And it doesn't feel any warmer now."

"Yeah, but you have me to hold you close as we walk." Seth put his arm around her as they stepped out of the bar. "I don't think Terry used to drink that much when we were in the service. He had two, maybe three beers to my one."

"He was downing them pretty fast. And when he started on the shots, I knew he was just going to be hammered." Cat shook her head.

"We haven't done this for a while." Seth glanced up at the clear sky. "And the moon is almost full. Maybe weird things are happening because of that."

"Maybe." Cat didn't want to remind him that people killed people, not werewolves dealing with the moon's different stages. But she could be wrong.

Chapter 18

The next morning, Cat spied Archer sitting in the living room when she came down the stairs for coffee. She paused at the bottom of the stairway and instead of getting her coffee in the kitchen, she grabbed a cup from the dining room, then went in to talk to Archer. She curled up in the chair facing him and sipped her coffee, waiting for him to look up from his laptop. She didn't have to wait long.

Archer looked up from the laptop and jumped back into the couch cushions. When he put his hand over his heart, Cat smiled. "Whoa. I didn't hear you come in."

"Sorry, I didn't mean to scare you. I just didn't want to bother you if you were writing." She sat her cup on the table. "What are you working on?"

"Oh, I'm not writing. I was going through all the pictures I took yesterday. There are some really good shots, but I have a lot of duplicates. And then there's these trash shots that I can't use at all. The problem with trying to replicate a historical event is someone always throws their trash around and ruins the shot." He pointed to his computer screen. "Come over here and see. There are five different shots where I have coffee cups, candy wrappers, and even a cigarette pack front and center. I wish I knew Photoshop. Do you think I could wipe these clean?"

Cat came over to the couch and sat next to him. "Let me see."

When he pointed out the cigarette pack, she froze. It was the same brand as Terry smoked. Not quite convincing evidence, but with the cut hand? Seth was going to have to admit there was a chance it had been Terry at the mining claim.

"Cat? What do you think?" A worried Archer stared at her.

She bit her lip. "Hey, can you send me these pictures? I think my uncle might be interested in seeing some of these."

"Seriously? To help solve the case?" Archer beamed. "That would be cool. But I'm not sure what you saw."

"I'm not sure it's important, but I want my uncle to see these." Cat picked up her cup. "Can you send those now?"

"Sure thing. Do you think it would be okay for me to try to fix these ones with trash in them?"

"Hold off for a bit. I think I know someone who could help. But let me reach out first. You never know what he might need for evidence tracking."

Archer nodded his head. "I know. I watch legal shows all the time. It's all about keeping the evidence secure so it can't be tampered with. I'll make me a copy of the file too so I can play with the copies and not the originals."

"Thanks, Archer." Cat walked into the kitchen and glanced at the clock. Was five in the morning too early to call her uncle? Had Shirley come back to the house last night, alone? She set her phone on the table and rubbed her eyes. These were all questions she shouldn't have to answer this early in the morning.

She heard a plate being sat in front of her and she opened her eyes. Shauna looked at her, concern filling her eyes. "Are you okay? How did the date go last night? I didn't hear you guys come in. Was it late?"

Cat held up a hand and dug her fork into the still-warm-from-the-oven blueberry coffee cake Shauna had sat in front of her. She took a bite, enjoying all the fresh fruit flavors. Then she washed it down with a couple of sips of coffee. "There. I'm better now. Last night was fine. I met two of Seth's crew. Joey, he was so sweet. And a big reader. Terry, on the other hand, is all guy. He barely spoke to me and when he did, he kept reminding me that I broke Seth's heart. Like I don't feel bad enough already."

"Oh, is that all?" Shauna went back to the stove, where she started stirring something.

"Yeah, no. And I think that his friend Terry is the guy who broke into the mining claim. And probably Chance's place." She picked up the phone. "And I need to call my uncle, but I'm not sure if I'd be interrupting something."

"If you're talking about Shirley, your uncle brought her back to the house about seven last night. We sat in the kitchen talking, and I fed her soup since she hadn't eaten." Shauna went and refilled her cup and sat down. "She's really worried about your uncle. She thinks he works too much and it's bad for his health."

"She's not wrong there." Cat looked at the clock again. "I guess this will wait until six. But then I'm calling, no matter what."

"Anything else have you in a tizzy?" Shauna leaned back in her chair, ready to listen.

Cat rolled her shoulders and glanced at the door. "Well, Seth and I finally talked about the ring he bought."

"Wait, what ring?"

Cat bit her lip, realizing she hadn't told Shauna what Sherry had told her about Seth's purchase in Germany. So she started with that conversation, told her about what Seth had not asked, then added in the piece that Terry had mentioned at the bar. "I'm not sure that any of it matters in finding out who killed Chance. And honestly, the emotion has me questioning anything I think I know."

Shauna stood and refilled both their cups with fresh coffee. "I think the exciting thing is Seth's thinking about asking you to marry him. Well, thinking about it again. I guess he'd planned to before when you—"

Cat held up her hand. "Don't say it, let me. When I married Michael instead."

"It's what happened. No shame in it. Now you just have to figure out what you want to do."

"Now? I like where we are. I like what we're doing. Yeah, maybe someday I want the little white church again and maybe kids. But not now. Who will remember to feed them when I'm lost in writing and Seth is rebuilding a roof somewhere?"

Shauna laughed. "Well, since I've had no luck with men, my plan is to live with you and your man the rest of my life, so I'll raise the babies. Or at least keep them fed."

"You're a good friend." Cat sipped her coffee. "So do you think he's the one?"

"Seth? I think you two are good together, but only you can make that decision." Shauna got up to check on something in the oven.

"No, I'm not talking about Seth. I mean Terry. Do you think he might have killed Chance?"

"There's no way that Terry would have killed Chance. He was part of our platoon." Seth stood at the door.

"Seth, I'm just asking a question." Cat stared into his devastated face. "Look, I'm sorry . . ."

"I've got to go. I told Joey I'd run with him this morning." He nodded at Shauna. "Don't hold breakfast for me. I'll eat in town."

When he disappeared out the back door, Cat sank back in her chair. "Well, I think I'm working myself out of that marriage proposal."

"Seth loves you. Couples fight. Especially about other people. You know that I hated Paul. He wasn't just Kevin's right-hand man, he was the bane of my existence. Every time we were about to go do something, just for us, he tried to stop us. Now, looking back, I realized he was probably just trying to break us up for the sake of his sister." Shauna sank into her chair. "And all my chattering isn't helping you, not one bit. What can I make for breakfast to make you smile?"

"Nothing, I'm not hungry. I'm going to go upstairs and work for a while. Tammy's arriving just before ten. Let me know when she's here and I'll help her set up. And Archer is up and in the living room." She glanced at the clock. "I'll call Uncle Pete after six. Then it's out of my hands."

"Calling him is the right thing to do, you know that." Shauna watched as Cat stood and refilled her coffee mug.

"Then why does it feel like I'm betraying Seth?" Cat shook her head. "Rhetorical question. Don't bother answering. This is my problem, not yours."

"But I'm supposed to feed the babies," Shauna said. When Cat didn't answer, she sighed. "Too soon to joke?"

"A bit. I'll see you around ten." She left the kitchen and made her way upstairs. She hoped she wouldn't run into anyone, but Archer had been awake. Who knew who else was up and writing or researching this morning? She made it all the way to her office without running into anyone. Then she locked the door, sat on the couch, and cried.

After she talked to her uncle, she felt even worse. But she hadn't been the only one to question Terry's whereabouts yesterday. The fact the guy was one of Uncle Pete's suspects only made her feel worse for Seth. Would this be the big fight that broke them up again? Why did they always run into problems? Maybe they weren't meant to be. Every time it started getting serious, crap happened. Just like every time she went on a diet, chocolate showed up in the house. Well, that might be because she'd bought it, but it was almost the same principle.

She was a pro at self-destruction. She was just going to have to face it. She would grow old and become the next Mrs. Rice, yelling at kids to get off her yard.

She opened the Word document and wrote for a few hours, knowing that what she wrote would probably be cut the next day. Writing while sad didn't bring out the best storyteller in herself. Even the word choices she made weren't appropriate for a funny satirist young adult or new adult book.

Finally, she gave up, closed the document, and spent the rest of the time looking for cute baby goat videos on Facebook. She shut the computer down at fifteen to ten and went downstairs. Tammy wasn't here yet, so she sat in the foyer, waiting.

The group came downstairs and, one by one, she directed them to the living room to wait.

"So I still have time to eat?" Brodie asked her.

She nodded, trying to put on the happy hostess face, but she really didn't feel it. "I don't know what's keeping Tammy, but you have until she gets here."

"Dude, you ate three full plates at breakfast. How can you stand to eat more?" Tristin followed him into the dining room.

Tammy pulled her book van in front of the house. She waved at Cat, then went to the back of the van, where she pulled out four boxes and put them on a hand cart. She then pushed the cart up the sidewalk and up the porch stairs. Cat held the door open for her.

"I'm so sorry I'm late. I left with plenty of time, but there was a road closed just up the street so I had to go around and then I got lost, so I was driving around the neighborhood for ten minutes. Finally,

I found Warm Springs and came back this way," Tammy rambled, as she dragged the boxes through the foyer and into the living room.

"No worries. Let me help you get set up." Cat followed her into the living room.

"Hey, Cat? Do you know if Shauna has more bacon?" Brodie blocked her way. "And we're almost out of juice."

She moved around him and pointed to Shauna, who was coming out of the kitchen with a cell phone in her hand. "I don't know. Ask Shauna."

"No problem. Shauna? We need bacon, man. Any chance there's still some in the kitchen?" He spun toward her, but Shauna just ignored him and walked around him toward Cat. "Shauna? Did you hear me?"

"Not now, Brodie." She grabbed Cat's arm before she could reach the living room. "Hey, I need to talk to you."

Running a hand through her curls, Cat turned back toward her. "Can't it wait? Tammy's going to have to leave to open her shop at noon, so we need to get this session started."

"No, Cat, it can't." She turned to the still-waiting Brodie. "Go in there and help Tammy set up and I'll make you some fresh bacon as soon as you're done."

"Deal." He sprinted into the living room, but stopped as he hit the door. "Don't forget OJ."

Shauna pulled Cat to the side of the stairwell, where the guests couldn't see her. "Your uncle is on the phone. There's been an accident."

"Is he all right? Don't tell me he's been shot. Well, he probably wouldn't be calling then, someone else would be, so I guess it's not that, but is Uncle Pete okay?" Cat's words fell over one another as she tried to form a coherent thought. "Please, no. Please, no."

"Hush now," Shauna said as she pulled her into a hug. "Be strong, it's not your uncle, but you need to talk to him."

Cat took the phone out of Shauna's hand. It could be her parents who were hurt. They would have used her uncle as emergency contact at their new condo in Florida. Her dad hadn't looked good when she'd taken a quick trip down to see them a few months ago. "Hello?"

"Cat, now listen, he's okay, just banged up a little."

Cat interrupted. "Dad? He's alive?"

"I'm not referring to your father. Honey, it's Seth. A pot of petunias fell off a rooftop patio and hit him midback. If Seth hadn't been watching, Joey could have been seriously hurt. I can't believe he didn't break a leg when he dove into him."

Cat could hear the sounds of the hospital around Uncle Pete's words. She felt numb and couldn't believe she hadn't even thought it might be Seth. Now that she knew it was, she felt cold. Seth was untouchable. Even in high school he hadn't been hurt throughout four years of football. "He's alive?"

"Yes, he's alive. Like I said, he's got some bumps and bruises from the fall. Would you or Shauna drive down to the hospital to get him? I can't leave until his friend comes around. I guess he hit his head pretty hard when Seth pushed him out of the way."

Relief gushed through her. "Yes, I'll be down

there in a few minutes. Thank you for watching out for him until I could get there."

"Seth's a good kid. Kind of like you are." Uncle Pete chuckled. "Look, I've got to go. The doctor just came out of the back and I need to see when I can interview Seth's friend. Maybe he remembers more about the incident."

She hung up the phone and handed it back to Shauna. "I've got to go."

"You're not going alone. I'll drive you to the hospital." Shauna led her to the kitchen door.

"But the guests. Brodie's bacon?" Cat needed to see Seth. To touch him and make sure that he was really fine like Uncle Pete had said.

"They'll understand. Let me just go tell Jocelyn what happened. She seems to be the most level-headed of the group. Sit down and I'll be back in a few minutes." Shauna pulled a chair out from the table and gently forced Cat down into it. "Stay right here."

"Okay." Cat felt numb. Her lips felt numb. Her fingers. And definitely her brain. It was like her world had shifted too many times in the last few minutes. She didn't know what to think. What to feel. So she just sat and waited. The clock on the wall ticked away the seconds that turned into minutes. Cat was just about ready to leave without Shauna when the kitchen door opened.

Shauna had Cat's purse, as well as her own. "Come on," she said, grabbing the keys to the car that were hanging on the row of hooks on the kitchen wall. "Let's go get Seth and bring him home."

Chapter 19

Walking into the ER waiting room, Cat stood by the door as Shauna went to find out where Seth was being treated. A cop stood on the other side of the door, but she didn't recognize him. As she stood there, Joey came out of a side door and headed to the exit. He stopped when he saw her.

"Oh, Cat. I'm so sorry. This is all my fault."

Cat shook her head. "You know Seth likes to play hero. He probably didn't even think twice before pushing you out of the way. He's like that." And it was one of the things she loved about him.

"I shouldn't have invited him to run with me. They must have thought he was Terry, so they went after him to shut him up. I should have just kept my mouth shut. I shouldn't have told Terry anything. But Chance, he was one of us. I should have stood up and told people then. Not waited so long."

"What are you saying?" Cat could see Shauna scanning the room for her, but Joey was blocking

Shauna's view. "Joey, you couldn't have known this would happen."

Joey didn't say anything.

"Wait, aren't you supposed to be in a coma? Didn't you hit your head?" Cat wanted to reach over to the cop on the other side of the door, but he was talking to a kid from the waiting room. She wanted to ask someone if they could see Joey too. Maybe she was imagining this whole thing. Maybe it was a dream. A nightmare.

"Just know I'm sorry." Joey stepped around her and out of the building.

Shauna waved to her. "Cat? He's back here."

Putting Joey out of her mind, she rushed toward Shauna. "Is he okay? What did they say?"

"They said he's back here." Shauna put a hand on Cat's back. "Let's go find out ourselves."

When they found the small room where Seth lay on a hospital bed, Cat's heartbeat went faster. He looked okay, but they had him hooked up to an IV and a blood pressure cuff. A quiet beeping noise filled the room. He turned his face from the television he'd been watching to the door. And smiled.

Cat's heart melted. He was okay. She rushed to his side and took his hand. "What happened? Are you okay? Joey said you saved him."

"He's awake?" Seth frowned and glanced at the television. "Pete was just in here a few minutes ago and said he was still out."

"I saw him in the waiting room. He's up and walking and fine. But he's worried about you. I don't know where he was going." Cat glanced at Shauna. "Maybe we should see if he's all right to leave? Maybe he's confused?"

"I'll go check in with the nurses' station." Shauna smiled at Seth. "Good to see that you're okay."

"Feeling a little foolish hooked up to all this crap, but yeah, I'm okay." He smiled back at Shauna. When she left, he reached out and pushed a strand of hair out of Cat's eyes. "Don't look so scared. I'm just banged up."

"Did you see what happened?"

Seth shook his head and squeezed her hand. "No, all I saw was the flowerpot flying down at Joey's head. I think it would have nailed him."

Cat laughed as she pulled up a chair to sit next to Seth. She wanted to keep touching him. To remind herself that he was safe. And alive. "Oh, my superman. Always on the watch to save others."

He leaned his head back on the pillow. "I have to admit, I'm feeling the pain here. If I want the good stuff, I'll have to stay over. So I told them I'd rather go back and have my girlfriend take care of me."

"Are you going to be able to make it up three flights of stairs?" Cat glanced at his legs. "Did they do X-rays? Is anything broken?"

"Yes, they did X-rays." He took a sip of water. "I'll be fine getting to my room, but I don't know if I'll want to drive the group to Outlaw tomorrow morning or not. We'll see what I feel like when I get up tomorrow. But if I'm still hurting, can you drive?"

"Of course, but I didn't realize you were going to Outlaw." Cat wasn't sure taking Seth home tonight was a good idea. Before she agreed with the plan, she wanted to talk to the doctor.

"Yeah, Jocelyn and Sydney tag teamed me the other day and asked if I'd take them up so they could see the ghost town. They haven't told Archer or Tristin, so don't ruin the surprise."

She shook her head. "You're a soft touch, you know that, Seth?"

"If I wasn't, I would have let Joey get hit by the flowerpot and I would have been the one walking out of the hospital pain free." He groaned as he moved. "Maybe I should see if I could get some sort of pill for this."

Cat pushed the button for the nurse. When the voice came over the speaker, she told the nurse that Seth needed something for pain, now.

"Someone will be right there." The voice broke off.

Cat glanced at her watch. "I'm giving them ten minutes, then I'm going and tracking down someone myself."

"You are a rock star." Seth closed his eyes and Cat could see the pain on his face. He just might have to spend the night in the hospital if he was hurting this badly.

Just then the door opened, but instead of the nurse she'd expected, Uncle Pete came into the room. He stepped closer to Cat.

"Are you sure it was Joey you saw leaving the hospital?"

Cat stood and put herself between her uncle and Seth. Lowering her voice, she answered the question. "Positive. I met him last night at Bernie's. He said he was sorry about Seth."

"What else did he say?"

She thought about the conversation and related it almost word for word to her uncle. "Then Shauna called me over and we came in to see Seth. Did you see a nurse out there? Seth needs something for the pain."

"I'll go get someone." Shauna disappeared out the door. Cat hadn't realized she'd been standing there all this time.

"What's going on? Why are you asking me about Joey?" Cat asked her uncle as he started to follow Shauna out of the room.

He took her hand and pulled her out into the hallway with him. Making sure they were out of earshot of Seth's room, he turned toward her. "Because up to about five minutes ago, he was asleep in his room and being monitored. Now, he's missing. The IV has been taken out, his blood pressure cuff is off, and his stuff is gone. I'm beginning to wonder if this thing was really an accident after all."

"What else could it be?" Cat glanced back at Seth. A nurse was standing over him and giving him a pill. Thank God for that. "Wait. You're saying someone intentionally hit Seth?"

"No, I'm saying someone tried to hurt Joey. And the fact he took off tells me he knows who would want him dead. Now we just have to figure it out before they succeed." He rubbed her shoulder. "Now, don't get all worried. We'll get Seth home; then I'll figure out this thing. But it would be better if he doesn't go out drinking with any of his old friends for a few nights. Maybe I can get someone charged with the murder before someone else gets hurt."

Cat watched the room as the nurse checked Seth's vitals. Then she started taking off the trackers. "Looks like they're getting him ready to leave."

Shauna met them outside the room. "The nurse says we can take him home as long as we get his meds from the hospital pharmacy. Your boy's a fighter, Cat."

She smiled. "He's stubborn, that's for sure." She glanced around the hallway. "Where can I grab a soda?"

"Down the hall to the left. Get me one, okay?" Shauna reached for her purse.

Cat waved her away. "I'll buy. I'm sure Seth will want one as soon as he's released anyway."

She gave her uncle a hug and made her way outside. She turned on her phone to call the house and it rang immediately. "Hello?"

"Hi, Cat, it's Sherry. I heard about Seth. I wanted to see if he was okay, but no one would tell me anything. I was going to just leave a message so if this is a bad time . . ." She trailed off.

Cat walked over to a vending machine that was set up near the exit, and started putting in change to get sodas. Might as well multitask as she talked. Cat slipped into a chair. She was so extremely tired. This was one retreat week she'd be glad to see in the done column. "He's fine. How are you?"

"I think I'm being followed. It's stupid, right? Paranoid? Why would anyone follow me?"

Cat frowned. "Maybe they think Chance told you something the night you met for drinks. Did he tell you anything that might be important?"

"No, we talked about the old days. About before he left for Germany. He told me he was sorry, but he'd gotten involved in something and just couldn't risk me being hurt. Then he and Prince left to go back up the mountain." She gasped. "Wait, what happened to Prince? I've been so lost in the past, I didn't even think about his dog. Is he okay?"

"The dog went to the shelter to be adopted."

Sherry sighed. "I need to go get the dog. I promised Chance if anything happened to him, I'd take care of Prince. I hope I'm not too late."

"Be careful. If you think you're being followed, you should tell someone."

"I did. I told you." Sherry hung up the phone.

Cat gathered up the sodas and headed back to Seth's room. Shauna would be wondering what happened to her. At least one good thing came out of the discussion. Chance's dog may have a place to live out his senior years. Cat didn't think that Sherry would let him go. Not now. She just hoped Sherry's husband was as understanding.

Seth was sitting up on the side of the bed. "We've been waiting for you."

"I got delayed." She glanced around. "Where's Uncle Pete?"

"He left to go track down Joey. Man, I think I'll pass if I get an invitation to a reunion in another ten years. This one's been nothing but trouble." He slipped on his jacket. "Let's go home. I'm going to lie on the bed and watch movies. Maybe I won't feel like I was hit by a car tomorrow."

"We can cancel the trip to Outlaw tomorrow." Cat handed Shauna her soda and gave one to Seth.

"Let me take the guests up. I haven't been up there for a while. You can stay home and play nursemaid." Shauna glanced at her watch. "I'm ordering pizza for a late lunch/early dinner. I'll pull out a batch of soup for later tonight. But I'm starving now."

"Me too." Seth rubbed his stomach. "I didn't have breakfast, if you remember."

Cat sat next to Seth on the bed. "Sounds good to me. Shauna, I can ride along if you want tomorrow morning."

"No, it will be good for me to spend some time with the guests. I haven't talked to most of them, just Brodie. And I'd like to get some pictures for cover ideas for the cookbook." She stepped aside and a nurse pushed a wheelchair through the room. "Here's your ride. I'll go move the car to the loading zone in front."

The nurse gave her directions on where to meet them. Then she handed a clipboard to Seth. "I've got some paperwork for you to sign before you can leave."

"I'll be out in the hallway. I need to call Uncle Pete." Cat kissed his cheek and left the room, dialing her uncle's number as she walked. When he answered, she quickly filled him in on what Sherry had said.

"So where is she now?" Uncle Pete asked.

Cat saw the nurse getting Seth into the wheelchair and figured she had only a few more seconds. "At the animal shelter. She's going to adopt Prince if they'll let her."

"Who is Prince?"

"Chance's dog. Sherry told him that if anything happened, she'd take care of the dog."

"Interesting. Maybe Chance was worried that something was happening. Maybe that's why he had the wall of pictures in his house."

Cat smiled as Seth and the nurse passed her in the hallway. She started following, still with her uncle on the phone. "Maybe. I think he must have told her more than just where he'd been all these years."

"I'll send an officer to watch her and make plans to talk to her again this afternoon. Look, tell Shirley that I'll call when I have a minute."

Cat paused at the exit door to the parking area. "Call me if you find out something."

"Sure, why not. You can come over and read my case notes when you have time too."

Her eyes widened. Her uncle never let her so far into an investigation. Maybe he was warming up to the idea. "Really?"

His laugh told her all she needed to know. "In your dreams. See you soon, and stay out of this investigation. I'm getting worried about what's going on with Chance's death. And you're not as quick to get out of the way as Seth is."

"Ha-ha." Cat opened the side door and climbed into the backseat. Seth was sitting in the front "shotgun" seat and grinning at her. "I'll talk to you later."

She climbed in and closed the door. "Do you need me to call in an order for lunch?"

"Already done. I had some time waiting for you. I take it you called Pete?"

Cat caught Shauna's gaze in the rearview. "Yep, he's more worried about us getting in the way than any news I could tell him."

"Which isn't a bad thing," Seth added. He leaned his head back and closed his eyes. "I think the only reason I'm awake is I'm starving."

Cat leaned back in her seat and made sure the seat belt was on. She watched the passing houses as they made their way home. As soon as they pulled into the driveway, a pizza truck parked in front of the house.

"You get Seth, I'll get the pizza." Shauna smiled as she headed toward the vehicle.

Cat went around the car, but he'd already opened the door and had started to the house. "You're making my nursing duties really easy."

"If I fall over, you'll be found negligent in the trial." He held the door open for her, then moved to the table, where he sat. "I can't believe I'm hurting this bad, yet nothing's broke."

"You're lucky it's just bruised." Cat grabbed a sealed bag filled with cookies and put them on a plate to sit in front of him. "Eat one of those until Shauna gets in with the pizza. I'm going to grab plates, then run out to the lobby and see if the guests are here or in town eating lunch."

"I'm betting in town." Seth glanced at the clock. "It's already one."

When Cat went into the hallway, she saw that Seth was correct. Everyone had gone to lunch. A piece of paper sat folded into a tent on the lobby desk. She opened it and read a note from Jocelyn. She'd taken her appointment of being in charge seriously. The note explained that after Tammy left, they'd locked up the doors and headed into town for lunch at Reno's and then a work session at the library.

She went back into the kitchen.

"Was I right?" Seth sat eating a slice of pepperoni deep dish.

"Spot on the money." Cat grabbed a slice of the combination she loved and set it on her plate. She took a glass from the cupboard and filled it with chilled water from the fridge pitcher. Shauna was trying to cut down on the number of disposable water bottles they used monthly. "They said they'd be back after dinner to do some word sprints if I was interested in joining them."

"They've become their own self-directed retreat." Shauna smiled as she grabbed a second slice of pizza. "Maybe we should have one of those a year and charge less. They can just come and eat breakfast and do whatever they want."

The more she thought about it, she wondered if it might work, especially on weeks where she was going to be on deadline. Shirley bounded through the back door.

"Oh, good, you're here." Her words came out in a rush. "Your uncle couldn't reach you by phone."

Cat looked down and saw that her ringer was still off from being in the hospital. She turned the volume back up. "What's going on?"

"He wanted to ask Seth if he knew where Joey was staying? The hotel doesn't have anyone under that name."

Chapter 20

"That's impossible. I met him in the lobby of the hotel just this morning to run." Seth set the slice of pizza he'd been working on down on the plate.

Shirley nodded. "What time? Maybe we can use their security system to grab a photo of him."

"Seven. I was a little early, so I sat and read the paper for a few minutes in the lobby." Seth rubbed his face. "Don't tell me all my old friends have been living under aliases. What happened in Germany?"

"That's the hundred-dollar question, now isn't it?" Shirley dialed a number on the phone and relayed the information to what must have been Uncle Pete. After she hung up, she glanced around. "Did the guests leave for lunch already?"

"Lunch, work at the library, then dinner. They said they'll be back this evening for word sprints if you want to join in." Cat pointed to the pizza. "Have you eaten?"

"Not yet. And it looks like Pete's going to be busy today." She sank into a chair as Shauna handed her a plate. "I knew dating a cop was going to be a time issue, but we've been lucky up until this week. Oh, well, it gives me time to write."

"Writers, you always look at alone time as a good thing." Seth ate the rest of his pizza in two bites. "I'm heading upstairs with a bottle of pain relievers. What time's dinner?"

"I'll bring you up some chili and cornbread about seven. Will that work?" Shauna glanced at the clock.

"Perfect." He kissed Cat on the head as he passed by her on the way to the door leading out to the hallway. "Sorry I'm bailing on you this week."

"The week's not over yet." Cat smiled. "I'm still counting on you to do the designated driver thing tomorrow night."

"I'll be there. Maybe not with bells on, but I'm not missing my free dinner out for anything." He nodded to the other two. "Ladies . . ."

And then he was gone. Shirley focused on her pizza. "Cat, if I wasn't way too old for him, you would be in big trouble keeping your boyfriend."

"That's what all the guests say." Cat smiled as she considered a mushroom that had fallen off the pizza. "It's a good thing you all go away after a week."

Shauna pulled out her planner. "Since I'm taking the group to Outlaw tomorrow, what time were they going to leave, do you know?"

"Tristin said something about nine. Sydney wants to be back to the house in order to get some work done before we go to dinner. She's working on a new blog series that she's releasing next month on ten places you have to visit before you have kids." Shirley folded her pizza slice and took a big bite.

"That's pretty specific. Is there something Tristin and Sydney aren't telling us?" Shauna lifted her head from making notes about the Outlaw trip in her planner.

Shirley shook her head. "I've tried to get it out of them, but they both just keep saying they aren't looking at having kids for a few years. Maybe Sydney has other plans."

"Well, since we're free and clear for a while, I'm heading upstairs to write." Cat glanced at Shauna. "Unless you needed my help with something."

"Nope, go ahead. Of course, you're going to have to watch Seth tomorrow while I'm hiking around Outlaw."

"Sure, ruin my Saturday." Cat set her plate in the sink and waved to the women as she went through the doorway to the foyer. If she planned it right, Seth might just be too busy watching college football to worry about where she was. Which would give her time to go talk to Sherry again. It was a long shot, but maybe she might have remembered something from her conversations with Chance. And she could use the excuse of going to check on Prince.

Instead of opening her Word document, she opened her digital picture storage program. She went back and opened the first picture of Chance's cabin. She went through the series once, then again. Nothing was jumping out at her. Maybe it was because she wasn't focusing on what Chance had been. She paused at the list of Covington professors on the wall. Three were circled. What was it about those three people, including Michael and the woman who used to be her best friend before the divorce?

She glanced at the third name, then opened her Web browser to Google the woman. Addie Callen was a professor in the history department. It looked like she'd been there for years. Her undergrad degree was from a small school in Oregon and her master's from Oregon State. Nothing that screamed she was related to any of the mob families that supported Covington as a safe place for their offspring to get a degree. Of course, Michael hadn't had connections either.

Cat frowned and studied the picture of Chance's wall again. Jessica didn't have connections either. Was that the entire reason their names were circled? Had Chance thought someone from the families had been after him? Was their lack of connection the reason why he circled the names?

She knew one person who might know. She looked at the Covington website and found that the other woman on the list, Addie Callen, had open office hours until three. If she didn't know Chance, that mystery may have just been solved. She tucked her notebook into her tote and headed downstairs to tell Shauna she was going to run to Covington to talk to a professor. Luckily, she wasn't in the kitchen. Cat signed out on the white board with a return ETA and grabbed her coat. Since Shauna hadn't signed out, Cat knew she was in the house or in the barn. Close enough in case Seth needed her.

She was two blocks away when she realized she

hadn't brought cookies. Cookies were a great way to get into someone's office. It opened the door to so many conversations. She'd just have to be charming and outgoing today. Two words that rarely anyone used to describe Cat.

The professor's office door was open when Cat arrived. She knocked, and an attractive blonde in jeans and a blazer looked up from her computer. "Come on in. Are you one of my students?"

"You're Professor Callen?"

The woman nodded and Cat entered the office, shutting the door after her. She moved some papers from one chair to another, then sat. "I'm Cat Latimer. I was wondering if I could ask you some questions."

Professor Callen stood and held out her hand. "Why, of course. I should have recognized you. I suppose you're researching a new book series? Pete didn't mention you were writing historical."

"Pete?" Now Cat was completely confused. This woman knew her uncle?

"Oh, dear. Maybe he hasn't mentioned me. We've only been on a few dates. He's very charming, your uncle. And busy, of course." She pulled a pen out of her hair and put it on the table. "Sorry, I'm chattering away. Please call me Addie. What can I help you with, Cat?"

Cat decided to put away the issue of Uncle Pete until she could talk to him. She'd come for another reason. "Thanks for seeing me. Did you know Chance McAllister?"

The look on her face when Cat mentioned the name told the story. She had indeed known Chance.

"What a horrible thing to happen. Chance was the most interesting man I'd met in a long time. His knowledge of Colorado history was unsurpassed, even by the professors on campus who focus on the local lore." She took a tissue out of her desk and dabbed at her eyes. "I focus mostly on western expansion, so our expertise crossed at times. He was always researching mining claims. Like he was going to make it rich with that plot of ground he had in the hills. Pipe dreams."

"This is going to sound weird, but did you ever visit his cabin?"

Addie shook her head. "He'd invited me up several times, but I'd felt uncomfortable with the invitation. You know how it is with single women. If we get a reputation, true or not, it can stay with you."

There went her theory. "Okay, well, I was just checking on something. Thanks for your time."

Addie stood and walked the couple of steps to the door and held it open for Cat. "I wanted to tell you I was sorry for your late husband's death. It's so hard to take, losing someone that young."

"Thanks." Cat wanted to add "but we were divorced," but sometimes it didn't help the conversation. Besides, let the woman think what she wanted about Cat's emotional state.

"Yeah, Jessica and I were just talking about how lovely a man he was." She reached out and patted Cat's shoulder. "Jessica explained how upset you were over the whole divorce thing. I'm so glad you were trying to patch things up."

Thanks, Jessica, for the lie. Cat shook her head, deciding not to clarify the situation. Then she realized what Addie had said. "How do you know Jessica?"

"We were on a professorial standard board a few years ago. Of course, Jessica wasn't really high enough in the pecking order to be part of the panel, but no one really cared. And she had connections, you know." She smiled. "Your husband was our chair. He was such a lovely man. Talked about you all the time. He loved telling stories about you fixing up the house. Then when you left, it was like the light dropped from his eyes."

Okay, so there was the connection. They'd all been on a board together a few years ago. And it had been right about the time of the divorce.

She needed to talk to her uncle and see if this woman was crazy or if she could actually have some useful knowledge to help find Chance's killer. And she needed to talk to him alone, without Shirley. "Thanks for seeing me. I've just been wondering about what Chance was working on. You know a writer's mind. We go all over the place."

"It was lovely to meet you. Please give my best to your uncle. I'm starting to think he's forgotten my phone number." She waved as Cat made her way down the hallway.

Cat figured she had two opportunities to find her uncle alone. Go down to the station now. According to Shauna, Shirley went with the group to the library to work. Or wait until tomorrow and make sure Shirley went on the Outlaw expedition. She decided she'd try today. That way, she might have it over and done with sooner than later. And it was a part of the investigation.

She left the campus and headed the two blocks to the station. She hadn't popped in to see her uncle for a while. And again, she wished she'd thought ahead and brought cookies. Entering the lobby of the station, she stopped at the reception desk and waited for the officer to get off the phone. Picking up a neighborhood watch pamphlet, she wondered if they should join the local group. Of course, Shauna might have already joined and the way she was, she was probably president of the organization now. Cat put the brochure in her pocket.

Before the phone call was over, her uncle's door opened and out walked Shirley and Uncle Pete. Cat's heart stopped. How could she bring up what she'd found out without him knowing that she now knew about his other girlfriend?

"Cat, what are you doing here? Shirley and I were just going out for an early dinner. Do you want to join us?" Her uncle nodded to the receptionist and as she covered the mouthpiece, he whispered, "I'll have my phone if anything pops. Does this need me?"

The woman shook her head. "Have fun."

They all stepped away from the desk to allow the call to continue in private.

Cat shifted back and forth on her feet. Then stopped when she saw her uncle's eyes narrowing. She decided to jump in. "So, I was at the college today and talked to Addie Callen."

Shirley frowned. "Why do I know that name?"

Before her uncle could respond, Cat jumped in. "It was one of the three professors that Chance had circled on his board. Along with Jessica and Michael."

"And you decided to follow up on this clue on your own?" Iron flowed through Uncle Pete's voice.

"Don't reprimand her until we find out what she knows. Besides, it was a smart call for her to go since she used to teach at the college. Make believe it was part of your plan. Your blood pressure will thank you for it." Shirley smiled at Cat. "Go ahead, dear, tell us what you found out."

Cat glanced at Uncle Pete, then focused on Shirley. "She said that Chance used to come and talk to her about Colorado history. Which makes sense from his library requests."

"Miss Applebome gave you his library card records? She told me I needed a warrant; then I got a thirty-minute lecture on the value of intellectual freedom and how what you read did not in any world make you a criminal." Uncle Pete glanced at his watch.

Cat could tell he was trying to get to the restaurant and out of the station before he would be called back on some emergency. Or he wanted to get her out of there before she spilled the beans. "Yeah, that's what I thought. And Miss Applebome didn't give me his records, a graduate student did because I said I was helping him with his documentation for his thesis."

"Smart." Shirley beamed at Cat like she was a prize pupil. "So basically, it was a dead end?"

"Not exactly." Now Cat could see her uncle shifting. She guessed it was where she'd learned it. "I asked her how she knew Jessica and Michael. Well, honestly, she brought up the fact that she was friends with Jessica, so I asked about Michael. They were all on some professor advisory committee together years ago."

Uncle Pete waited, but when Cat didn't go on, he frowned. "And this is the only connection?"

"According to Addie, yes. But maybe Chance knew Addie from his research and got her to talk about the professors to see if any of them were connected." She sighed and lowered her voice, stepping closer to her uncle. "What if he was afraid that the mob was after him for some reason. Maybe he was circling the people he could trust."

"Three professors out of the entire school? That's a little paranoid."

Cat shrugged. "Maybe he was just starting his elimination process."

"As a theory, it's not the worst I've heard." He opened the door. "But if we're going to make our reservation, we have to leave. Are you coming to dinner with us?"

"No, I've got to get back to the retreat. We're doing a closing session with word sprints this evening." She followed them out of the station. "Were you going to interview Addie? Or did I just ruin your plan?"

"She was on the list, but there are so many others ahead of her." He glanced at Shirley. "I appreciate the information, Cat."

As they walked away, she heard Shirley mutter, "Now, that wasn't so hard, was it? She's only trying to help."

Cat was too far away to clearly hear her uncle's response, but she got the drift. She'd wait for Shirley to be out of town to have the rest of the conversation with her uncle. Because if she let the chips fall, her uncle might be the one who was in danger of getting himself killed, by Shirley.

Chapter 21

Cat had a full house when she started the retreat roundup, as she liked to call the ending session at seven that night. Shirley had just come in from dinner. Brodie and the two couples were sitting in the living room, drinking coffee and chatting. She'd checked on Seth, who had been sleeping when she peeked into his room, but according to Shauna, he'd eaten a big bowl of chili and two grilled cheese sandwiches just before Cat had arrived home.

Cat liked the feeling of having the house full. And somehow, she thought the house liked it as well. She sat down and curled her legs up underneath her. Her cup of hot chocolate sat on the table in front of her. "Welcome to our last session. I wanted to thank you all for an interesting retreat this week. First, because we still have a day left, at least what's open between your trip to Outlaw in the morning and our closing dinner tomorrow night, I wanted to hear from you what you expected and didn't get. We'll see if we can fit it in."

"I know we talked about sitting down one-on-one and talking about my contract. Can we do that before the Outlaw trip tomorrow?" Jocelyn pointed to the dining room. "I'll buy you breakfast and we can go into the study to talk."

"The breakfast is part of our retreat fee." Archer tapped his wife's arm. "Besides, she lives here."

"It was a joke." She kissed him on the cheek. "Sometimes you don't get modern humor."

"Sometimes you're not funny." He sipped his coffee.

"Sure," Cat stepped in before it turned into a fight. "I'll meet you at eight in the dining room?"

"Sounds great." Jocelyn leaned back. "Who's next?"

"Wait, you have a contract and you didn't tell anyone?" Sydney set her cup down. "I thought we were friends."

"We are, or I wouldn't have mentioned it now. I didn't want you to see me differently." Jocelyn grinned. "I'll tell you more about it after Cat and I talk and I know it's legit."

"So, I wanted to talk about how to finish a book." Tristin leaned forward, blocking the stares between his wife and Jocelyn. "I know I said I love shorts, but that was just to keep Sydney here from freaking out. I've decided by this time next year, I want to have a book to shop to an agent."

"That's so cool." Sydney forgot her staring contest with Jocelyn and took his arm. "I didn't know you wanted to write a book."

"I started it in college, but well, life happened."

He grinned at Brodie. "This is a lesson for you. Don't let life push aside your dreams."

"We can talk about the writing process tonight." Cat glanced around at the other guests. "Anything else on the need-to-do list?"

Brodie raised his hand and waited for Cat to nod before speaking. "So, I've been working on this fantasy/YA novel this week. I'm not done, but I've loved working on it. How do I keep writing the novel when I go back to school?"

Cat frowned, unsure of the question. "What do you mean, Brodie? Don't you have a writing schedule already?"

"I do, but that's for my thesis book. And it's not genre fiction. My advisor will freak if I tell him this is what I really want to write." He sank back in his chair. "You all were great at encouraging me to write it, and I love the story. But Professor Enders? He's going to be less than enthusiastic about the whole thing."

Cat nodded, understanding. It hadn't been that long ago that she'd been writing one thing for grades and another for her amusement. "I was there, in the same spot. I chose to serve two masters, which meant the book I sold, the genre fiction one, took at least a year longer to write. I say go with your gut. Tell Enders what you are doing and have him read what you have so far. I think you'll be surprised at his reaction."

"Besides, if he doesn't like it, you just do what you need to and get your degree. Then you write and submit the book you love or the next one. Writing words into stories gives you the chops to write a better book the next time," Shirley added.

"I've written three books so far, and I think the one I'm writing now is the one that might get me that agent."

"It only takes one," Tristin added. "Besides, it's good practice for when you're working a full-time job doing something stupid and you write at night to get the passion work done."

"You're saying our career is stupid?" Sydney sipped her coffee, studying him.

Tristin shook his head. "No, that's not what I'm saying. But you and me, we're lucky. I could be a lawyer and hate my work but feel trapped because of the money. We get to turn our hobby into our job. I just want something more. To see if I have the fiction chops too."

"Or a police officer," Shirley said. She picked a cookie off the tray and took a bite. "I loved my job, but I always felt like something was missing. Now that I'm retired and writing, I know what I missed all those years. This is my true calling. The work just gave me plenty of research materials."

After making sure there were no other questions, Cat did one more round robin to list off on a flipchart what everyone had accomplished this week. She was amazed at the high word counts, even though the group hadn't been working at the house much. She totaled it up. "By my calculations, and forgive me, math is not my strongest skill, you all did amazing this week. I think that total is higher than last month's group."

"We're good at getting our work done so we can play." Sydney smiled. "And we all agreed we wanted to make time for the trip to Outlaw tomorrow. It's still on, right? Even with Seth's accident?"

"Shauna's taking you, so meet down here at nine tomorrow morning. You'll spend the morning at Outlaw, then come back here in time to get ready for dinner." She glanced around the group relaxed on the living room furniture. "So let's get started with these questions."

An hour later, they were done and the group was on their first word sprint. Cat bowed out and went to the kitchen.

"Are you done already?" Shauna looked up from her computer. "I'm working on adjusting a recipe. My beta tester thought it might be better with a substitution. I'm getting ready to make a new batch of the cookies right now and thought the group might enjoy some before bedtime."

"I'm sure they will. They're doing writing sprints so they should be another hour or two in the living room." She glanced at the loaf of banana bread on the table. "Can I slice that and take some up to Seth?"

"I was just up there with a plate of treats. He's doing good, but I think he was going right back to sleep after I left. He needs the rest to heal. A normal person would have probably been kept overnight in the hospital."

Cat glanced at the banana bread again. "Then can I have some? I probably should have eaten some more chili. I'm hungry."

"I can make you a sandwich." Shauna started to stand, but Cat shook her head.

"Nope, two slices of this and a glass of milk and I'll be fine. Besides, I'm beat as well. If Seth's okay, I'm heading up to crash too. Maybe a bubble bath first, then I'll read."

"Did you tell them about the change of driver tomorrow?" Shauna watched as Cat put two slices of the bread on a plate.

"Yes, and I told them you'd be leaving at nine. I can freshen the rooms if you want me to." Cat poured herself some milk, then sat down to eat.

"No, it's the last day. I did a full refresh today so all I'll need to do is replace towels and dump trash tomorrow. I can do that when I get back. Besides, tomorrow's brunch is already ready to go. I made quiches for the guests and for us." Shauna stood and started gathering the ingredients for her recipe do-over. She turned and watched Cat. "You know Seth's fine, right? He's just a little banged up."

"I'm just wondering why someone tried to hit Joey with that flowerpot in the first place. Was it accidental? Or is this all related to Chance's murder?" Cat finished off the last bite of the banana bread. "I know, all questions that can't be answered. Or at least not until Uncle Pete finds Joey."

"Seth's not in danger."

The way Shauna said it made it sound more like a question than a statement. Cat sat the empty plate and glass in the sink. Then she grabbed a bottle of water to take upstairs. Pausing at the door, she made eye contact with Shauna. "That's the working theory. But honestly? I'm not so sure anymore."

The next morning, Cat got up and dressed before her alarm went off. She knocked quietly on Seth's door, but when he didn't answer, she opened it a crack to see if he was awake. He laid curled on the bed, eyes shut and his blond hair a mess over his face. Cat could see his chest rise and fall with steady breathing. She shut the door quietly and went downstairs to meet with Jocelyn.

She was already in the dining room, reading the paper and eating a slice of quiche. Cat poured herself a cup of coffee and filled a plate with snacks. She'd eat breakfast in the kitchen with Seth and Shauna. "Come on into the study, where we can talk without being interrupted."

They made their way to the study. Jocelyn folded the paper and sat it on Cat's desk. "I'm always interested in the news at different places. Your paper is so cute; there's a lot about the college and craft boutiques at the local churches. One article was even an interview with a past alumnus who's working at a movie production company out in Los Angeles."

"You were busy this morning." Cat took a bit of the cinnamon roll she'd grabbed off the sideboard. "Running into town and getting the paper all ready."

"What?" Jocelyn set down her coffee cup. "Oh, no. That's your paper. The paperboy delivered it around seven this morning. Of course, I shouldn't call him a paperboy. He was a grown man."

Cat stared at her. "We don't get the paper. Shauna likes to run into town in the morning and pick one up. That way she gets to talk to her friends at the store. But she doesn't go on retreat weeks." Cat sipped her coffee, considering the folded paper on the desk. "Maybe it was someone new and we got Mrs. Rice's paper."

"That would explain it." When Cat looked at Jocelyn with a questioning glance, she continued. "The guy looked confused. When I came downstairs and saw him out on the porch, he seemed to be looking at the house number and inside the windows. I went over and opened the door. I guess he didn't see me because he must have jumped back two feet. He shoved the paper at me, then took off down the sidewalk."

"Weird." Cat sipped her coffee. "Tell me about your contract. Who is it from? An agent or a publisher?"

After they'd gone over the details and Cat had explained what Jocelyn needed to look for before she signed, Cat left her in the study to work on her questions for her agent. Luckily the contract was from a large, well-known romance publisher, so Cat felt confident it was standard for that house. But still there were some clauses that Cat would have questioned if it had been her contract. Like length of copyright. She smiled as she reached the kitchen door. It looked like Jocelyn was going to be published. She'd have to find out what her expected release day was so she could reach out then. Shauna was at the sink, looking out the door. "Have we ever sent flowers to a retreat graduate who released a book after attending?"

Shauna thought for a moment. "I don't think so. I think we've had a few that we sent e-mails to to congratulate them on the release. But flowers, that's a great idea. Who's getting published?"

"Jocelyn." Cat explained the situation and asked Shauna to put it in the follow-up file so they wouldn't forget. She shook the paper at her. "Here's the paper. I think there must have been a substitute and we got Mrs. Rice's paper."

"She doesn't get the local paper. She gets *The Wall Street Journal*. And it comes via the post office." Shauna glanced at the paper on the table. "How did this get here?"

"Jocelyn says she scared off the paperboy." Cat refilled her coffee cup. "Ready for your trip to Outlaw?"

"Wait, do you think we need to call Pete about this?" Shauna pointed to the paper. "I'm not excited about leaving you alone here."

"I won't be alone, I have Seth." Cat sipped her coffee. "Besides, I just think someone was probably substituting for the regular guy and got our address mixed up. It's just a paper, Shauna."

"If you say so." She shivered and cupped her hands around her cup, even though it didn't feel cold in the room.

"Look, I'll keep the doors locked. And if I hear something, I'll call the station. Uncle Pete has enough on his mind without worrying about this." Cat leaned back in her chair, studying Shauna. "So are you ready for this?"

"I think so. I packed a picnic basket full of treats and a few sandwiches and chips for an impromptu lunch, just in case we are there longer than expected." Shauna tapped a pad of paper with a pen as she listed off her to-do list. "And I filled two thermoses each of coffee and hot chocolate. I was just going down to grab a cooler out of the basement for sodas and waters. Am I forgetting anything?"

"Maybe blankets in case you get snowed in?" Cat

suggested, and watched as Shauna started to write it on her list.

Then she set down the pen. "You're messing with me."

"I am. Seriously, I don't think we took this much food with us when it was a full-day excursion in summer."

"Yeah, but they served you lunch. And if something had happened, like a flat tire, you would have had people right there to help. I'll have to wait for a rescue with five other people. At least we can mark food off our worry list if that happens." Shauna glanced at the clock. "I probably better go get ready. Do you think Seth will be down for breakfast anytime soon?"

"I figured he would have already been down." Cat stood and went to the door. "I'll deal with Seth's breakfast. You go get ready. Let me know before you leave. And try to have fun."

"I'm very fun. I'm just also very prepared. Just in case," Shauna called after her.

Cat knew she would go get the cooler, pack it, and put it in the car before she went upstairs to get ready. Cat went upstairs to work for a few minutes before waking Seth.

When she glanced at her watch, the morning was flying by. The group had already left and she still hadn't gotten Seth's breakfast. She hurriedly shut down her computer and sprinted down the hall to Seth's room. Knocking on the door, it swung open. He wasn't asleep on the bed. She stepped inside and looked in his bathroom. Towels were on the floor and she could smell the powerful scent of the bar soap he used. But no Seth. She grabbed the towel and absently hung it on the rack before heading downstairs to find him.

He was in the kitchen, dressed and looking normal. There was no indication that he'd even been hit by a flowerpot the day before. Cat breathed out and walked into the kitchen to join him.

"You just missed the gang. Shauna got everyone out of here fifteen minutes ago. She's pretty efficient at moving people along. Of course, she bribed them with warm muffins she already had waiting in the car." He pointed toward the coffeepot. "Can I get you coffee?"

"No, I'll get my own coffee. I was supposed to get you breakfast. I guess Shauna took care of it?" She filled a cup and sat at the table next to him.

He leaned over and kissed her. "No, I told her I'd wait to eat. But I think we should go have breakfast at The Diner. I'm craving one of their Big Apple Omelets."

"The ones with biscuits and gravy and hash browns in the middle?" Cat's mouth watered, even with the carb overload warning signs going off in her head. "I'm game. We never get to sneak out on a retreat week. This will be our third date this week."

"We're delegating better." Seth glanced at the clock. "Do you need to get something? We can walk. I feel like I need some light exercise after yesterday's adventures. Or if you need to, we can take the truck."

"You're asking because I'm in worse shape than the guy who was in the emergency room yesterday?

That makes me feel so special." Cat sipped her coffee. "Are you paying? Otherwise, I need my wallet."

"My idea, I'll pay. And I'm only asking because I knew it would rile you up." He stood and headed to the kitchen door. "If you don't need anything, I'll go lock up the front. Shauna and the guests will be gone for at least four hours and we'll be back before then. I hate leaving the door open if no one's here."

Cat sipped her coffee as she waited for Seth to return. She had to admit, she kind of liked the slower pace of this retreat. Maybe she was getting better at relaxing and just letting things happen. The group discussion last night had proved that the production for the week had been just as high as prior retreats. The group had finally bonded. And there had been some breakthroughs in the writing for at least Tristin. Talking about writing with other writers let the ideas and the commitment flow. She always came away from these discussions excited to go back to work on her own projects. Somehow she felt like she should be paying the retreat guests for motivating her too.

But that wasn't going to happen. Seth came back into the kitchen, moving slowly but already in his casual, but not work, coat. He paused at the door. "What are you smiling about?"

"Just thinking how much I love my life." She finished off her coffee and put the cup in the sink. "Let's get going before the phone rings or someone shows up."

"Shirley's with Shauna and the group, and your uncle is working Chance's murder. I don't think there's anyone who would show up." Seth moved toward the back door.

"Really? You want to tempt fate and not get your omelet?" She slipped on her coat.

He opened the door and waved her outside. "Sorry, I was thinking we were normal people. Hurry and let's get out of here."

Chapter 22

Cat's phone rang just after they'd ordered. She glanced at the readout. "Shauna. I better take this."

"Don't tell me she got stuck." He glanced over at the kitchen. "Maybe we could get it to go and you could drive so I could eat?"

"Let's just see what's going on before we get our food boxed up. It could be nothing." Cat answered the call. "Hey, Shauna, what's going on?"

"Just reminding you to feed Seth. He's up and looked good today. But I don't want him not to eat. He needs food to heal." Shauna's voice came over the cell loud enough that Seth heard her words and gave Cat a thumbs-up sign and leaned back. "By the way, his friend Joey pulled into Outlaw, just after we did. He said he was looking for Seth."

"That's weird. Why didn't he just call? Do you think he followed you out to the site?" A bad feeling sank into her stomach and she saw Seth sit up in his chair. "Is he gone now?"

"Yeah, he took off right after talking to me. Archer was crazy excited to get some pictures, so we started our tour right after he left. But then I started thinking about it and Seth, and figured I'd give you a call just to make sure you're aware." Shauna lowered her voice. "Is he the one whom Pete's looking for to question? Should I have called your uncle?"

"Don't worry, I'll call him." Cat leaned back as the waitress set her breakfast plate in front of her. "When did you see him?"

"About nine thirty. It didn't take us long to get up here," Shauna responded. "Are you sure everything's all right? We can come back. We've seen about half the town and now Archer wants to explore the blacksmith's shop, but if you need us . . ."

"Actually, Seth and I are eating breakfast at The Diner. No need to come back. I'll call Uncle Pete and let him know that Joey's been spotted. If you feel safe, continue the tour. Archer's probably having a blast."

"He's in ghost town heaven," Shauna agreed. "Okay, but let me know if you need something."

"Will do." Cat hung up the call, then texted the information to her uncle. She set the phone away and started eating. When she realized Seth wasn't eating, she waved her fork at him. "I thought you were dreaming about that omelet. What's wrong? Not enough gravy?"

"You sure you don't want to go up to Outlaw and check on Shauna?"

"You heard her. He's already gone and besides, she has three guys there to help out if something happens. Besides, it's not like Joey threw the pot. You pushed him out of the way. He probably just wants to thank you."

"Without having to answer Pete's questions. Yeah, I can understand that. I don't know what Joey's involved in, but I hope it's not gambling. The guy was always looking for that next score, or bragging about how he just knew the right horse to bet on." Seth picked up his fork and took a bite. "Wow. This is as good as I remembered."

Cat watched amused as he dug in to the overstuffed omelet. She had ordered a normal ham and cheese omelet with a side of biscuits and gravy. With the hash browns on the side, she didn't think she'd be hungry until tomorrow. Which was a bad thing since they had the end of retreat dinner tonight. Oh, well, she'd just have to force herself to eat again. Her life certainly didn't suck.

They'd just finished eating and were waiting for the waitress to bring back Seth's credit card when Cat's phone rang.

"Shauna?" Seth sat up straight, looking around to find their waitress.

Cat shook her head. "Nope, Uncle Pete."

"Really?" He waved over the waitress, who was refilling coffee cups.

"Hey, I just sent you a text." Cat answered her uncle's call directly without a fluffy greeting. He was probably calling about the text anyway.

"I saw it. Shauna okay?" Uncle Pete was just as direct as Cat was in her approach. Probably a family trait.

"Yep, they're fine. And Shirley's with them if something feels off. Where are you?" Cat finished off her orange juice as she watched Seth sign the charge slip.

"I am standing in front of your house. Your alarms went off about the same time as Mrs. Rice called in a possible break-in. Where are you? I take it you're not in Outlaw with Shauna and the group."

"We're at The Diner." Cat stood and directed her next words to Seth. "We've got to go. Someone broke into the house."

"No, someone *tried* to break into your house. The alarm system kept them out, and Mrs. Rice yelling from the sidewalk, cell phone in hand, scared him away." Uncle Pete sighed. "Look, just get here as soon as possible. I swear, this week has gone from bad to worse."

Cat tucked her cell in her pants and dropped some money on the table. "How fast can you walk?"

"I'm not an invalid, Cat. I'll keep up. Let's just get going." He motioned to the door and they left The Diner and headed out to the street at a fast pace.

Cat glanced at him as they crossed the street. He didn't look out of breath, yet, but she'd keep an eye on his condition as they walked. She'd seen the way he'd sat at The Diner, like he'd been hurting from the original stroll into town. Now, he'd be pushing it. "Look, it's not going to change anything if it takes us five or ten minutes longer to get there."

He put a hand on her back. "Thanks for worrying, but I'm fine. Let's just get home."

They power-walked to the house and when they arrived, met Uncle Pete and Mrs. Rice in the kitchen. Cat watched as Seth almost fell into a chair, and grabbed him a bottle of water out of the fridge. Then she poured herself a cup of coffee. "I see you found the hide-a-key. What's going on?"

"Well, I was coming over to talk to Shauna about the pages she'd given me this week and I saw a man trying to crowbar open your back door." Mrs. Rice shook her head and then grabbed a cookie from the plate in the middle of the table. "These are good, but she really should learn to use a higher-quality chocolate chip."

Uncle Pete rolled his eyes, but his voice was soft when he spoke. "Mrs. Rice. Tell us about the man you saw. Can you describe him?"

"Of course, I can." She snapped at Uncle Pete. "Didn't I just go through all of this with you? I swear, men don't listen."

"I mean, could you go through it so Cat and Seth could hear your description. They might know the person." Uncle Pete rephrased the request.

"Oh, I get it." She turned to Seth. "Anyway, the man was shorter than you. He had on jeans and a Wisconsin Badgers sweatshirt. I'm assuming that's some sort of sports team? Then he ran away when I held up my phone and told him I'd called the police and he needed to leave."

"Did you see his face?" Cat wondered if having on a Wisconsin sweatshirt was enough evidence, but she was already convinced that it was Joey.

He'd been wearing the same sweatshirt yesterday when he'd talked to her at the hospital.

Mrs. Rice glanced at Cat, then turned back to Seth, answering the question. "No, I didn't see his face. And he had his hoodie pulled up over his hair so I couldn't even see that. If I hadn't been on the phone with the station, I could have taken a picture with my phone. Did you know phones could do that now? My grandson bought me this smarty phone for my birthday. I can even look up recipes on it if I need to."

Cat wanted to explain to the woman that she could have taken a picture and stayed on the phone with the police, but she didn't have the energy. She looked at Uncle Pete. "You think it was Joey?"

"Could he have gotten back from Outlaw that fast?" Seth asked.

Uncle Pete turned to Mrs. Rice. "Thank you so much for your time. I'll have one of my officers walk you home."

"I need to get home to Mr. Peeps, anyway. He's probably all worked up." Mrs. Rice stood and moved to the door. Then she came back and pushed a pile of papers at Cat. "Give those to Shauna, would you?"

The room was quiet until after she left; then Uncle Pete leaned back into his chair. "The woman drives me batty and calls in everything that happens, but this time I think she saved your house from being broken into. Any idea what Joey might have been looking for?"

"How do you know it's Joey?" Seth asked.

Uncle Pete picked up a cookie, then bit into it, enjoying the flavors. He looked at Seth after he finished eating the treat. "Really? Okay, because

Joey was wearing that same sweatshirt yesterday at the hospital. It's not like we have a lot of Wisconsin fans here in Aspen Hills."

"I saw him in the same hoodie too." Cat looked at Seth. "Is there something you're not telling us?"

"Joey got in trouble before he went into the army. Some relative of his talked him into driving for a break-in. He's always the first person authorities look at when things go bad." Seth stood and got himself a cup of coffee, throwing the now-empty water bottle in the recycling. "He's a good guy."

"I'm not saying he's not, but why would he be breaking into my house?" Cat studied Seth.

Seth shook his head. "I don't know. It's been weird. Terry and Joey were both asking a lot of questions about Chance and him living here. Hell, once I thought Terry was going to call me a liar when I said I had no idea Chance had holed up in the mountains. He's right, though. I should have known. What kind of friend doesn't know his buddy is living less than ten miles away?"

"A buddy who didn't want to be found." Cat rubbed his hand. "Look, even Sherry didn't know until a few years ago when she hit the grocery store one night instead of her normal shopping time."

"Wait, Sherry knew?" Uncle Pete turned to me, flipping through his notebook. "When did she say that? She told me she was unaware that he was living here."

"When Shirley and I went to talk to her, she said that she'd run into him at the store. So they went to have coffee to talk." Cat shook her head.

"Well, I'm going to have to have another talk with her." Uncle Pete glanced around the kitchen. "I'm going to leave an officer here for a couple of days. Especially since you have guests in the house."

Cat nodded. She didn't want to have someone watching over them, but she didn't want to put her guests in danger either.

"And there's one more thing. We tracked the deposits into the Dwight Washington account. They were being made from a security company. One that has contracts in Europe. And the same one that Joey and Terry are currently employed at."

"Joey works at a plant. And Terry? He's working for a golf course," Seth responded.

Uncle Pete shook his head. "Yeah, that's true. But both also get a two-thousand-dollar deposit once a month from this same company. And according to records, they were on leave when the jewelry store burned down. The store put in a claim for over fourteen million in lost diamonds."

"You think the three of them stole diamonds, then set the place on fire? Why would they do that?" Seth turned on Uncle Pete. Although even Cat could see his anger dissipating into grief and pain.

"I don't know, but it might give us a motive for why someone would want to kill him. Maybe he was talking about giving the stones back. Maybe they thought he'd gotten a bigger share. There's a whole bunch of maybes that I can't ask about because I can't find these guys. If you know anything, Seth, you need to tell me."

"All I know is I don't know my friends very well."

Seth sipped on his water. "Chance was friends with the jeweler. He took me there to buy a ring for Cat."

"Maybe he didn't have a choice, Seth. Either way, he's seemed to have paid for that one mistake for a long time." Uncle Pete stood to go. "I've got to get down to the station and get a BOLO out on this guy. Please keep your doors locked."

"Will we see you tomorrow night for dinner, then?"

"Yeah, I'm hoping so. Although every time I try to make plans with Shirley, something comes up this week. I'm going to have to pay for her flight out here just to make up for the lousy week we're having." He stood and adjusted his hat on his head. "I'll talk to you all later. If you remember something or find out something new, please call. I don't want you forgetting something important that might get you all hurt. You're just lucky that Mrs. Rice was heading over here to talk to Shauna. Things could have been a lot worse."

Cat watched her uncle leave the kitchen; then she paged through the stack Mrs. Rice had left. "I never expected this."

"Expected what?" Seth leaned over and glanced over the top sheet. "It's just a recipe with a few handwritten notes on it."

"Exactly." She glanced up at Seth's and laughed at his confusion. "Fiction writers use beta readers to make sure their story is understandable and doesn't jump the shark, so to speak. Cookbook authors use something like that. They have someone test the recipes before they publish them. Just in case. Shauna is using Mrs. Rice as her beta reader."

"That's a bad thing?" Seth still looked confused.

Cat shrugged. "It's not good or bad, just surprising. I didn't think Shauna was close enough to Mrs. Rice to ask her to get involved."

"But according to my mom, Mrs. Rice was an amazing cook. Maybe Shauna just found the right button to push with the woman." He glanced at the clock. "I hate to do this to you, but do you mind if I lie down? I'm beat after all the excitement."

"Go lie down. I'll wake you long before dinner so you can get ready. Are you driving tonight?"

He shook his head. "Nope, Shauna has taken over the designated driver role for the night. Just make sure she remembers when we get to the restaurant. The girl loves her margaritas."

She watched as he made his way slowly out of the kitchen. He might not want to admit pain, but at least he was taking care of himself. Cat stood and locked the kitchen door, glancing out at the lone police car sitting in front of her house. Uncle Pete hadn't been kidding.

Feeling a little spooked, Cat ran downstairs to make sure the cellar door was locked and then to the front door. She texted Shauna to let her know the place was locked up and if she needed to be let in, to text her. She watched the phone, but no answer. Either they were on their way back home and Shauna's phone was tucked into her purse, or they were in a dead zone. Either way, she should hear from them soon.

Then she grabbed a book from the shelf, choosing carefully so that it wasn't a mystery, and settled in the living room to read. The doors were locked.

Seth was upstairs sleeping. And there was a police car in front of the house. She should feel safe. The problem was she didn't feel that way.

She set down the book and went to the dining room to grab a couple of cookies. Stress eating for sure, but she'd give herself some grace today. The week had been crazy. She went back into the living room, setting the book aside and taking out a notebook. In the middle of the page, she wrote, *Chance*. She circled the name. Then she made shoots going out from the circle and wrote down all the possible things that could have led to his death. Since the guy who had his credit card didn't kill him, it most likely had to do with whatever happened in Germany. The time period where Seth didn't have much recollection and what he did remember seemed incorrect. Seth never believed gossip, but he'd always believed what his friends had said. So they'd made up this story about how Chance died, and even Seth believed it. The truth lay somewhere either north or south of what he'd been told. Joey was the key, she could feel it. But what did Joey know? And what did they think Seth knew?

That was the sixty-four-million-dollar question. And she still didn't have an answer. Not yet.

Chapter 23

Cat tried to go back to reading after she'd filled a page full of leads that went nowhere. Many that Uncle Pete had already cleared from his real list of suspects. Maybe she'd pull Shirley aside before dinner and see if she had anything to add to the list. Heaven knew that Cat wasn't making any progress.

She set the book down and went into the kitchen to look at the pages that Mrs. Rice had dropped off. She wondered why Shauna hadn't mentioned working with the neighbor; then she sighed. She knew why. Cat was always complaining about Mrs. Rice. Shauna probably thought that Cat didn't like her . . . which was true. But they didn't keep secrets like this from each other. As soon as the writers were gone, she and Shauna were going to have a chat. Cat wanted Shauna to know that she could tell Cat anything, even things she didn't like.

Maybe Sherry and Chance had been like that. A couple where they could tell each other anything.

Had Sherry really not known about Chance coming home? Had she just gotten tired of waiting and decided to marry someone who wasn't playing dead? Sherry had been anxious to get to Chance's dog. Maybe a little too anxious?

She picked up her phone and dialed while pouring a cup of coffee. When Uncle Pete answered, she sat at the table. Then she told her uncle what she was thinking. When she finished, the line was quiet. "Uncle Pete?"

"I'm here. Just trying to play out the scenario in my head. If what you think is true, I need to get Sherry into protective custody and not just have someone watching her place."

"Wait, you put a tail on her?"

"Let's just say after they tried to break into your place, I figured Sherry's house wouldn't be far behind. And she's got those three little girls. I would have never forgiven myself if something had happened."

Cat could hear the pencil tapping on his desk. "What's wrong?"

"I just don't see the end game. I know whoever is behind this thinks Chance had something. But what could it be?"

"Who knows after all this time? Maybe he overheard something from his higher-ups."

Uncle Pete snorted. "And they waited ten years to silence him? Not likely. And before you ask, yes, I checked on all of his commanders. No one is high enough up in the army or political food chain to worry about something they said in the past."

Cat heard noises in the foyer. "Well, that's all

I've got. Are you meeting us over at the restaurant? Do you want me to save a seat for you?"

"I doubt I'll get away tonight. The mayor wants to chat and whenever that happens, it's never quick. I swear that guy thinks everything I do is going to affect his reelection chances." Uncle Pete paused. "You all be careful tonight. Not too much alcohol consumption and if it feels wrong, just don't do it."

"Yes, sir." Cat laughed.

"I'm serious. I have a bad feeling about this case. All I want for Christmas is to get it solved and off my desk. Then I could relax just a bit."

"Uncle Pete, Christmas is two months away." Cat glanced around the empty kitchen. And she hadn't bought one gift yet.

"Go play with your writer friends. Tell Shirley I'll call her later." He clicked off without saying goodbye.

Shauna came into the kitchen and stopped short when she saw Cat. Then she walked over and hung the keys on the key rack by the back door. "What are you doing sitting here? I would have thought you'd be tucked in your bed reading."

"I just got off the phone with Uncle Pete. I wanted to run some scenarios by him." Cat picked up the pile of papers. "So we had a couple of visitors while you were gone."

"Really? Who?" Shauna went to the fridge to get a soda.

"Well, we think one was Joey. He was trying to break in."

Shauna sat in a chair and stared at Cat. "Joey? The guy who was at Outlaw looking for Seth?"

"Yep, Seth and I went to grab some breakfast and the house was empty."

Shauna opened the bottle and took a drink. "So how did you know he tried to break in?"

"Mrs. Rice was on her way over to see you and scared him away. She called the police and stayed on the line until he ran away." Cat slid the papers toward Shauna. "I really don't blame him. Mrs. Rice scares me too."

Shauna glanced down at the pages, then blushed. "I was going to tell you, but you two don't get along and I didn't want you to feel bad."

"Why would I feel bad?" Cat asked.

Shauna took the pages and put a clip on them before tucking them into her desk drawer. "You are the real author, but she's such an amazing cook. I wanted her to taste test the recipes. To see if they would work. You'd just look at the words."

"You needed a different type of help. I get it." Cat sipped her coffee. "I just don't want there to be secrets between us. I'm sorry I made you feel like you had to keep it from me."

"I should have told you. My bad. Do you forgive me?"

Cat glanced at the clock. "Definitely. I hear you're our designated driver tonight. Uncle Pete wants us to keep a lid on our alcohol because he's thinking this isn't over yet. The people who killed Chance are looking for something."

"And they think Seth might have it now?" Shauna seemed to read Cat's mind. She laughed when Cat looked surprised. "You're not the only one who can put clues together. When Joey took off out of Outlaw that fast, I wondered what he needed Seth for.

He made it seem all casual, but he sure put up a plume of dust driving out of there."

"Let's get this retreat over and the guests home safely. Then maybe we can figure out what the heck is going on around here." Cat stood and dumped the rest of her coffee out. "I'm going upstairs to get ready. Keep the doors locked if you go up before I get back down. I'll wake up Seth and have him get ready too."

"No man left behind." Shauna opened her laptop. "I'll check my e-mails and watch out for the guests. It's like having our own little security detail."

By the time Cat had gotten dressed and replaced Shauna, Jocelyn and Archer were down in the living room, waiting.

Jocelyn held her hand up when Cat came into the room. "I know, I know. We're way too early. But I'm so excited. I don't think Archer and I have gone out to dinner so much in forever. It's nice having a social life. At home we're so busy with the jobs and then the writing that we never see each other."

"We live in a three-bedroom house, dear, there's not much room for either of us to totally disappear." Archer put his arm around his wife and turned to Cat. "But it is nice to get out. We're going to have to continue this when we get home. What do the young ones call it? A date night?"

Jocelyn's eyes widened. "Are you kidding me? Really? We can go out once a week?"

This time it was Archer's eyes that widened. "Once a week? I was thinking every so often, like a few times a year."

"I think maybe there's a compromise in between." Cat stood at the door to the living room, watching the front door. The back had been locked up and, she had to admit, so had the front, but she felt better watching, just in case.

"You expecting visitors?" Archer asked, a tone in his voice that made Cat know he was saying much more behind that one word.

She sighed and left her post. "The door's locked. Someone's going to have to drive a car though those locks to break in. A tall car at that because they have to go over the porch."

Jocelyn waved her over to the couch. "Come sit down and tell us what's going on. You look strung tighter than a cello."

"I would have used a banjo in that comparison, but the sentiment's the same." Archer stood and stepped toward the door. "Do you need me to watch the front?"

"No, I'm just a little nervous today. Seth should be down soon and then we'll get everyone settled into the car for our night out." Cat put on a fake smile that she didn't feel. Fake it till you make it time. She slipped into a chair. "Tell me what you think about Jocelyn's contract? Feeling proud or a little jealous?"

"A high tide floats all boats." He didn't sit down, but instead took Cat's spot standing in the doorway. He leaned back casually, like he was just waiting to leave, but Cat could see the tension in his stance. "I'm willing for her to become wealthy and successful so she can keep me in the style I'm sure to become accustomed to."

"You wish." Jocelyn smiled fondly at her husband. "We've decided I'm going to say yes. Thanks for talking me off the ledge on this one. There's so much to learn on the legal side. Then you have to figure out who to trust."

"Trust your agent. If you can't, then you need a new agent." Cat tried not to watch Archer. It was bad enough that one of them was hyperalert. "And I've only heard good things about your agent. If there were issues, you'd probably hear whispers. It's not for certain, bad things happen, but you can't focus on that. Just be aware of what you expect and if it varies, have her explain. That way she knows you're watching the business end of the relationship as well as the authoring part. It's your money. Make sure you get your share."

"You have such good advice." Jocelyn beamed. "So many people in my critique group are so hung up on what they're missing out on, they don't see the opportunities that are available."

"Or they really don't want to do the work. Didn't that one woman bring back the same manuscript she's been working on for the last two years when she was up for critique last week?" Archer continued to watch out the door.

"And we told her the same thing. I swear, I'm typing up the notes and when she's up for critique again, I'm just handing them to her. It will save us all an hour of listening to the same story and the same excuses." Jocelyn laughed, then focused on her husband. "Is there something out there?"

"Actually, yes."

The women stood and moved quickly toward the door. Archer held his hand out, holding them back.

"Slow down, you're going to scare him away." He moved slowly into the room. "Cat, you first."

She glanced out but didn't see anything. Then her eyes dropped to the bottom of the glass window in the door. Ali stood there, stretching his kitten body up on the door and making himself as tall as possible. Two other kittens were playing on the porch with him. "I was afraid that they'd start to wander."

"How cute." Jocelyn moved toward the door, but Cat beat her to it. She picked up the three kittens and glanced around for the fourth. "I'll take them back to the barn. You have on dress shoes and it's a little muddy out there. Tell Seth and Shauna I'll be right back."

"I'll go with you." Archer and Jocelyn locked gazes.

Nodding, Jocelyn stepped back. "I'll lock the door after you. Nothing special about this lock, right?"

"Seriously, guys, I'll be fine. I'm running the kittens back to the barn and then I'll be right back."

"No, you're not going alone. If you don't want Archer to go, I'll go with you." Seth stepped between Archer and Jocelyn. "The lock is a deadbolt. We'll be back in less than five minutes. If we're not, call the station and have the officer in that car out there paged so he can come check on us or assist if necessary. Don't hang up the phone until we're back, and don't open the door to anyone but us."

"Seth, this is a little excessive," Cat complained, but she felt his hand on her arm moving her out of the doorway. "I'm just getting the kittens out of the front. I don't know why they even came out here, they usually stay out by the barn."

"And you don't think that's strange?" Seth closed the door and pointed through the glass at Archer, who promptly threw the deadbolt. "We've had the kittens two, maybe three months and they've never wandered this far away from the barn."

Cat picked up the last wanderer and walked down the stairs. "You think it's a trap to get one of us out of the house?"

Seth waved to the officer who was watching them. Then he pointed to the back of the house, raising one of the kittens as they passed. The officer nodded. Cat was impressed at the amount of information a few physical movements could convey. It wouldn't be long before the officer would come looking for them.

"I think that's what I would do if I wanted to get someone out of a locked house." He scanned the back of the yard. "We might have already scared him away if he's watching, since we made contact with the officer. At least, I'm hoping so. I was really looking forward to a chicken burrito tonight."

"This is so weird. I'm not used to being under surveillance. Why do you think they are after you?" She didn't look directly at Seth; instead, she watched the kittens play in her arms.

"Not a subject I want to discuss at this point, but if I had to quickly guess? They think I have something. That Chance gave me something. The thing is, he didn't. The last time I heard from him was when he went to the jewelry store to pick up the ring I'd had designed for you. Then he sent it back here to Sherry for safekeeping."

"Sherry had my ring?" Had Sherry told her this? Or did she say that Chance had mentioned the ring.

Seth smiled. "I couldn't very well send it to you. It would have ruined the surprise. And we both know my mom can't keep a secret to save her life."

Cat laughed quietly. "That's for sure. She came over the week before I was supposed to marry Michael three times. Just to check in on me, was her excuse. I think she was trying to see if there was a chance I'd change my mind."

"We Howards, we don't give up easily. My mom really liked the thought of having you in the family." He paused at the barn door. "Stay here a minute, let me glance around before you come inside."

"But what if the bad guy is out here, waiting for me to be alone?"

Seth grinned. "I guess you're on your own with that then. Did you keep up with your martial arts training?"

Cat wished she'd started the practice up again when she'd moved back home. Shauna had started going a few months ago and was getting into amazing shape. "Monday I'm signing back up for classes."

Seth took the third kitten and entered the barn. A few long minutes later, he reappeared. "Nothing out of place. Angelica and the other kitten were sleeping in a corner. The three escapees weren't even missed."

"Maybe they did just get out." Cat scanned the area around the barn and the adjoining field. It looked normal to her.

"Let's get back before Archer thinks we've been gone too long and calls in the cavalry." Seth took her arm and led her back to the house. "Honestly, this whole thing has me a little spooked. "I'm glad your uncle left one of his toy soldiers here to protect us."

"Daryl isn't a toy soldier. He's a nice guy. He's dating one of the secretaries over at the college. She loves my books."

"I take it you met him?" Seth waved to Daryl, who was watching from the car.

Cat laughed. "Are you kidding? Me? Think about it."

"Shauna." He walked up the porch steps and motioned for Archer to let them inside.

"Yep, she even took him coffee and a box of treats, just in case he gets hungry." Cat slipped inside, then considered the gathered group. "Looks like we're ready to go to dinner. Just as soon as Shauna comes down."

"I'm here." Shauna came out of the kitchen. She had on a royal-blue pantsuit. Cat felt totally underdressed standing next to her. Shauna saw Cat's lips twist. "No judging. I haven't been out at night for at least a month. I want to look pretty."

"Well, you hit that mark," Brodie said from the back. When everyone turned around to see who'd spoken, his face turned a bright red. He dropped his gaze.

"Shall we go?" Cat asked, desperately holding back laughter to spare him further embarrassment.

Chapter 24

Getting everyone at the table at the same time at the restaurant had been a major chore. Between bathroom visits and Jocelyn and Sydney's fascination with the attached gift shop, Cat had been munching on chips and salsa for a while, waiting for the group to get together so they could order real food. Now, they were finally all at the table and the waitress was getting their food orders.

"I'll have the beef burrito plate, rice no beans. And a virgin strawberry margarita," Shauna said, handing the woman her menu. Then she leaned toward Cat. "Now I have to tinkle. I'll be right back."

"Whatever." Cat was just happy that their food order would be done before the kitchen closed. She turned to Seth. He looked pale. "Are you feeling all right?"

"A little tired, but I'm good." Seth pushed her

hair behind her ears. "Don't worry about me, play with your friends."

Just as he said that, a waiter came up to the table. "Mr. Howard? I hate to tell you this, but someone hit your car."

"What else could go wrong tonight?" Seth stood, then waved Cat back down into her chair. "Let me figure out how bad the damage is. If we can just drive it home, I'll take it to the shop tomorrow to see if it's safe to drive on the airport run."

"Maybe we're just stuck here forever," Sidney announced, leaning into her husband. "I love our room. We could live there. I'll do local tours to pay our way."

"But what would Curly and Moe do without us?" Tristin put an arm around his wife. He smiled at the others at the table. "They're our dogs. They're going to be mad enough that we brought in a pet sitter for the week."

"Sometimes we get to take them with us on our trips." Sydney started telling a story about how they'd visited Mount Rushmore last summer.

A hand fell on Cat's shoulder. "How bad is it?" she said as she turned, expecting to see Seth.

"Terry sent me in to tell you to keep your mouth shut, especially to your uncle." Joey shook his head. "I'm sorry, Cat. We need to talk to Seth. I'll have him back as soon as possible. I promise you. I owe him that much for saving me yesterday. Our boss, he doesn't like screwups." He headed toward the door.

"No, you are not just leaving after telling me that," Cat muttered as Joey walked away. She stood to follow him. "Tristin, call nine-one-one and get my uncle over here."

"Wait, what's going on?" Tristin asked.

Cat heard the question, but she'd already taken off to follow Joey out of the dining room. He turned his head and saw her. He sped up, keeping his head turned and watching her, but then he ran smack into a waiter with a tray of drinks. The crash of the glass on the floor had everyone's attention.

"Stop that man. Don't let him leave," Cat yelled at the host, who was bringing a couple into the dining room.

The host, who Cat knew from town, was a line-backer for Covington College and a townie working to pay tuition. He dropped the menus and lunged for Joey. He would have caught him too, except for the momentary distraction when the woman behind him screamed.

Cat dodged around the sobbing couple and the host, who was now getting up off the floor where he'd landed. And then she stopped dead in her tracks when she hit the lobby.

Seth had Joey in a headlock. Another man lay on the floor with Shauna standing over him. A man dressed in a suit and tie was on the phone. "Yes, officer, I said we need assistance. One of our guests was attacked, but now his attackers are under control."

Shauna grinned at Cat. "I think I broke a heel when I kicked him."

"And you may need to send an ambulance," the frantic manager added.

It took five minutes for the first squad car to arrive, but Uncle Pete was there in three. He took out cuffs and handcuffed Joey before sitting him down on a bench. He knelt to the still-unconscious man. He glanced up to Seth. "Isn't this your friend Terry?"

"He's not my friend anymore. The jerk tried to kidnap me. If Shauna hadn't come out of the restroom and high-kicked him, I would have been in some van with a bag over my head. What the heck was he thinking?"

Uncle Pete stood and walked over to Shauna. "You did that with one kick?"

"I've been working out at the gym once or twice a day. It's helping with my stress level." Shauna held up her broken pump. "And who do I bill for a pair of replacements. I just got these in New York."

"I'll let you talk to his lawyer when he wakes up and makes the call. Although I don't think he's going to be in any position to pay you anytime soon." Uncle Pete pulled a blue jewelry bag out of his pocket and sprinkled some of the contents into his hand. The rocks sparkled.

"Ooh, pretty." Shauna reached out to pick one up, then stopped. "Can I touch?"

"Sorry, evidence. I just wanted to show you all what this was all about. Apparently when Joey and Terry came to find Chance for his share of the diamonds since they'd run out of their part of the money, he told them he'd lost them."

"His share of what diamonds?"

"Chance helped us rob the jeweler in Germany. He took his share and then, when he went off on that last mission, we thought his diamonds had blown up with him. We knew he was living off the grid and figured that he hadn't had a reason to spend his share, so we came to divide up his share in thirds again. It wasn't like he had bills." Joey closed his eyes. "Don't look at me that way. It was all Terry's idea."

"What did the jeweler get out of this?" Cat looked at the stones twinkling in the dim lights.

"He got half of the diamonds and all the insurance money. That's why he was paying us monthly. To keep us quiet. But do you know how hard it is to live off of a lousy two grand a month? I had to sell off my diamonds just to survive."

By the time they'd finished dinner and returned home, the guests were beat. They'd gotten the story out of Shauna and had chatted nonstop on the way home about the situation. Brodie paused at the bottom of the stairs. "I don't understand why they killed him?"

"Apparently, according to Joey, they didn't mean for it to go that far. They heard someone coming up the trail and thought the guy would call the police, once he saw that Chance was hurt. It wasn't until later that they'd found out that the other guy didn't actually find Chance until it was too late. The mountain valleys can echo footsteps from miles away." Seth filled in the missing pieces for Brodie.

"I don't understand how anyone could do that to a friend What is wrong with people?" Brodie slipped up the stairs, not waiting for an answer.

"I have to agree. I don't understand the reasoning. They were supposed to be friends. More like brothers, if I read the situation right. And they let someone else die, for what? A little cash?" Cat headed to the kitchen. "I'm getting a beer. I'm not sure I'll sleep tonight."

"I'll have one with you. But just one. Since the car didn't really get hit, I've still got airport runs to make in the morning." He went to the fridge and pulled two bottles out. "Where did your uncle find the diamonds? In Chance's cave?"

"The treasure is where your heart is." Cat smiled and took the beer. "Not his cave, but with Sherry. He'd sent it to her with your ring. She'd just kept it safe for him all these years."

"Love, it makes you do crazy things. Like hide several million dollars in diamonds for your ex-boyfriend." He leaned back in his chair, letting his head hang. "If I fall asleep here, will you carry me upstairs to bed?"

"Three flights? Are you kidding?" Cat sipped her beer and just relaxed. The retreat was over. Uncle Pete had found who murdered Chance McAllister. And they were home. All was right in the world.

Shauna had set dinner in the dining room. The roast chicken's crisp skin glistened in the candlelight. Cat smiled as she put a pile of real mashed potatoes on her plate, then made a hole in the middle. She filled the crater with a generous serving of gravy. The six of them were busy filling their plates and conversation had slowed.

Mrs. Rice glanced around the room. "I appreciate being invited over for dinner. When my kids were young, we used to fry chicken every Sunday after church."

Cat smiled as the woman told the table about her memory. It was sweet, not something that she'd expect from the nosy neighbor. Maybe she'd misjudged her. "We love having you. We should have done this a long time ago."

"I'm sorry I didn't fry the chicken. I was a little busy this afternoon. I have some news. I got an e-mail from three agents who want to talk to me about the book." Shauna wiggled in her seat. "The house may have two authors living here soon."

Rounds of congratulations sounded around the room. Cat loved the warmth of the moment. Her family was together. She'd gotten over her fear of Shirley taking Uncle Pete away forever. Shauna was finally crawling out of her funk. She and Seth were in a better place than they'd ever been. And Mrs. Rice . . . well, the woman did have a positive side, Cat noticed, as the woman chatted with Shirley.

Shauna broke into her thoughts and passed her the corn. "Hey, Pete? I ran into someone in the store who said to tell you she was expecting a call from you. Haven't you let her down easy yet?"

"Let me guess, Addie cornered you?" Uncle Pete finished carving the chicken and held out the plate with the meat to Seth. "That woman has turned one coffee date six months ago into an obsession. I'm afraid to go on campus anymore. She's crazy."

Shirley laughed. "You shouldn't be so charming. Everyone falls for that ruse."

Cat snuck a glance at Seth, who was laughing. Cat could tell that everyone including Shirley had known about Addie's obsession with her uncle. She should have realized that her uncle wasn't dating two women at the same time. He had more integrity than that.

"You look surprised, Cat." Uncle Pete set the now-empty platter on the sideboard. "Don't tell me you believed her version of reality."

"No, of course not." Cat blushed. Trying to get the attention off of her, she turned to Shauna. "So did you ever tell Jake you wouldn't be investing with him."

"Actually, I did invest with him." Shauna laughed at the intake of breath from around the table. "Don't worry, I told him I was trusting him with all my worldly possessions of five thousand dollars and he better not lose it for me or I'd never talk to him again."

"You really shouldn't have done that." Cat wondered if it was too late to get the funds transferred back to Shauna's account. "Wait, you only gave him five thousand? You were left a lot more than that."

"He wasn't listening to me, so I gave in. Besides, only you, me, and Kevin's lawyers actually know how much I really got. He bought it and now won't answer my calls. I'm afraid he's lost it already." Shauna picked up her fork. "There's more than one way to skin a snake."

"That's the truest thing I've heard for a long time." Seth held up his glass. "To Shauna and the rest of my crazy family. Thank you for helping Cat see the errors in her ways."

"Hey now, I'm not the problem." Cat held out her glass.

Seth snapped his fingers. He picked up a paper bag from where it had sat on the floor under his chair. "You're right. You're not the problem. I totally forgot about something."

Uncle Pete set down his glass. "It's going to be a while. These two are always trying to one-up each other. Who knows what Seth has in that bag?"

"No time like the present to find out." Seth stood, moving the chair away from the table. He dropped on one knee, then held up a ring box.

Cat's breath caught and she could feel her heartbeat through her chest. She put a hand over her heart to keep it inside. This wasn't happening.

"Cat Latimer? Will you marry me?" He held up the ring. "You don't have to say yes right away, but if you do, you don't have to pay your handyman anymore. Well, after the ceremony. Before that, we're just single people in love."

Cat couldn't talk. Tears fell. Finally, she nodded and let Seth slip a ring on her finger. The ring that had started this entire investigation. He stood and took her in his arms.

"We don't have to do this fast. You know my mom and yours will want in on the planning, so don't say I didn't warn you."

She giggled into his chest. "Maybe we could elope?"

"Or just put the actual wedding off for a while." He kissed her. "Like three to five years?"

"Sounds perfect." She glanced around the room. "He put a ring on it."

"About time," Uncle Pete grumbled, then raised his glass. "To my lovely niece and my favorite of all her boyfriends, Seth. May they find time to explore everything, good and bad. And get out of my hair."

The group laughed as they toasted and then the feast began. Cat relaxed knowing that she had people she could count on. Not all of them were at the table, but these five, including Shirley, were a big part of her life.

Her happy, joyous, messed-up life. And she wouldn't change any of it. Not one thing.

Enjoyed Cat's adventures?
Don't miss the rest of the series,
available now.
And be sure to check out other series
by Lynn Cahoon:
the Tourist Trap Mysteries
and
the Farm-to-Fork Mysteries,
available now wherever books are sold!